'I loved it. The plot is twisty and the issues being dealt with here are big scale but told beautifully through Emily. Her envy and confusion is so real as to be palpable and of course, all too relatable. Creepy and weepy.'
Niki Mackay

'Claire's thrillers are twisty like tornadoes!'
Liz Nugent

'Fantastic, fluid and engaging, a 2019 hit!'
Jo Spain

'A brilliant and hooky read.'
Fionnuala Kearney

'A first-rate psychological thriller. Emotional and twisty, with excellent characterisation.'
Patricia Gibney

FORGET ME NOT

Claire Allan is a former journalist from Derry in Northern Ireland, where she still lives with her husband, two children, two cats and a hyperactive puppy.

In her eighteen years as a journalist she covered a wide range of stories from attempted murders, to court sessions, to the Saville Inquiry into the events of Bloody Sunday right down to the local parish notes.

She has previously published eight women's fiction novels. Her first thriller, *Her Name Was Rose*, was published in 2018 and became a *USA Today* bestseller, followed by *Apple of My Eye* in 2019.

When she's not writing, she'll more than likely be found on Twitter (@claireallan).

Also by Claire Allan:

Her Name Was Rose
Apple of My Eye

avon.

FORGET ME NOT

CLAIRE ALLAN

Published by Avon

A division of HarperCollins*Publishers*

1 London Bridge Street,

London SE1 9GF

www.harpercollins.co.uk

A Paperback Original 2019

3

A catalogue record for this book is

available from the British Library

ISBN: 978-0-00832-191-8

This novel is entirely a work of fiction.
The names, characters and incidents portrayed in it are
the work of the author's imagination. Any resemblance to
actual persons, living or dead, events or localities is
entirely coincidental.

Set in Bembo Std by Palimpsest Book Production Limited,
Falkirk, Stirlingshire

Printed and bound in Great Britain by CPI Group (UK) Ltd, Croydon CR0 4YY

MIX
Paper from
responsible sources

FSC
www.fsc.org
FSC™ C007454

This book is produced from independently certified FSC™ paper
to ensure responsible forest management.

For more information visit: www.harpercollins.co.uk/green

For Julie-Anne, Vicki & Fionnuala

Prologue

I disappeared on a Wednesday afternoon, in June, right in the middle of the heatwave. I was there one minute and the next I was gone. You might think it hard to disappear in broad daylight. To be visible and then, just seconds later, to be invisible. To have a life, and then moments later to have lost it. It wasn't hard at all.

It was much too easy.

They found my shoes. Well, one of them, turned upside down and covered in dust. They found my car, unlocked. The driver's window down. My keys in the ignition. My weekly shop melting and rotting in the boot. Cooking in the unspeakable heat.

They found my bag, my purse, my bank cards. My phone. The memorial card with my mother's picture on it and some rhyming words of comfort, which were supposed to make me feel better about the fact she'd died of breast cancer in her sixties.

They found traces of blood – mine – on the ground outside. Minute droplets. They found traces of unidentified seminal fluid on the back seat, too. Not my husband's profile. Evidence of a sexual assault, maybe?

Or maybe not.

Scuff marks on the ground, the ground kicked up. Vomit on the patchy, faded tarmac. Smeared fingerprints – mine.

Signs of a struggle.

Half a packet of Wotsits crisps, crushed into the floor of where the rear seats are. An empty Fruit Shoot bottle – black-currant – under the passenger seat. An ankle sock. Pink trim. A booster seat in the front of my car.

Signs I was a mother.

'She wouldn't leave the baby,' they said. The baby was three. Blonde curls and blue eyes. Cupid bow lips. A dimple in her left cheek. I wouldn't leave the baby, they were right. Not unless I had no choice.

I'd been given no choice.

Wednesday, 6 June

Chapter One

Elizabeth

Even with every window open, this house is still too warm. It's only half past five in the morning and I know there will be no reprieve from this heatwave. It didn't cool more than a few degrees overnight and I've not slept properly in days. Izzy looked at me mournfully, big brown eyes, pleading for the chance to run about outside before the heat becomes oppressive. I feel sorry for her – even though she's shed her winter coat, it's much too warm for her. Like me, she's become a virtual prisoner in our home.

We'd changed our walking routine a few weeks before. Setting out early now. Before six. Doing our best to avoid the full heat of the sun, though the temperature didn't seem to drop much overnight. This heatwave was stronger than any I remembered in my lifetime. Even warmer than 1976. That morning I was tired, though. My bones ached and I felt every one of my sixty-seven years, and then some. Still, I'd be back at home within an hour, I reasoned, and I could spend the rest of my morning doing what I had planned – baking bread for my grandchildren, who were coming here after school. I eyed the bananas on the worktop – brown spots seeming to multiply with every hour that passed. I might even throw a quick banana bread in the oven. With chocolate chips. The children would love that.

I had to leave the dough for the bread to prove for another hour anyway – wrapped in clingfilm in the airing cupboard – so I had no excuse but laziness and the persistent ache in my left arm. It hadn't been the same since it had been broken eighteen months earlier and was, according to the doctor, unlikely to improve further. I'd just have to work through it.

'Come on, then,' I called to the dog, who started to wag her tail with great enthusiasm. 'You win. Just like you always do.'

She bounced her way down the hall, deliriously happy at seeing her lead in my hand. Patting my pockets to make sure I had everything I needed with me – phone, keys, poo bags – I opened the door then watched as Izzy bounded to the end of the garden before stopping, looking back at me and waiting. She was a good dog. She made me leave the house at least once a day, which was a positive thing. I could quite happily have never left the safety of my own home. I preferred my own company. Peace and quiet. My solitary routine. But fresh air was good for body and soul. Or so they said.

I clipped Izzy's lead to her collar and off we set along Coney Road, narrow, quiet, just far enough from the main roads of Derry to feel as if we were in the middle of nowhere. We'd walk half an hour out on the road and half an hour back, taking in some of the back roads, maybe slip into the country park for a bit.

Striding out, I didn't put my earphones in. I preferred to be able to hear what was around me. To keep my wits about me, just in case. I doubt I posed an attractive prospect to any would-be kidnapper, rotund and in my mid-sixties, but nonetheless, you never could be too careful. People who wanted to hurt others would do so regardless.

I was glad I'd brought a bottle of water with me. It didn't take long for me to feel too hot. I chided myself for bringing a jacket. Even though it was light, it was still too heavy for this weather. Everything was too heavy for this weather.

I slipped it off and tied it around my waist. There was a beautiful calm to the morning. The sound of birds tweeting. In a while the city would start to wake up and the rat race would begin again. I was so glad to be out of that now.

After a while, I let Izzy off the lead. She ran on, occasionally stopping to look back at me, teeth flashing a bright canine smile, before setting off again. Occasionally, she'd spot a rabbit or a bird and would speed off up the road, or into the fields to chase them – bounding as she ran. It was then I felt guilty for wanting to stay inside and not walk her. This was where she was at her happiest.

She never wandered far enough that I couldn't see her. She'd reach a certain point and stop, then turn her head back to me as if to say: 'Come on, old girl! Keep up.' She'd wait patiently until I was closer, then set off again.

We walked on until she started barking, running to the hedgerow, yelping and spinning around – running back to me and back to the hedgerow again.

'What is it, girl?' I asked as I followed her, wondering what it was she'd uncovered this time: an old ball, ripe for throwing into the field for a prolonged game of catch, or more likely a bone, or the remains of an animal that she'd then roll in, necessitating me wrestling her into the bath when we got home.

Only as I got closer, I saw her pull at something bright. Orange. Fabric. Whatever it was, it was heavy. She pulled and struggled with it, yelping all the time. Despite the heat, I felt a chill run up my spine. I wanted to turn around and run, but Izzy was becoming more and more distressed.

The orange object took shape before my eyes. Sharpened. Came into focus. As did a hand, bluish grey. Izzy pulled back. I noticed her white paws, which just minutes before were brown with mud, were now a dark red. Her barking had become whimpering. I wanted to run but I couldn't. I was frozen to the spot.

I pulled my phone from my pocket, took a deep breath. Forced myself to keep walking. Before I even reached the crumpled wreck of a body curled in the hedgerow, I'd dialled 999. Asked for help. Police, yes. Ambulance, yes. Was the person breathing? I didn't know, I wasn't close enough, but I had to be now. I had to get close. I saw a face, blue, a gaping neck wound. Fibrous tissue, muscle and cartilage all on display. An arm that lay at a strange angle. Dried blood. Fresh blood.

Surely this figure before me was dead. Surely no one could survive such butchery.

'It's a woman. A girl,' I blurted down the phone.

'Is she breathing?' The voice on the other end of the line was the calm to my panic.

'I don't think so.'

I got down on my knees, repulsed by the sight in front of me but knowing I at least had to check. I had to do what I could. I bent my head down over her body, my ear to her mouth – senses primed to pick up even the slightest whisper of breath. I took her poor, cool wrist in my hand – tried to feel for a pulse. I was shaking. Trying to push away the memories of another time. Other girls. Other men. Other children. Cold and grey and mutilated. This was why I stayed away. The thumping of my heart drowned out all noise, even the yelping of the dog at my feet.

But there it was. The faintest pulse. Thready. Slow. The softest exhalation. Short. Shallow.

'She's alive,' I said to the operator. 'But only just. Be quick.'

I untied my jacket, placed it on her – as useless as it probably was. Even though it was already hot, she was so cold. The bleeding from her neck wound had been profuse but it had slowed now. I lifted the jacket, moved it and pressed against the wound, almost afraid that I'd press too hard, that my hand would slip inside it.

'Help's on the way,' I said, for my own benefit as much as for that of the unknown woman in front of me. 'If you can hang on, help is on the way. I'm Elizabeth and I'm not going to leave you. I'm going to be here until the paramedics arrive. So if you could do me a favour and just hang on, that would be great, lovey. It really would.'

I took her hand in mine. Could barely countenance how it could feel so cold and still have life in it.

'You're not alone,' I told her, trying to reassure her.

I wondered who she was and who she belonged to. She wasn't wearing a wedding ring. There didn't appear to be much at all distinguishing about her. It was hard to tell the true colour of her hair, matted as it was with mud and blood. If I had to guess, I'd have put her in her mid to late thirties. But it was hard to tell given how bruised and battered she was. Her toenails were painted bright green. It looked so gaudy against the mottled, discoloured skin of her feet – the large areas of raw flesh, gravel-speckled flesh where it looked as though she'd been dragged along the ground, her ankle pointing in the wrong direction.

Someone had wanted this woman very much dead. Someone had left her here. On this quiet country lane, bleeding out.

I could hardly believe she was still alive.

'You keep fighting,' I told her. 'You hold on and keep fighting.'

I was shivering then. Shock was kicking in. My muscles were seizing. I rubbed my arms, tried to release the spasms. Kept an eye out for any traffic that might pass. An ear out for the sound of sirens. Any sound of an approaching police car or ambulance.

I both wished I'd stayed at home and was grateful I was here – at least she had a chance. However small. I put my ear to her mouth again, listened for those shallow breaths. Almost imperceptible but still there. I heard a small gurgle. A rattle. The words 'Warn them' carried on the last of her breaths.

Then she was silent. Still.

And I could hear the sirens approaching.

Chapter Two

Rachel

I saw the news on Twitter first: 'Body of woman found on Derry outskirts.' It linked to a short article in the *Derry Journal* saying little more than the headline. Police were at the scene. The Coney Road, from Culmore Point onwards, was closed until further notice. There would be more on this story as it broke.

I felt a shiver run through me. Was it a hit and run, maybe? Oh, God, I hoped it wasn't a paramilitary attack. No one wanted a return to those days.

No matter the reason, someone would be getting bad news. I shuddered. This woman – she could be a mother, a sister, a friend. Some poor family was about to have their whole world turned upside down.

It was just another reminder that life was short – too bloody short – and as clichéd as it sounds, we don't know what lies around the corner for any of us. If I'd known this time last year what the following twelve months would bring I might have run away or hidden under my duvet and refused to come out.

I would have wanted to hit pause, but of course I couldn't.

The world kept turning anyway – even though I felt mine had ended with the death of my mother – sixty-five. No age at all. Breast cancer.

I hated that when I talked about her to new people now, the conversation always seemed to wind its way round to how she died. Like it defined her. That final, stupid, too-short battle. Surely everything else she'd done in her life should have mattered more?

I slid my phone back into my bag and along with it I buried my emotions for now. I had to get in front of a classroom of thirty demob-happy youngsters and keep them focused.

At lunchtime, in the staffroom, I pulled my phone from my bag again. Switched it on and looked at it. No substantial updates from the *Derry Journal* except a photo from the scene – dark hedgerows, bright sunshine. In the distance, beyond the bright yellow, almost festive police tape, there was an ambulance and what looked like the top of one of those white forensic police tents.

Local political representatives were expressing their 'shock and sadness', all of them saying it was important not to jump to conclusions until the police had more information. All the police had said so far was that the road would remain closed for some time and that they were appealing for witnesses in relation to the 'fatality'.

'We're appealing for anyone who travelled along the Coney Road on the evening of 5 June or the early hours of 6 June who may have seen any unusual activity to come forward and speak to police.'

I clicked out of the link, tried to join in the chat around the table. The looming end of term meant it wasn't just the pupils who were feeling giddy at the thought of the long summer break. Still, this news story had brought a sombre feel to the classroom.

'It's awful,' I heard Mr McCallion, one of the geography

teachers, say. 'I heard, from someone who knows these things, that it looks like a murder. A particularly gruesome one at that.'

'What?' Ms Doherty, our young, quirky, opinionated art teacher chimed in. 'Like, is there any kind of a murder that isn't gruesome? The two tend to go hand in hand,' she said with a roll of her eyes and a smile that showed she was amused at her own wit.

'I don't think us gossiping about it is very appropriate,' I snapped.

I couldn't help it. The feeling that some poor woman had lost her life shouldn't be the subject of staffroom banter. Maybe my own grief had made me raw to it all. Ms Doherty said nothing, but the look she gave me spoke a thousand words. She thought I was a killjoy, a fuddy-duddy. Someone bereft of 'craic'. She hadn't known me before my mother died. Before I'd been changed, utterly.

My phone beeped again with a text message from one of my oldest friends, Julie:

Have you heard anything from Clare? She didn't go into work today. I called round her flat but there was no answer and her phone is off. You know, it's not like her – and there's been that woman found . . .

Julie was always prone to drama and tended to jump directly to the worst possible conclusion about everything, but this time a nagging, sickening feeling started to wash over me. Julie, Clare and I had remained the very best of friends after we'd left school. While I'd trained to teach English, they'd both joined the Civil Service and worked for the Pensions Department on Duke Street. They didn't do anything without the other knowing.

I immediately tried calling Clare myself, I don't know why. I hoped for some sort of rational and reasonable explanation as to why she wouldn't have got Julie's call. When it went straight to answer service, I wondered who else I could call to try to find her. It would be a bit hysterical to call the hospital, wouldn't it? I mean, she was a grown woman. She could be anywhere. She might be with her parents. Out with another friend. She'd been seeing someone lately, someone she'd admitted to developing deep feelings for. She could be lying in post-coital bliss in his bed right now, being decadent and loved-up for once in her up-to-now sensible life. I almost envied her, if she was. I couldn't remember the last time I'd been post-coital anything, never mind blissed-out.

I was about to call Julie back, when my phone rang and her name popped up on the screen. I answered, said hello, expected her to tell me Clare had just rolled into work, hungover but happy.

I hadn't expected the breathless, sobbing, gasping, almost screaming cry of my friend.

'It's her, Rachel. It's Clare. She's dead.'

Chapter Three

Elizabeth

I was sitting in front of the kitchen range, shaking. I winced at the sweetness of the tea I'd been given for the shock.

I had just been too late. Even if I'd got to her an hour before, it would probably still have been too late to save her. She shouldn't really have survived for as long as she did – her wounds were so severe.

'Mrs O'Loughlin, if we can just go over your statement one more time,' the kindly-faced police officer said to me.

He'd been lovely. So gentle in his manner. So sorry for what I'd been through, even though I wasn't the victim here. Not at all.

'I'm not sure I've anything more to tell you,' I said, placing the cup on the kitchen table, the shake in my hand more pronounced than it normally was. 'I can't think of anything more.'

My brain was trying to process the trauma. I knew that. In my younger years I'd worked as a theatre nurse. Cared for many survivors of catastrophic traumas – the de facto warzone that Derry had been during the Troubles meant I saw more than most. Heard more than most. Lost limbs, blast wounds, burns, gunshots, a child who couldn't be saved, whose body was broken beyond repair by the impact of a car bomb.

Images were coming at me now. Fast. Horrific. I shook my head to try to get rid of them, but they didn't go. They wouldn't go and now I had these flashes of that woman, her orange T-shirt and linen trousers – blood-soaked, mud-soaked, wet through. Her eyes, flickering, closed. That wound, jagged, vicious, intentional. The soft warmth of her last breath on my cheek. How gentle it had been for someone who was taken from the world so violently.

'And you saw no traces of anyone else along the road? No cars passed as you were out walking?'

I shook my head. It had been so quiet. Blissfully quiet.

'It's a quiet road at the best of times, especially at that hour of the morning,' I told him as one of his colleagues offered to refill my teacup.

'I imagine,' he said. 'And she just said those two words? "Warn them"? Nothing more at all?'

'Well, my hearing isn't as sharp as it used to be, but no, DI Bradley, she didn't say anything else. I don't think she had the strength. The poor girl. Do they know who she is yet? Who she belongs to? Her poor, poor family.'

'I believe they think they've identified her,' he said, his soft blue eyes sad. 'But I'm afraid I can't give you any further information until she's been formally identified by a family member. You know how it is.'

I nodded. I did, indeed, know how it is, and how it was. I'd stood with family members myself as they'd identified bodies of their loved ones. A matter of procedure. A formality that sometimes felt unspeakably cruel.

'And you've never seen this woman before?'

I shook my head, rubbed my arm to try to ease the aching muscles. 'I don't often get out and about, apart from walking Izzy there. My health isn't what it used to be. And I don't tend to bump into too many people when I'm around these roads and fields.'

16

The handsome DI Bradley nodded again, closed his notebook and sat back in his chair.

'Mrs O'Loughlin, I appreciate this has been exceptionally traumatic for you, but we really appreciate your time and the information you've been able to give us. Have you any family members who can call over and sit with you? You've had quite a shock.'

'My son-in-law will be visiting later. He always comes on a Wednesday with my grandchildren. Makes sure I've everything I need.'

That reminded me that that bread was still proving in the airing cupboard and the bananas were still overripe in the bowl. I didn't have the energy left in me to make banana bread any more. The children would have to make do with fresh bread and jam. It had been good enough for their mother when she was little.

He handed me a card with his details. Told me to call him if I could think of anything else. Any detail at all.

'If there's any way we can be a support to you then please get in touch. We'll have someone from victim support get in touch to talk to you about your experience, help you through the trauma.'

'Detective Bradley, victim support have no need to be wasting their limited resources on me. I'm tougher than I look, you know!'

He smiled. 'Well, I imagine you are, especially with all the help you've given to people in the past, but we all need a little help from time to time,' he said.

I didn't argue. There was little point. But I knew I wouldn't talk to anyone from victim support. I'd just file the horror of this morning's find with all the other horrors in my mind. They were my cross to carry.

Chapter Four

Rachel

I moved through the early afternoon in a haze. I considered crying off to the head but what good would that have done? I'd just have ended up sitting and thinking about the unthinkable. Not that staying in my classroom stopped that. As much as I tried to focus on my work, I couldn't. It was stupid of me to ever think that I could have.

My friend was dead. Someone I'd known for thirty years, from the first day we'd sat together on the newly polished floor of the assembly hall in St Catherine's College, our too-big green pinafores and coats swamping us as we nervously waited to be divided into our form groups.

We'd clicked over a mutual dislike of geography and Kylie Minogue, and we'd stayed friends since. We didn't live in each other's pockets, but we were there for each other through everything life threw at us. When Julie had postnatal depression, when Clare's marriage had crumbled just days before her third wedding anniversary and when I'd fallen to pieces after the death of my mother. The girls had held me up, literally at one stage, as grief took the legs out from under me and I'd fainted. They'd welcomed the steady stream of mourners to our home, directed them to where my mother's body lay so that they could pay their respects and then offered a cup of tea afterwards. They'd made sure everything ran smoothly, while I'd sat, ashen-faced and bowed with grief, by the side of the coffin, unwilling to move – struggling to let go of my beloved mother.

How could it be that Clare was gone now? That her body had been found by the side of a road? The police weren't saying murder yet and I hoped, perhaps naively, that it wasn't murder. That it was an accident. Although I couldn't think of any possible excuse for her being on that road, alone in the early hours of the morning.

I didn't know how she'd died. Didn't know when she'd died. All manner of horrors kept dancing through my head until I couldn't hold in my pain and my fear any more. I simply lifted my bag, left my Year 12s open-mouthed and walked out of the classroom midway through a discussion on the book *Of Mice and Men*.

I walked to the head's office, my legs shaking – the grief hitting me from the ground upwards, weakening me, diminishing me.

'You'll have to send someone to deal with my Year 12s,' I muttered. 'I've got to go home. I've had bad news.'

Sheila, my deputy head, looked me up and down. 'Are you okay, Rachel?'

I didn't trust myself to speak. I didn't want to say the words. It was so completely, utterly, surreal. You never expect to have to say those words to anyone. Those are words for TV shows and movies, not for school offices on sunny June days as the school secretary eats an ice cream and talks about her forthcoming holiday.

I just shook my head as a surge of something powerful, painful and overwhelming rose up inside me. She was dead. My friend. I'd be sitting by her coffin next. And if Mr McCallion was right, it was a 'gruesome murder'.

19

The shock rose up inside me until I had to run from the room to the staff toilets and throw up until I could barely breathe.

I was aware of someone, Sheila most probably, behind me. I was embarrassed she'd hear me retching, sobbing and trying not to scream. She sat down beside me, put her arm around my shoulder and pulled me into a hug. It should have been awkward. It certainly wasn't professional. But it was just what I needed in that moment. It gave me time to find my breath again, to slow the shaking.

'That body,' I told her. 'The one found this morning? It's a friend of mine. One of my oldest friends.' I stumbled over my words. My tongue felt too big in my mouth. The sentences too alien. 'People are saying it's a murder, Sheila.'

She hugged me a little closer, told me that of course I could go, but she wasn't happy about letting me drive given that I'd had such a shock.

'Do you want to call Paul?' she asked.

I shook my head. I didn't want to call my husband. I wanted, no, needed to go and see Julie. She was the only other person who could possibly understand.

'I need to see my friend. Our friend. Julie. She works with Clare. Worked. I suppose. We all went to school together.'

I knew I was rambling and talking too much, but I couldn't seem to stop. Nor could I stop shaking. Once it had started, it became severe. Teeth chattering, legs jiggling. As if I had no control.

'Maybe we should get you a cup of hot, sweet tea or pilfer a bottle of whisky from the summer fair tombola – for the shock,' Sheila said.

I shook my head. I knew she meant well, but I couldn't stomach it and I just wanted to go. It was the adrenaline, I imagined. The shaking and the sickness and the pounding of my heart.

'Well, let's get you to your friend, then,' she said and helped me to my feet. 'I'm so, so sorry you're going through this,' she offered. 'It's awful.'

I nodded because I didn't know what to say, and despite the sickness and the pain in my chest, it still didn't feel real. I didn't know just how awful it was to become. Once I knew how she died, I knew it would only be worse. But for that moment I just kept thinking of my friend, hair tied back in a ponytail. Embracing life again in a way she hadn't through her thirties. My friend smiling from her Facebook page. My friend who had the most contagious laugh in the world.

My friend who was dead.

Julie was perched on the edge of her sofa, her knees tight together, her body stiff with shock. She lit one cigarette off the end of another and continued smoking. Her hand shook as she brought the cigarette to her lips. Her eyes closed on the inhalation and as they did, a tear escaped, running down her already streaked face.

She looked wretched. Old. I'd never looked at one of my old school pals and thought we looked our age before, but Julie did in that moment, in that room. Her usually neatly preened hair was messy, strands of copper escaping from her ponytail, frizzy and unkempt. Her make-up was mostly gone, washed away by her tears and the rough way she pulled the sleeve of her cardigan across her cheeks to dry her face. Her skin would be red and sore later, I thought, as if that would matter. As if that was important in the grand scheme of things.

I'm not sure what I expected. Perhaps that we'd run into each other's arms and cling on, sobbing like lost souls. That didn't happen. Julie looked at me through glazed eyes and just shook her head while I sat down at the opposite end of the sofa, my adrenaline gone and a weariness washing over me.

'Do you want a cup of tea or coffee, or something stronger?' Julie's husband, Brendan, asked me.

It had been him who'd let me in, who'd hugged me awkwardly at the door and who'd warned me that Julie was 'in a bad way'.

'I'm on the vodka,' Julie spoke, her voice hoarse.

I noticed the tall glass, half full of a clear liquid and ice cubes, on the floor by her feet.

'I'll stick with tea,' I said, knowing I'd have to deal with the girls later.

How would I tell them? Tell Molly her godmother was gone? I felt something in my stomach contract.

'Probably the wise choice, I just . . . I just needed to block it out. Or something,' Julie said. 'Oh, Rachel, I can't believe it. I can't get my head around it.'

'How much do you know?' I asked her.

She took a deep, shuddering breath. 'Ronan called me. He was in bits, Rachel. Could barely talk. He said the police had just called to their parents' house, asked about distinctive marks, hair colour, clothes, that kind of thing. They'd found a bank card or something stuffed into her trouser pocket.' Her voice broke as she spoke. 'They've got to go for a formal identification. Can you imagine that?'

A sliver of hope surged inside me. 'So the body hasn't been identified yet? They could be wrong, Julie. Someone could have stolen her card or something. It doesn't mean it's her.'

Julie sighed, dragged on her cigarette again. 'It's her, Rachel. They had jewellery – that bracelet she always wears. They described the tattoo on her wrist. The identification is just a formality. It's definitely her.'

The feeling of that sliver of hope disintegrating almost broke me in two. 'But maybe . . .' I offered to no one in particular, the sentence dying on my lips as I realised how futile it was.

Julie just shook her head. 'I wish. I really, really wish. I can't stop wishing and hoping, but Ronan was as sure as he could be. He's going with their parents. He says he's not sure his mother or father will be up to the task of identifying her. He might have to do it.'

My heart ached for Ronan, Clare's older brother by eighteen months. As much as he'd roll his eyes at us and our giggling, melodramatic, annoying teenage ways, he'd been almost as much a part of our gang back then as any of us were. He and Julie had even shared an ill-fated snog at the youth club Halloween disco once. It was such a drama at the time. Drama. We hadn't known the meaning of the word.

This wasn't how our lives were supposed to go. Julie, Clare and I – we were meant to live to a ripe old age and become our own version of the Golden Girls. This wasn't meant to be how it ended. I wondered whether I should have a drink, after all. Numb the senses. Dull the edges, just as Julie was doing.

'Do they know what happened?' I asked, not sure if I was ready for the response.

Julie's hand shook more as she took another sip from her glass, shuddering slightly as the vodka slid down her throat.

'It definitely wasn't an accident,' she said. 'He didn't have details – I'm not even sure that I want to know them. But the police are treating it as a murder inquiry. I imagine it'll be all over the news by teatime.'

Brendan walked back into the room and handed me a mug of tea, but my hand was shaking too much to hold it. I sat it on the coffee table in front of me and looked at my friend. I couldn't speak. I didn't know what to say. It was taking all my strength to keep breathing normally.

'She was so happy, Rachel. I don't know when you last spoke

to her, but she was so happy. Said she felt her life was finally going in the right direction. She was finally over that bloody break-up and was ready to move on. It was the brightest I'd seen her in years. I don't understand it. Who would do this to her? You know Clare like I do; she wouldn't ever hurt a fly. I don't understand . . .' She finally gave in to her tears, her body shaking.

I thought of the last time I'd seen her. It was about three weeks before. We'd met for a hurried brunch one Saturday. She'd been so happy – glowing, in fact. Told me she believed more than ever that it was absolutely true that life began at forty. She was happy in work, hoping for a promotion, and she'd met someone.

I wondered about him. Did he know? Jesus, could he have done it? We knew so little about him. Had the police spoken to him yet? Did they know who he was? Clare had always been coy about him when we'd talked. Said she didn't want to 'jinx' it. But she'd met him through a dating app and they'd been out a couple of times.

'He's a real gentleman. Not a player, like so many of the men on those sites. He seems genuinely interested in a relationship,' Clare had said.

I'd warned her to take it slowly. She was a romantic at heart – threw herself into relationships too easily. Allowed her heart to be broken. She'd reassured me. 'We've not even slept together yet,' she'd whispered, blushing. 'But I'm enjoying the snogging sessions.' She'd sounded so upbeat. Young. Innocent. I'd been almost jealous of her *joie de vivre*.

'Joy of life'. How quickly things had changed. I sat, numb, looking at Julie.

'Have the police spoken to her new man?' I asked.

Julie shrugged. 'I don't know. Maybe. If they can find him, but you don't think he'd be behind it, do you? He was making her happy.'

'There's something about it all that I don't like. Did she ever tell you who he was?'

Julie shook her head. 'She said we'd meet him soon enough. I wasn't going to push further. . . Oh, God!' She doubled over again. Another gut punch. 'What if they don't find him?'

'There'll be stuff on her phone. Her computer. They'll find something,' Brendan piped up. 'But don't jump to conclusions. Let the police do their job.'

'I can't breathe thinking about it,' Julie said, tears falling thick and fast.

I felt useless. I couldn't ease her pain. I couldn't make sense of any of this. I just hugged her while she cried.

The sound of sobbing was nipping at me. It was too loud. My head was too full. My heart was too sore and yet at the same time I felt as if I were reading lines from a script. No one had these types of conversations in real life. No one. I dropped my head to my hands, covering my eyes, blocking out the glare of the sun through the window.

The doorbell ringing pulled me back to the present. I sat up, moved closer to Julie so that I could hug her as she cried. It seemed such an inadequate gesture.

I heard a man cough as if to announce his presence, and turned round to see Brendan standing with a man in a suit and a uniformed police officer.

'This is DI Bradley,' Brendan said. 'And his colleague Constable King. They wanted to talk to you, Julie. And probably you, too, Rachel, come to think of it.' He turned to inform them that I was one of Clare's oldest friends, too.

'Rachel Walker?' the policeman asked and I nodded.

'Yes, it's good to have you here too, then.'

I nodded again.

Julie and I shifted apart. She pulled the cuff of her cardigan across her face again to dry her tears – her skin now red and angry.

'I'm very sorry for your loss, Mrs Cosgrove, Mrs Walker,' Bradley said, looking at both of us in turn.

'So, it's definitely her?' I asked, knowing even as I spoke that it was a stupid question. He'd hardly be here if it was someone else.

'A positive identification was carried out a short time ago,' he said.

I felt my body sag and Julie grabbed my hand. Brendan invited the two officers to sit down on the armchairs on either side of the room. DI Bradley took the seat closest to us and pulled out his notebook.

'We're trying to speak to as many people as we can, as quickly as we can, to try to gauge Ms Taylor's last movements. Her brother, Ronan, gave one of my officers your details. He said you were very close to the deceased.'

I shuddered at the use of the word 'deceased'. It seemed wrong. I felt angry. He shouldn't be reducing who she was to how her life ended.

'We are . . . were . . . very good friends with Clare. Yes,' I said.

Julie just nodded.

'And can I ask, both of you, about the last time you either saw Ms Taylor or spoke with her? When was the last time you received any communication from her at all, be it a text message or social media chat?'

Julie spoke first.

'I saw her yesterday. At work. We work in the same building – the pensions office. Or we did.'

'And how was she? Did she talk of her plans for after work?'

Julie shook her head. 'It was a busy day. We just had a brief chat at lunch. Mostly nonsense stuff. About the book she was reading and holiday plans. I said I'd call her later and maybe we should go for a drink at the weekend.'

'And you?' he asked, turning to me. 'When was the last time you spoke to her?'

'I think we had a chat on Facebook a few days back. It was something and nothing. I think I asked her how things were going with her new boyfriend. Hang on, I should have it here on my phone.'

I noticed the glance pass between Bradley and his colleague at the mention of a boyfriend, and I rifled in my bag to pull out my phone, scrolling through my messages to find the last chat I'd had with Clare.

God, if only I'd known it would be the last chat I'd have with her, I'd have said more. It would have been more heart-felt than a simple exchange of gossip. I handed my phone over.

'Do either of you know the identity of this new boyfriend?' DI Bradley asked.

I shook my head before looking to Julie. I wouldn't have been surprised if she did know, given how close they were, but she was looking downwards.

'I don't,' she said. 'I'm so sorry. Clare was so scared of jinxing it, she wanted to keep it to herself for now. It was all fairly new, you see. Do you think it's him? You do, don't you?'

'We're at the very early stages of the investigation. At this stage we've no clear suspects, but nor have we ruled anyone out. How new is fairly new?' DI Bradley asked.

'Maybe a month, six weeks at most. Something like that.'

We were interrupted by a knock on the door. Brendan popped his head around and spoke.

'Sorry, love. I'm just going to go and pick up the kids from school. I'll take them to your mother's house, keep them out of the way for a bit.'

Julie nodded, her eyes darting to the packet of cigarettes on the coffee table. She clearly wanted to smoke another one.

I glanced at the clock on the mantlepiece and realised with a start that it was almost three o'clock and I usually picked Molly up from daycare at three thirty on a Wednesday. I needed to go, too, or I'd be late.

'Actually, DI Bradley, I need to go, too. I have to pick my little girl up from crèche, and I need to collect my car from work first. I'm sorry, my husband's working in Belfast and there's no one else who can collect her.'

'Okay,' he said. 'But could you call into the station at some stage in the next twenty-four hours if at all possible? We'd like to take a full statement and get a copy of these messages, Mrs Walker.'

'Of course,' I said, taking his business card from him. 'I'm sorry to have to rush off.'

I was lifting my coat from the arm of the sofa, when Julie spoke.

'How did she die?' she asked, her voice small. 'What happened?'

Constable King shifted a little uncomfortably in her seat. 'At the moment we can't say too much while we await a post-mortem examination, but it looks as if the cause of death was severe blood loss brought about by knife wounds.'

I felt my stomach tighten again. My legs weaken. I thought of Molly standing at the door of the crèche, some brightly coloured painting in her hand ready to be shoved in my direction with a smile. I thought of how we usually sang nursery rhymes all the way home in the car. How my evenings, which I'd considered so completely dull and ordinary, could never be so again.

I desperately needed to speak to Paul, but more than that, I ached to speak to Michael. Michael who could distract me from any pain, who could help me block the horrific reality of what had happened. Michael who was my guilty pleasure, and my darkest secret.

Chapter Five

Rachel

'Mammy, why are you sad?' Molly blinked at me, her bottom lip trembling as I undid her seat belt and lifted her from her car seat.

I'd been trying to act normal for her; clearly, I wasn't doing a very good job.

But just how do you tell a three-year-old something so catastrophic has happened? She trusted me implicitly to protect her from all the bad in the world. This would prove to her that I wasn't infallible. That bad things happened. Horrible things. And while it's a lesson we all have to learn, I didn't want to be the one to take the innocence from my baby girl.

'I'm just a bit sleepy,' I lied, kissing the top of her head. 'You know how you get really grouchy when you need a nap? It's a bit like that.'

She looked at me for a moment, her blue eyes staring out from under the mop of tight blonde curls surrounding her face. I swear she could see right through me – knew I was lying – but just chose not to challenge me. Not this time.

'Okay, Mammy,' she said. 'Let's go see Daddy and Beth.' She took my hand in hers and pulled me towards the front door.

'Daddy's working in Belfast still,' I told her, 'but Beth should be home and I bet she's ready for cuddles from her best girl in the world.'

Molly beamed at me, delighted to have her place as best girl in the world reinforced, and I let us into the house, calling upstairs to my older daughter that we were home. I really needed her to take Molly out from under my feet for a little, just until I called Paul and then, of course, Michael. I should have been seeing him that night, at the creative writing class I tutored, but I'd hardly be teaching that night. Not after what had happened. It would have been wrong. Everything felt wrong, even the most mundane tasks.

Beth appeared at the top of the stairs, still in her school uniform, but her hair was loose around her shoulders and she was wearing her fluffy slippers instead of school shoes.

'You called?' she asked, giving me the same inquisitive look her little sister had just moments before.

'Beth, could you mind Molly for a bit? I need to make a few phone calls.'

'Mum, what's going on?' she asked, walking down the stairs towards me. 'Trisha Donnelly was on Snapchat telling everyone you'd just walked out of class today. What's up? Is it Dad?'

She was twelve years older than her little sister, but she looked just as vulnerable as she walked down the stairs towards me.

'Mammy says she needs a nap, 'cos she's a sleepyhead,' Molly said, throwing her padded jacket on the floor and grabbing her favourite teddy bear from the hall table.

Beth raised one perfectly shaped eyebrow. 'Mum?' she asked again.

'It's not Dad. Dad's fine. I'm going to call him now, but please, Beth, could you just mind Molly for a little? Put on a

DVD or something. Just make sure I get a little peace.' I heard the wobble in my voice and inwardly crumbled.

'You're scaring me, Mum,' Beth whispered as if Molly didn't have the ears of a bat.

'Darling, please, I'll explain it all shortly. But don't worry. Everything's okay.'

I felt awful lying to her, but this wasn't something you just blurted out. Truth being told, I didn't know how to say it. How to find the words.

Reluctantly, she led her little sister into the living room and I climbed the stairs to our bedroom, where I sat on the edge of the bed and took my phone out. It was Paul's number that I dialled first. It rang three times before he answered. On hearing his 'hello', I felt my composure slip.

'Paul,' I said, my voice breaking. 'You need to come home. Something really awful has happened. I need you here.'

'The girls?' he asked.

'They're fine,' I assured him. 'It's Clare. Paul, have you seen the news about the body found at Coney Road?' I realised I'd started to shake.

'Yes, I saw it . . . but, God, no, Rachel,' Paul said, his voice low. 'It's not Clare? It can't be.'

'Police confirmed it this afternoon,' I said, my voice breaking. 'It was murder, a knife wound.'

I finally gave in to sobbing as I heard my husband try to soothe me down the line.

'I'll be home as soon as traffic allows,' he said. 'I can't believe it, Rachel. This is awful.'

I couldn't even speak to say goodbye, so I just ended the call and curled up into a ball on my bed, burying my head in my pillow so that my daughters wouldn't hear my sobs. I didn't want to alarm them. I wished there was someone here to hold me and soothe me as I cried.

I knew I should have wished for that person to be Paul, and in a way I did. But more than that, I wished it were Michael. I needed him. My body physically ached for the comfort he could give me. Knowing that I wouldn't see him tonight was hard, when I just wanted him to hold me and tell me everything would be okay in the way only he could.

I tried to slow my breathing, to regain control of my emotions, and I dialled his number, saved in my phone as Michelle. Just in case, I'd thought, long before I realised just what I was getting myself into.

'Hey, you,' his voice, smooth, comforting, came down the line. 'I'm looking forward to seeing you later. Can you get away for coffee afterwards?'

At this point normally we may have laughed at the word 'coffee', knowing that it was about more than coffee. We'd not slept together. Not yet. But it was, we'd both realised, only a matter of time before we couldn't hold out any longer. Before I took the final step, which would brand me a cheat forever.

'I won't be there tonight,' I told him. 'I've texted them and asked for a substitute to be sent in.'

'Does that mean you'll be pretending to be there and we might just have more time together if I skip class, too?'

I so wanted to say yes. I so wanted to be led astray by him. I wanted to be distracted by him, taken away from the horror that had been unfolding all afternoon.

'Michael,' I said, loving even the sound of his name, 'I wish it were that simple. My friend's dead.' I gulped back a sob, closed my eyes and tried not to picture how she may have been found. 'That poor woman out on the Coney Road. It's Clare.'

'Oh, Rachel,' he soothed. 'I'm so, so sorry. I wish I could do something to be there for you. Is there any chance we could see each other even for five minutes?'

I shook my head, told him no. 'Paul's coming back from

Belfast now. We've got to tell the girls yet. And the police want a statement, so I've got to go to the station, too. It's all just a nightmare. I can't even. . .'

'It's okay,' he soothed, his deep soft voice washing over me. 'You know I'm here for you whenever you need me. You do believe that, don't you? You know how I feel about you, Rachel. I'll do whatever you need me to do to help.'

'I don't know what's going to happen – these next few days, I just don't know. . .'

He sighed. 'Don't worry about the next few days. Just take it a day at a time, Rachel. An hour at a time if you need to. I'll be here when you're ready, whenever that may be. Even if it's just for five minutes.'

'I wish you were here now,' I breathed down the phone.

'Me, too,' he said. 'More than anything. I hate that I can't comfort you.'

I heard footsteps on the stairs, recognised them as Beth's. She was no doubt done with waiting for me to tell her what was going on.

'I've got to go,' I whispered into the phone and hung up, just as my daughter walked into the room, chewing on her lip, her eyes, clear blue like her sister's, wide with concern.

There was no way to hide the fact I'd been crying. My face, I knew, would be puffy and red, my eyes bloodshot. The bed was crumpled from where I'd thrown myself onto it.

'Mum, I'm scared. . .' she said, walking towards me.

I gestured for her to sit down beside me and I pulled her into the biggest hug I could.

'Oh, my darling girl, I need you to be brave, okay? But there's been some really awful news.'

Chapter Six

Elizabeth

By teatime it was all over the news. This murder. How a dog walker had discovered the body of 41-year-old Clare Taylor, a civil servant, that morning.

They didn't say on the news that she'd still been alive when the dog walker had found her. I was grateful for that. People didn't need to know all the sordid details of everything. It was bad enough I knew them. I doubted the image would ever leave me.

Izzy sat forlornly at my feet. The house was quiet again. The grandchildren and my son-in-law had gone home. I hadn't told him it was me who'd found the body. I didn't want him worrying. He worried about me enough. I didn't want any fuss. I'd rather just forget about it as much as possible, if the truth be told. It would have been different if Paddy were still alive. I'd have talked everything through with him and he'd have helped me to make sense of it in the way only he could. I'd been blessed to have been married to him. I only wished I could have had him in my life for longer.

An image flashed on the screen. A beautiful woman. Chestnut hair – the colour mine used to be before the grey took over.

She was smiling at the camera, the faces of two others in the picture blurred. She looked nothing like the person who'd died in front of me. Nothing like that grey figure, covered in mud, almost translucent owing to blood loss. Her face twisted in fear.

That policeman who'd been out to see me earlier was speaking. Describing the crime as 'particularly depraved'. Appealing for witnesses. Answering questions from the media. Or not answering them. It seems Clare Taylor was a well-liked woman. Police had no idea what the motive might be. How could there be any justification for this kind of attack? How could one human inflict this kind of suffering on another?

My muscles still ached. I'd taken a warm shower – too warm for this heat, really – to try to ease the stiffness. Still, I thought, I was alive. I could think and feel, even if I sometimes wished I couldn't.

Clare Taylor. I think my daughter went to school with a few Clares. It was a very popular name the year she was born. Laura would have been just a little older than this woman, if she were still here. We'd have just celebrated her forty-second birthday. But both of them were gone. Before their time. Both horrifically. I wondered what this Clare's story was. What her life was like. If she'd left behind a grieving husband, as Laura had. If there were two children left completely lost without her. I wondered if there was a mother out there who felt as if she'd let her daughter down, as if she more than anyone should have been able to save her.

I decided I'd contact that police officer, ask if there was any way I could meet this Clare's mother. I wanted to talk to her. To assure her that her child hadn't been alone when she died. That someone was with her, trying to keep her warm and comfort her. I knew that would mean something. I know I'd have loved to have heard that after my Laura died.

Normally quite content with my own company, or at least

with the company of just Izzy, I felt unsettled. My house didn't feel quite so safe and secure any more. Knowing that something so horrific could happen so close to me had unnerved me.

I got up and walked around the old farmhouse, closing all the windows and locking the doors. I tried to recall the days when there was always someone coming or going. The blaring of music from the children's bedroom. Paddy coming in and out of the kitchen door, filling me in on what he'd been up to in the milking shed, or down in the back fields.

Now, there was no noise and no movement bar the smallest of breezes trying to push its way through the dusty window with little luck. The air was stifling, stagnant.

'What do you think, Izzy?' I asked the dog, who didn't seem to think very much at all. 'Am I being a selfish old woman wanting to meet her family?'

Izzy trotted off in the direction of the cool kitchen floor, not that I could blame her. I followed her. It was still too early to go to bed, even though a deep, all-embracing tiredness had engulfed me. Instead, I sat down on the armchair beside the range cooker and looked out of the window over the fields. Bathed in sunshine, the sky blue with not so much as a whisper of a cloud, it seemed almost unthinkable that something so brutal had happened so close by on such a beautiful day.

It was only then that I allowed myself to cry for poor Clare Taylor and my poor Laura, who should have been able to bring her children to see me herself but who'd never do so again.

Chapter Seven

Rachel

Did I feel guilty that I texted Michael from my car just after I left the police station and asked if I could call round to his? Yes. Of course. But my need to see him had grown as the hours had passed.

Beth had been devastated; hysterical. Her cries still echoed in my ears. Molly had teetered up the stairs upon hearing the commotion and had stood, open-mouthed, her teddy hanging from her arm, tears spilling over from those beautiful blue eyes down her cheeks.

I'd told Beth I'd handle how we told Molly what had happened, but that I needed time to find the words. So both Beth and I had just hugged her, reassured her through our tears that we were just sad about a 'grown-up thing' and that everything was okay.

I'm sure she didn't buy it but, thankfully, being three, she could be distracted by the allure of colourful TV characters and ice cream for dinner. Beth worried me. Her reaction was so visceral, as if any sense of innocence at the world she still possessed at fifteen had just been ripped from her.

She'd cried until she threw up and then she lay facing me

on my bed while I stroked her face and tried to comfort her. But how could I? I couldn't say everything was okay – because everything wasn't okay. A woman she considered her aunt had been murdered. It would colour everything in her life from now on. She'd carry it with her.

I held her until I heard the front door open and the call of Paul from the bottom of the stairs, followed by Molly excitedly telling him she'd had three different flavours of ice cream for her tea. Her trauma was forgotten, or buried at least. I hoped it would stay there.

I didn't cry when I saw Paul. I suppose, just as I'd expected to break down when I saw Julie, this surprised me. He sat on the edge of our bed and hugged a still-snivelling Beth, soothed her in the way he used to soothe me. Reassurances whispered into her hair, promises that he'd look after her. I drank in the tableau of father–daughter love in front of me and I felt another piece of my heart get chipped away.

When did Paul and I stop meaning everything to each other? When did the sight of him stop soothing my heart?

'I've to go to the police station, make a statement,' I said, breaking their moment.

'Surely you don't have to do that tonight?' Paul asked, his face tilted, brow furrowed. He nodded surreptitiously towards Beth, as if to tell me she needed me more than the police did.

'I want to do whatever I can to help,' I said. 'I want this man found, Paul, and soon. They want to build a complete picture of her life.'

'But it's weeks since you saw her,' he said.

'We talk, Paul. You know that. She's one of my oldest friends.'

I was starting to feel irritated now. I felt myself tense. I knew I was being terse with him and it wasn't right – not in front of Beth. Not now.

'Of course,' he said, almost apologetic. 'You do what you need to do. Should I come with you?'

I bristled again. 'No,' I said. 'I think it's best you stay with the girls. I don't think Beth here is in any state to mind Molly. Are you, Beth?'

My beautiful daughter blinked up at me, her eyes red and puffy. In that second she looked very much like my little girl again, not the young woman she'd blossomed into. My heart ached for her. She shook her head.

'Okay, then,' Paul said. 'I'll stay here with the girls. Maybe once Molly's in bed, we can order in some Chinese food?' he said to Beth, who nodded.

'I'm going to get a shower and change into my pjs,' she said and stood up.

I hugged her and told her that I loved her before changing into a linen skirt and white T-shirt.

'Dressing up for the police station?' Paul asked.

'Hardly,' I said. 'But my blouse is a bit stained, with tears and make-up from our beloved daughter, and I just want to be comfortable. I'm hot and sweaty, and I don't know how long I'll be there.'

Suddenly, I was very tired. And hungry. I realised I'd not finished my lunch, or eaten anything since, but I wasn't sure I'd be able to keep anything down now if I tried.

'Well, hopefully they won't keep you too long,' Paul said, standing. 'I'm really, really sorry this has happened,' he said, pausing to look me up and down before leaving the room.

I'm sure he was talking about Clare, but he could just as easily have been talking about the ongoing disintegration of our marriage.

As it happened, I wasn't in the police station all that long. Less than an hour. I didn't have much to tell them, really. I just let him copy all the messages from Clare from my phone then talked about her life and if there was any way she could have enemies.

Even the thought of Clare Taylor having enemies was laughable. She was the most easy-going person I knew.

Of course they asked again about her new man, but I couldn't tell them much more than what I'd told them at Julie's. He was handsome, according to Clare, and kind-hearted. He'd insisted on paying for dinner on their first date. But that was about it. I didn't have his name. There weren't any pictures of them together anywhere. I didn't know where he worked or even where he was from. I'd assumed he was a Derry man, but I didn't know for sure. We'd just never had that conversation. Clare had always been one to play her cards close to her chest and that was okay.

'Maybe I'll introduce you all at our annual August barbecue,' she'd told me, 'if it keeps going well.'

They asked me how Clare got on with her ex-husband, James. Was there any residual animosity between them?

I told them that as far as I knew, they rarely spoke. They'd both moved on since the divorce – which was as amicable as could be in the end. There'd been tears and a lot of soul-searching. She'd been hurt when he'd told her he didn't love her any more, of course she had. And then angry when she'd found out he already had someone else lined up. But when all was said and done, they'd simply grown apart. He'd never, to my knowledge, been violent towards Clare and I didn't think he was the kind of man who would be. There was no reason to suspect that he'd have murdered his ex-wife. But then again, the notion that anyone at all would want to murder Clare seemed completely absurd.

I felt as if I was being singularly unhelpful, unable to give the police anything to go on. Any questions I'd asked, they didn't really answer. Everything was 'too early to tell', or they weren't 'at liberty to say'. They'd assured me no stone was being left unturned, that every avenue was being explored.

They used all the clichéd terms that police could use, which just made it all feel even less real. As if we were all acting in a TV show, saying our lines. A grisly-faced detective would show up at any minute and swear at his underlings before declaring there'd been a murder, in a thick Scottish accent.

It was impossible to get my head around the idea that somewhere my friend was lying cold, dead, carved up by a pathologist. I shook that image from my head each and every time it pushed back in and tried to focus on what the police were saying.

By the time I left, all I wanted to do was to feel something tangible. Michael replied to my text message almost immediately – telling me that of course I could call round. He looked forward to it. He hoped I was okay.

A wave of something I couldn't quite put my finger on washed over me. It was desire, mixed with affection, mixed with guilt. I looked at myself in the rear-view mirror, glad I'd fixed my make-up and brushed my hair at home. My look still screamed middle-aged teacher, but it was presentable. I didn't look as haggard as I had earlier.

Guessing I could probably spend an hour at most with Michael before any suspicion was aroused, I set off, eager to get to him as soon as I could.

Michael lived in a house close to the Irish border at Ballyarnett. It was an old house that he was midway through renovating. Still a bit ragged around the edges, there were more than a few half-finished projects on the go; the kitchen was minimal and due to be replaced by something sleek and modern, the bathroom was basic but work had begun on replumbing, and a new floor had been laid in the living room. Half of the house's rattling old windows had been replaced with double-glazing. The whole thing was starting to take shape, but Michael didn't seem overly bothered about getting it done quickly. 'I'd rather take my time and do it right,' he'd said. And being a single man living alone he had the luxury of being able to do that.

We didn't spend an awful lot of time there, anyway; in fact, I'd only been to his house a handful of times. Most of the time we'd spent together had been walking through the nearby country park and sitting in my car, talking and kissing, of course. His kisses took me to somewhere where I felt like an unburdened teenager again.

I rang his doorbell and he answered within seconds – a sight for sore eyes. Standing there in his jeans and a red T-shirt, his dark hair messy and curly, unshaven but with deep green eyes that looked at me with such concern I felt myself melt into them. He pulled me into a hug, a hug that I didn't let Paul give me earlier. He told me he was so, so sorry for what happened. That he wished he could make it better for me.

He poured me a glass of wine, which I knew I shouldn't drink because I had the car with me, but I gave in to the temptation anyway. Just as I gave in to the temptation of his kiss – his lips full, soft, determined. His hands roaming. His body pushing against mine. It was wrong, but it felt right. It felt as if it was the perfect thing to do – to allow my nerve endings to fizz into life as a big two fingers up to death.

I needed to feel alive. I needed him. So when he wordlessly led me from the kitchen up the stairs to his bedroom, I didn't hesitate. When he took the wine glass from me and sat it on his bedside table – before gently pushing me back onto his unmade bed, his eyes filled with longing – I responded by reaching for his belt and unbuckling it, desperate to feel as alive as I possibly could.

'Are you sure?' he asked as I unzipped his jeans, reached my hand inside, desperate to touch him.

I couldn't speak. I could only nod. I desperately needed him. I knew this was taking whatever it was we had to the next level, that there'd be no going back once we did this, but I was powerless to stop. Life was just too short not to get what I wanted any more.

We lay curled together afterwards, in the fading light of his room. Still half-dressed. Passion had taken over. The need to have him. I could feel his heart beating in his chest against my back as he held me.

'I wish you didn't have to go,' he said, kissing my shoulder. 'I'd love to have you to myself all night. To be there for you.'

I took his hand in mine. Revelled in how strong it felt. 'I wish I could stay, too. I don't want to go home and face reality.'

He pulled back a little and I rolled onto my back, looking up into his eyes.

'Then don't go home, Rachel. Stay here, with me. This is real,' he said.

'You know I can't stay,' I said. 'Beth was so distraught. Molly's so confused . . .'

'And him?' Michael asked, avoiding using Paul's name as if saying it would conjure him into the room between us. 'You have him, too.'

'Yes, he's there. But it's not that simple. You know it's complicated,' I said as I reached up and stroked his face, tried to convince him that I cared. Properly cared.

I knew I was just sounding like a serial cheat now. Spouting the oldest line in the book. It couldn't have been further from the truth. I'd never been tempted to stray before I met him. Not even once.

'It's not fair of me to ask, not now,' he said. 'I'm sorry.' He turned away, sat up and started getting dressed. 'Do you ever think, though, Rachel, especially at times like this, that you have a right to be truly happy? If you tell me that you're happy with him and all he has to offer you, then that's fine. I'll find a way to deal with that.' He turned to look at me while putting his T-shirt on. 'But I don't think you are happy and you don't deserve to be miserable for the rest of your life. You don't know what's coming next, none of us do. Clare would agree, I'm sure.'

I showered when I got home, washing away any scent of Michael and what we'd done; let my guilt at having slept with another man wash down the drain along with the soapy water. I slipped into fresh pyjamas and lay down on top of the bed, it being too warm to climb under the covers. Exhaustion washed over me. I was just about to switch off the bedside light, when Paul walked in and sat down on the edge of the bed at my feet.

'I'm sorry if I've handled this all wrong,' he said. 'I just don't know what to say. I can't get *my* head around it, so God knows what it's like for you.'

'It's awful for me,' I said, pulling myself up to sitting. 'I don't know how to deal with it either, Paul. My head hurts, and my heart hurts, and I don't know what actually happened, or how. I don't even know if I want to know – the very thought of it. That someone did this to her on purpose. They said blood loss, you know. That they thought she bled to death, and my mind just keeps going over and over that. And whoever it was, whatever monster did this, left her on the side of a road like a wounded animal.' I pulled my knees up to my chest and hugged them as my voice began to break; I was just so tired now and confused about how I felt about everything. 'She didn't deserve this, Paul. And her poor family – her mother and father, Ronan – how will they cope? I'm not sure I could even begin to.'

Paul shuffled up the bed and pulled me into a hug. I felt guilty as I allowed him to comfort me. Not only at what I'd done that evening, but also that I was letting this man hold me when my feelings increasingly lay elsewhere. I wasn't being honest with him. The hug felt awkward at first, but then it was as if my body remembered how we fitted together, Paul and I. How we knew each other inside and out and, selfishly perhaps, I gave in to the softness of his hug, breathing in the familiar smell of him. I wondered, did he feel the same as I did? That we were falling into old roles, our awkwardness masked by the tragedy we were going through?

'Do you know what happens next?' he asked, still holding me close.

I shook my head. There would be a postmortem, if it hadn't already been carried out. Beyond that I didn't know. I hadn't experienced this before.

'I'd like to go and see her parents tomorrow, maybe see if Julie can come, too. I want them to know they aren't alone in this.' I pulled back from him and looked in his eyes, tried to read his face.

He nodded, tilted his head to the left slightly. 'Hmmm, as long as you don't feel they'd be too overwhelmed, you know, with loads of people arriving at the door.'

'We all grew up together. We were in and out of each other's houses as if they were our own. We're not just "people" showing up for a look at their misery, you know.'

I was being sharp with him again. I knew it and I hated myself for it, but I wondered at how little he actually understood me. How could he not know I'd need to be there, with them? How was it that he no longer seemed to understand me at all?

'That's not what I meant,' he said wearily.

'I know, I'm sorry,' I replied, deflated. The moment between us was gone. The closeness of our hug shattered. 'I'm tired,' I told him again and he moved to allow me space to lie down.

'I'm going to watch TV for a bit,' he said, leaving me alone in the darkness of our room.

Thursday, 7 June

Chapter Eight

Rachel

The following morning felt just as surreal as the previous day. We tried to keep things light as we got Molly ready for daycare, even though I wasn't going to work. I couldn't face it. I wouldn't have been able to concentrate even if I was there. My sleep had been terrible, broken and filled with nightmares, and my head was thumping. Still, I wanted to keep things as normal as possible for Molly.

I threw back two paracetamol with my morning cup of coffee while Paul helped Molly into her favourite sandals. Beth was still asleep, having cried herself to sleep the night before. I'd already texted Julie and told her I'd call round after I dropped Molly off. We'd head to Clare's parents from there.

It was something I felt I needed to do, but it wasn't something I particularly relished. I was scared to see their grief up close. But there was something innate in that Irish-ness of having to be helpful following a death, how we could all spring into action, making sandwiches and tea, leading mourners through the house to view the remains and offer condolences.

There was no floral wreath or black ribbon on the door of the Taylors' house, but the blinds were closed – more, I guessed, to try to ward off any intrusive members of the press than anything else.

After parking the car, Julie and I were set upon by a small but determined group of reporters hoping to get a topline to run with, or to strike gold and get an interview with Clare's family.

I felt them swarm around me and while they were polite, it felt overwhelming. How did we know Clare? Were we related? Was there any more information? Was there any truth in the rumour that the police were hunting her boyfriend? Could we just, please, ask her parents to speak to them? Did we have a picture they could share?

Julie blinked at me, her eyes wide with panic. I clasped her hand tight in mine and politely told the reporters that I wouldn't be answering any of their questions. Thankfully, the sight of a policeman at the door of the house was enough to stop them following us up the garden path. He looked us up and down, sizing us up.

'We're friends of Clare's,' I said. 'Close friends. Ask Ronan or Mr and Mrs Taylor.'

He asked us to wait where we were while he went inside to check. We were expecting him to return, but it was Ronan, pale and exhausted-looking, who opened the door and let us in.

'I'm so, so sorry,' Julie said, throwing herself into his arms.

He didn't speak for a moment, just hugged her back as they both cried. I stood awkwardly; there was an intimacy in their hug that made me feel like a third wheel.

When they pulled apart, Ronan gave me a hug, too, and I whispered my apologies for his loss. Never had words seemed so woefully inadequate.

'My parents are upstairs, sleeping. It was a bad night, so we got the doctor to give them something first thing. I've told them they've to keep their strength up,' Ronan said.

'You've been here all night?' I asked.

He nodded. 'I didn't want to leave them. They are so lost.'

'Any more news?' I asked as he ushered us into the kitchen.

Empty teacups were piled by the sink, testament to many visitors. Used to making herself at home, Julie emptied the teapot of cold tea and put on the kettle to make another. I filled the sink and started to wash up.

Ronan sat, shaking his head, staring into the middle distance. Trying to find the words he needed.

'They still won't tell us much,' he said eventually. 'They have to "protect their investigation".' He shook his head. 'The postmortem was done last night. Did you know, they don't do them here? They had to take her up to Belfast. We can't even be with her, or near her, and they can't release her body. Not "at this stage of the investigation".' He made quote signs with his fingers. Parroted what he'd been told. 'We can't bring her home. Can't make any arrangements. They can't tell us when we'll be able to.'

Julie sat down across the table from him then reached out and took Ronan's hands.

'And yesterday. Did you see her?'

I stood, back to the sink, watching them. A tear rolled down Ronan's cheek, which he brushed away quickly before taking a shuddering breath. Here was this grown man. This guy we'd all seen as cool and funny and untouchable in so many ways, and he was broken in front of us. My heart physically ached for him.

'Mum couldn't face it. Da and I went in together. They had her well covered up, you know, up to her chin almost. We were told they did that so we didn't see the worst of her injuries. I don't know if that just made it all worse. If I'd seen them, maybe I wouldn't be imagining all sorts of horrors now.'

Or maybe he'd be plagued by the real horror of what he'd seen, I thought, but I didn't speak.

'I was still hoping, you know, until the last minute, that it wouldn't be her and at first . . . God, it didn't look like her. I thought they'd made a mistake. Her hair was all wrong, too dark. And her face seemed . . . I don't know. It just wasn't an expression I'd ever seen her pull. But Da gripped my arm so tight and I felt him buckle then he let out this noise like I've never heard before, and I knew it was her.'

I watched Julie squeeze his hand, rub his arm with her other hand. Tears ran unchecked down her face.

'We've seen dead bodies before, right?' he asked, looking at Julie and then up at me.

And of course we had, many times. It's part of our culture to bring our dead home, wake them over the course of a few days and nights, spend time with them, ensuring they're never left alone until they make their final journey.

'She didn't look like anything I've ever seen before. She was blue. Not even grey but blue and bruised. I could see the bloodstains on her ears, her face. Her hair was matted with blood. That's why it looked all wrong. There was this huge graze on her cheek, as if she'd been dragged along the road. It was just a horror show.' He broke down, gasping to gain his composure, while I tried to quell the nausea in the pit of my stomach. 'We weren't even allowed to touch her. I couldn't hold her hand or kiss her forehead. I had to hold Da back . . . He wanted to hug her, but the police said it might interfere with evidence. Evidence? That's all my sister is now. She can't be touched by any of us until after the autopsy. I've never seen a man look so broken,' Ronan said.

I realised I was crying too, and shaking. I wanted to shake the picture he'd just painted from my mind, focus on being there for him instead, but it was so hard.

'They can't get any information on the man she was seeing,' he said. 'They couldn't find her phone. Her laptop was gone from her house. Why would that be? You know Clare. She always had that bloody phone on her. They're going to access her phone records, see if it throws anything up.' He looked up again. 'Are you two sure she didn't give you any details that might catch him?'

I shook my head. I wished I did know more. I wished I could point the police directly at him. I wished I could go and take him on myself. Ask him if it was him. Show him exactly what I thought of him.

'So they definitely think he did it, then?' Julie asked. 'That's who they want?'

'Who else could it be?' Ronan asked. 'You know Clare . . . knew Clare. She didn't have any enemies.'

Julie shrugged. 'Could it have been random?'

He shook his head. 'I don't know. Maybe. But with the missing phone . . . something's not right. They need to find this guy and quick. God knows if I find him first, the police won't get a look-in.'

Ronan looked exhausted, as if he wouldn't have the physical strength to take anyone on. I wondered if he'd had any sleep at all.

'How are you holding up?' I asked.

He gave a short, cold laugh. 'I don't know what side's up. I feel so helpless. I can't make it better. I'm trying to be here for my parents as much as possible, but you know, Jenny needs me home with the kids, as well. It's hard to get the balance right.'

'I'm sure Jenny understands,' Julie said. 'Your parents need you.'

'My kids need me, too,' he said, pulling a face as if he were mimicking the words of his wife. 'I know they do, you know. But I'm only one person and I can't split myself in two.'

'You have to be careful you don't burn out,' I told him.

'That's what Patricia says. The family liaison officer. You'll meet her soon, no doubt. She was just calling at the station and then she said she'd be over. She says I've to keep myself strong and well.'

Julie nodded. 'She's right.'

'And the media camped at your door? I assume she'll deal with them?' I asked.

'We're planning what to do, if we need to do a TV appeal, that kind of thing. It's all so strange. As if it's happening to someone else but at the same time, I know it's happening to us. I just wish I knew why.'

'The police asked me about James,' Julie said. 'You don't think it could be him, do you?'

It had been four years since Clare's marriage had officially ended, following two years of repeated attempts to patch things up and try again. It was James who'd made the final call to walk away once and for all.

I shook my head. 'I don't see it. He wanted out – she'd have given him her whole life and more. It was his choice to end things when push came to shove. They both worked through it and isn't he with someone else now, anyway?'

'Maybe he wasn't happy about her seeing someone new,' Julie offered. 'He didn't want her but he didn't want anyone else to have her.'

'I wouldn't put it past him,' Ronan said bitterly.

But no, I knew in my heart it wasn't James. He had no reason to hurt her. He was no saint, but he'd been a part of our gang of friends for ten years – surely we'd have known if he had the capability to snap like that? Grief was clearly making Ronan clutch at whatever straws he could see.

'In so many of these things, it's the husband or the partner or whatever. We'd be stupid to discount him,' Ronan said while Julie nodded.

'Well, I'm sure the police'll speak to him, but I think it's more important to find whoever this mystery man was that she was seeing. Don't you all think it odd not one of us had met him, or knew his name even? And where is he now? His girlfriend's been murdered. If he has nothing to hide, why hasn't he come forward?'

Ronan shrugged. 'I don't know. I don't understand any of it. Maybe he's married and coming forward would risk his marriage.'

'If he's married, and is cheating, I've no sympathy for him,' Julie sniffed. 'I hope he gets hauled in front of the media. Scumbag.'

A shiver ran through me. What would they think if they knew about Michael and me?

Chapter Nine

Elizabeth

I lifted my keys and told Izzy I wouldn't be long. She looked at me mournfully, wanting to go on an adventure with me. But this wasn't much of an adventure. This was just something I felt I had to do.

I'd been the last person to speak with Clare Taylor. If I could bring an ounce of comfort to her parents, it was only right that I did so.

I hadn't been able to speak to DI Bradley that morning. He was busy, which was hardly surprising. But I had been able to speak to a friendly-sounding woman called Patricia Hopkins, the family liaison officer, and she'd okayed it for me to call round to the Taylor household. She'd be there to meet me, she said. 'I think it really could help them greatly to know their daughter wasn't alone when she passed,' she said, which is exactly what I'd hoped she'd say.

Still, my heart was thumping when I arrived outside their house and saw the street lined with cars. There were huddles of photographers and reporters standing around, dressed in summer frocks and short-sleeved shirts. There was an air of informality to it that I didn't care for. I saw some laugh as they talked to each other, slugging from bottles of cool water. I knew they were only doing their jobs but it felt ghoulish. They were waiting for a soundbite of misery. I'm sure they couldn't have enjoyed it all that much, either. I'd seen reporters over the years breaking down under the pressure of covering some of those horrific atrocities.

I nodded an acknowledgement in their direction, wondered if they'd come running to me for a statement. Then again, they didn't know who I was. What I'd seen. How I'd held her hand. If only they knew, they'd be all over me. I kept my head down, hoped that the natural invisibility that seemed to come with being a woman of a certain age would stop me from beeping on their radar.

They say you know you're getting on in years when policemen and doctors start to look unconscionably young. The uniformed police officer at the door of the Taylors' house looked as if he had yet to start shaving. He'd a nervous disposition about him, a natural air of suspicion in how he looked me up and down. It was laughable, really. It was hardly as if I posed any kind of threat to him.

I introduced myself as Mrs O'Loughlin, asked to speak with Constable Hopkins, the FLO – as Patricia had directed.

He nodded and opened the door, directing me through.

'Patricia, Mrs O'Loughlin's here,' he called.

I was surprised and a little reassured to hear his voice had broken.

A short woman, with cropped dark hair and a friendly face, walked out of the kitchen and reached her hand out to welcome me. Her handshake was firm and I wondered whether or not she could feel my own hand trembling in hers.

'Thank you for coming, Mrs O'Loughlin. I'm sure it'll be a real help to the Taylors to hear from you.'

'Please, Constable,' I said, 'call me Elizabeth.'

She nodded with a small smile. 'I will do, and you must just call me Patricia. I'm here as support for the family at this very difficult time. We like to keep things informal. It helps everyone.'

I nodded and followed as she led me through to the small kitchen where three adults, two women and a man were sitting around the table drinking tea. I guessed they were all around the same age as poor Clare had been. Were they siblings, or cousins?

They looked at me and to Patricia as I stood awkwardly, waiting for an introduction.

'Ronan,' she said, 'this is Elizabeth O'Loughlin, the lady who was with Clare yesterday morning when she passed.'

The man in front me, his eyes red-rimmed with exhaustion, got to his feet and crossed the room. He stretched his arms wide and pulled me into a hug. I could feel him shaking, heard him say 'Thank you' over and over. I felt like a fraud. Sure, what was there to thank me for? I'd done nothing. I hadn't saved her. Maybe if he knew I was a nurse who didn't save her his welcome wouldn't be so warm.

'Ronan's Clare's older brother,' I heard Patricia say, just as I heard the two women who'd been sitting with him excuse themselves.

'We'll give you some space,' one of them said.

I wanted some space just then. Needed some air. I felt guilt and sorrow wrap around me just as Ronan's arms did.

'Maybe you'd like a seat, Elizabeth,' I heard Patricia say and Ronan pulled away from me.

Patricia just looked at me sympathetically. She'd known I was feeling overwhelmed, or she was familiar enough with horrible events like these to assume that I would be.

'Thank you,' I said, sitting down on one of the pine kitchen chairs.

'Tea or coffee?' Patricia asked.

'Tea, please,' I said as Ronan tried to compose himself, wiping his eyes with a tissue.

'I'm sorry,' he said. 'I'm sorry, I just don't know how to thank you enough.'

'I didn't do anything, really,' I said, feeling my face blaze. I didn't like being thanked for my woeful inadequacy.

'She wasn't alone, at the end. . .' he said. 'The police told us you were holding her hand. Had put your jacket over her. That means a lot.'

I nodded, not trusting myself to speak.

'Did she say anything? Did she speak at all?' he asked.

I was aware of Patricia close by. She'd asked me not to reveal what Clare had said to me. That it was sensitive to the case. I didn't want to lie – that felt wrong – but I had to do what Patricia had asked, so I shook my head. I watched Ronan deflate in front of my eyes. Watched as Patricia took in every detail of our exchange.

'She wasn't really conscious, slipping in and out, you know . . .' I told him. 'I doubt she'd have been too aware of anything around her at that stage.'

'But you held her hand?' he asked.

'I put my coat over her and called the emergency services, then I held her hand. Pleaded with her to hang on. She was just too ill.'

I felt a tear roll down my cheek. Saw images of her poor, mutilated body flash before my eyes. I shuddered. Patricia placed a cup of tea in front of me.

'It's a great comfort to my parents to know someone was with her,' Ronan said.

'Mr and Mrs Taylor are sleeping at the moment; it was a bad night for them,' Patricia explained.

'I can imagine,' I said softly.

Although that wasn't quite true. I didn't need to imagine. I knew exactly how it felt to lose a child in the most horrific of circumstances.

Chapter Ten

Rachel

I was exhausted, physically and emotionally, by the time I got home. I'd picked Molly up from crèche and had done my best to pretend everything was normal, but I could feel my facade slipping.

Spending time with Ronan, and then his parents, had been harrowing. It had made it too real. Mrs Taylor was the kind of woman who was always impeccably dressed and made up. She used to give us girls make-up lessons when we were teens – warning us against the dangers of going overboard on the rouge or choosing the wrong shade of lipstick. I'd never seen her without her make-up before – not even when I'd had a sleepover at Clare's. Yet, there she'd been, her face pale, devoid of its usual glam look, her hair pulled into a loose bun, wearing a pair of black trousers and a jumper that seemed to swamp her. She'd looked so small, so vulnerable that it had shaken me, but at least she'd been able to talk to us. Mr Taylor – this big teddy bear of a man with a booming voice and an even louder laugh – just sat silently, staring into a mug of tea that he didn't once lift to his lips.

Julie had been silent on the drive back to hers. I'd been

grateful for it. There wasn't much we could say to each other. We both knew how awful this was.

But when I'd picked Molly up, I'd plastered on a wide smile and pulled her into a hug that was probably a little tighter than it should have been.

'Why are you hugging me so tightly? Mammy! You're hurting me!'

I loosened my grip and she squirmed away from me. I wanted to pull her back into my arms, but I didn't. I thought of Mrs Taylor, though – all the times she must have held Clare to her and never imagined that this was how things would turn out.

How could anyone have imagined this?

Beth was already home when I opened the door. If I wasn't mistaken, I could smell the makings of a bolognese on the hob.

My eldest daughter walked into the hall to greet me. Still in her pyjamas, her eyes still red, it was clear she was still hurting. All I wanted to do was protect her.

'I've put some dinner on,' she said, shrugging in that awkward way teenagers do.

I knew she was trying to make life easier for me and I loved her so much for it. I pulled her into a hug. The same tight hug I'd given her little sister before. Beth didn't wriggle away, though; she just hugged me harder.

'I love you,' I whispered.

'I love you too, Mum,' she answered, without a hint of her usual teenage sarcasm.

When we pulled apart, she took Molly into the living room to put the TV on for her while I walked through the kitchen to check on dinner. A bouquet of flowers, in hues of red and purple, sat in a vase on the table.

'Beth? Where did these flowers come from?'

Beth popped her head out of the door. 'They were delivered earlier. I meant to text you. They're from your work, I think.'

I was touched by the gesture of my colleagues. I walked to the table and lifted the little white envelope from the arrangement. Opening it, I saw a message that made my heart soar then sink in quick succession:

Thinking of you at this difficult time
All our love,
Michelle and all your colleagues at NWRC

'Michelle' – I knew immediately the flowers were from Michael. It was a nice gesture but a risky one. I knew he was just reaching out and after what we'd done the night before, I knew that things had shifted between us. But this was outside of my comfort zone. Paul would never have heard me talk about a 'Michelle', either in my day job or at my nightclasses. He'd wonder why 'she' put her name specifically on the card. He could ask questions. Get suspicious.

I was both touched and angry with Michael for putting me in this position. Beth had seen them. Paul could have. He might have, for all I knew. He was working from the Derry branch that day and hadn't returned to his bolthole in Belfast. He might have come home at lunchtime to check on Beth.

I swore under my breath, contemplated ripping the card up and binning it, but then I remembered just how Michael made me feel. Desired. Wanted. Loved. Special. It had been such a long time since anyone made me feel special. I put the card back in the envelope and slipped it into my handbag.

I'd send him a text. Thank him but remind him of the need to be careful.

I didn't want to risk Paul finding out, largely because, I realised, I didn't want to risk having to give up Michael. With everything that was happening, I needed him in my life more than ever.

Friday, 8 June

Chapter Eleven

Rachel

There was a moment when I woke up the following morning when everything was as it should be. Nothing had changed. I lay in the early morning sunlight and listened to the gentle snore of the man I'd married beside me. Passing thoughts of the summer holidays went through my head. Having two children so far apart in age had made it hard to find a holiday that would suit them both. We'd opted for a villa with a pool and allowed Beth to ask a friend along.

I smiled, thinking of Molly – who'd already thrown a couple of dolls and a swimming suit into her Trunki suitcase. Yes, she'd been a bit of a surprise when she'd arrived. The result of too much wine, a missed pill and caution being thrown to the wind. But she was so precious to me. And to her daddy, too. I'd give him that much. He was a doting father. It was almost as if he'd taken all the love and attention he used to give me and simply transferred it to his beautiful baby girl. I supposed she was easier to love than I was.

I yawned, glancing at the alarm clock. It would go off soon. The day would begin. And that's when it swooped in again. The reality of what was happening. I'd have to go back to work.

They'd only be understanding to a point – and I couldn't let my pupils down – but the very thought of it intimidated me. My head was too full of the horror of what was happening in my life to stand in front of a classroom and pretend to be normal. This wasn't normal.

I sat up, turned off the alarm clock before it beeped and made my way downstairs to make a coffee. I'd take this time to myself to gather my thoughts before the rest of the household woke.

Sitting at the kitchen table, coffee cup in hand, I scrolled through my phone. It was filled with messages about Clare, questions – people I'd barely spoken to in years wanting all the juicy gossip. Facebook wasn't much better. A grief fest. Everyone who'd ever seen Clare before making a claim on her and how much they'd miss her.

There were no new leads from the police. There'd be a press conference in the afternoon. I wondered if Ronan and his parents were preparing to make a statement, after all. Would they be like those poor families you saw on TV, blinking and crying in front of all the flashing lights and cameras. Stunned by their grief and this horrendous way of getting fifteen minutes of fame.

Michael hadn't replied to my message. The one where I'd thanked him for the flowers but urged discretion. I didn't like that. It made me nervous. I chewed on my thumbnail as I contemplated calling him to make sure everything was okay. But it was barely gone seven in the morning and it would be risky to have a phone conversation in the house at this time. What if the girls woke? Or Paul?

I thought of Michael's words to me just after we'd slept together. How he'd asked me whether I thought I deserved to be happy. Had what happened with Clare not shown me how life was short and I should grab at happiness?

It wasn't as simple as that though, was it? I had daughters. A house. A job. A reputation. A mortgage, for goodness' sake. I deleted my messages to 'Michelle' – I'd been selfish for wanting him . . . for needing him. Other people relied on me to be there for them. To be strong and stable. Even when things weren't always going well.

For better and for worse, that was how it went, wasn't it? Had I been looking for an easy escape from the harder times – fooling myself with romantic notions for a man who hadn't even messaged me back?

I slipped my phone into my bag, finished my coffee and wondered quite what the hell I was doing with my life. Wondered if I was just a stupid woman enduring a midlife crisis and justifying my selfish actions to myself in whatever way I could. Maybe this was how it was supposed to be. After so many years of marriage. So many years of raising children and being sensible. Maybe I was stupid to expect anything more than simply working together like a team, managing the house and the family we'd created together. Stupid and vain and desperate for male attention. Why couldn't I just be content with what I had?

Chapter Twelve

Elizabeth

I'd had that nightmare again. The one where I was with Laura but not with her. I'm watching her go through the last hours and minutes of her life and it's as if I'm watching from behind a screen. I keep trying to reach out to her, but my hand only ever gets close. I never make contact. I can only ever reach out with my bad arm – the one that doesn't work properly. No matter how much I try to use my other arm, it won't move.

I call to her to wait for me, but she disappears, or the scene changes, or it gets too dark. I'm watching her as she tries to phone me, reaches my voicemail but doesn't leave a message. I'm shouting at her to speak. 'Leave a message, Laura! Let me hear your voice one more time!'

Maybe if I'd got a message, things would have been different. I wouldn't have ignored a message the same way I'd ignored a missed call. I'd promised myself I'd call her back later, but I never got the chance. In the dream, she doesn't hear me shouting. I'm stomping my feet, and banging cupboard doors and shouting until my throat hurts and my stomach constricts with the effort of it. I'm throwing things – hoping if I don't reach her, don't touch her, they will. They'll distract her. They'll get through to her.

I'm begging and pleading and shouting as I watch her walk out of her house, away from her husband, away from her children, away from me. I'm praying to Paddy, imploring him in his heavenly seat to get through to her. Pleading with a dead man, as if that would ever work. 'Please, Paddy. Stop her. Stop our girl. Let her know she can't leave me. It's bad enough you're not here.'

I run to the door to follow her, but I can't open it. It won't open. The locks keep disappearing and changing and locking again, and all the time I'm screaming at her not to go.

That was how it usually went. It had been different this time, though. I'd crumpled to the floor, shouting and crying, and turned to see Clare Taylor sitting at the bottom of the stairs shaking her head. She was smiling – a weird, twisted kind of smile. It unnerved me. Her hand reached out to mine, just as I'd tried to reach out to Laura. I expected not to quite get close enough. I expected us just to miss each other, just as I always missed Laura's hand. But I felt Clare's hand, in my dream. It was holding mine, squeezing it. I looked in her eyes and she told me again to 'Warn them' – I just didn't know who 'they' were.

I woke with a start, a cold sweat drenching me despite the heat. My breathing was laboured. I didn't want Clare in my dreams. I wanted Laura. I wanted to hold *her* hand and feel *her* hand. Not this woman I didn't know. I didn't want the trauma of what I'd shared with her to take my daughter from my dreams – no matter how harrowing those dreams had been. At least it had been Laura in them. At least she'd been alive in my imagination.

I sat up, aware of the first signs of light in the sky outside. I hugged my knees to me, looked to the empty side of the bed. I'd never get used to it. Paddy being gone. It had been seven years and still I never allowed so much as my foot to slip over to the space where he once lay. This house had known too much loss and too much pain. I sat and rocked myself until my heartbeat settled.

I'd call that DI Bradley as soon as was appropriate and I'd ask him more questions. Ask him if he was warning anyone. Surely I had a right to know that? I shouldn't have to carry that burden on my shoulders alone.

'The investigation is at a very sensitive stage,' Patricia had told me after I'd sat drinking tea with the Taylors – both of them too numb with shock to talk to me. 'I know that our methods might seem a little strange, but please bear with us,' she told me.

I'd nodded. Agreed. Because that was what I did. I nodded and agreed with people – did what I was told. Meanwhile, I was being haunted in my dreams by that poor woman and I'd never forgive myself – ever – if anyone else got hurt.

DI Bradley led me through a series of dull and uninspiring corridors until we reached a small and equally uninspiring office. It was tired-looking; dank and depressing. I saw he was tired, too. In fact, he looked exhausted – his shirt wrinkled. His face unshaven. The room had a musty smell to it – as if someone had slept there, grabbed a few hours when they could.

'You look done in,' I said as I sat down.

'It's been a busy forty-eight hours, Mrs O'Loughlin. Busy and frustrating.'

'You'll have to be careful not to burn yourself out,' I said.

I'd seen it before, police officers chasing a case until they had nothing left to give.

'I'll be going home in a bit,' he said. 'Grab a couple of hours' kip, get a shower. Be back here for the press conference. Now, what can I help you with? Have you remembered anything else?'

I shook my head. 'No, it's not that. I'm very grateful you've taken the time to see me. I just feel uneasy about it all. I know maybe I've no right to keep asking what's happening, but that poor girl told me to warn people and I've made myself sick with worry that I've not been able to warn anyone. Patricia – Constable Hopkins – asked me not to say anything to the family.'

He pinched the bridge of his nose and sat back in his chair. 'I know this must be very difficult for you. We're asking you to stick with us. Just as it's important that information gets out there, it's important that some information is held back – for the sake of the investigation. I'm not at liberty to go into it all, but we have good operational reasons.'

Frustration niggled at me. 'But what if someone else gets hurt? Won't it be my fault then? I mean, it's bad enough now, knowing I couldn't help her. I don't want to feel worse if something happens to someone else. And I felt awful lying to her family yesterday – telling them she hadn't said anything. I mean, they'll find out eventually, won't they? They'll think me a liar. I don't understand why they haven't been told.'

'This is a complex investigation,' DI Bradley said. 'We have to play our cards close to our chest at the moment until we're able to identify a clear suspect. We have concerns that revealing her last words could, in fact, place you in a position of some jeopardy.'

My heart thudded. 'Me? Why?'

'Because if there are more people out there who this killer might target, you warning them might make him, or her, unhappy.'

I felt sick. Why had no one mentioned to me before that I could possibly be in danger? Didn't I have a right to know?

'We're doing our best to protect your identity. We've not released any of your details to the press; nor have they been discussed outside the confines of the incident room.'

He must have noticed the colour draining from me. The police may have kept it under wraps, but I'd been to see the Taylors. Had they been warned to say nothing about my identity? And those two women who'd been drinking tea with Ronan in the kitchen. Who were they?

'Mrs O'Loughlin, at the moment we have no reason to believe at all that you're in any danger,' DI Bradley said, cutting through my thoughts. 'We intend on it staying that way, but we're reviewing the situation as often as the need arises.'

I nodded, but I couldn't push down the nausea increasing in my stomach, nor stop the thudding of my heart. I'd have to check all the locks in the house. Get that security light in the yard fixed. It had broken at least six months ago and I'd kept meaning to get it looked at.

'The investigation's proving more complex than we thought,' he said. 'We hope the press conference later will jog some memories or bring some more information to light. We just ask that in the meantime you trust us and trust what we're doing.'

I was hardly in a position to say no.

As I left the police station and walked out into the hot morning air, the brightness of the sun in my eyes, I felt a growing sense of unease wash over me. I cursed myself for going for my walk on Wednesday morning. I should have stayed inside. Things would have been easier if I'd just stayed inside.

My body tensed, my muscles aching. Stress, they say, makes every ache and pain flare up. Fibromyalgia, the doctor told me. On top of the nerve damage from my fall. Physical pain to match the mental anguish I lived with every day.

As I walked my ageing, aching body back to my car, part of me hoped that whoever it was that had brought this horrific end to Clare Taylor would come back and end my life, too.

Chapter Thirteen

Rachel

The press conference was timed to hit the evening news. Paul questioned whether or not it was wise for me to watch.

'It's not going to tell you anything you don't already know,' he said, but of course he didn't know that for certain.

'I'm just trying to protect you from further upset,' he said, when I told him I felt I had to watch.

'My upset isn't going to go away, Paul. That's not how it works,' I snapped at him.

'I just don't see why you have to torture yourself with the details,' he said. 'Once you hear things, you can't un-hear them. They'll stick with you.'

'All of this is going to stick with me anyway,' I told him.

I already couldn't imagine a time when I could close my eyes and not think of what had happened. I didn't see things the way he did. The more I knew, the less my mind would wander. My imagination could be a dark place. How did he not know that about me? After all these years.

'Well, I'm going to take Beth and Molly out for an hour. I don't want Beth being upset more than she already is.'

His intentions were good, I saw that, but he was naive to

think that Beth wouldn't access the press conference feed when she got the chance from her phone or tablet. The reality of the modern world was that we couldn't protect her from it. Nonetheless, I agreed with him. I wanted time to absorb it all by myself. I didn't need his commentary, his tutting and judgement.

They left and I poured a glass of red wine before sitting down in front of the TV. The press conference started, and I saw Ronan and Mr Taylor sitting behind a table alongside Patricia and two men, who I presumed to be police officers. A uniformed officer spoke, detailing where the investigation was and asking for the help of the public in tracking down Clare's killer.

'We're in the process of checking phone records, CCTV evidence and other information brought to us by the public, and we're confident that the person or persons responsible for the horrific murder of Clare Taylor will be caught and brought to justice,' he said.

He went on to urge anyone with information about Clare's movements in her last few hours or who may have witnessed anything out of the ordinary in the area surrounding Coney Road on the night prior to her death to come forward.

'No matter how inconsequential the information may appear, it could help us close the net on this dangerous killer quicker,' he said.

I listened to the words of the policeman, but my eyes were constantly on Ronan and Mr Taylor. Their gaze never left the table in front of them. I watched as Mr Taylor wiped his eyes repeatedly. Watched as Ronan looked forward and held up a picture of my beautiful friend – in which she was smiling to the camera, looking carefree and happy.

He read from a prepared statement: 'My sister, Clare, was a bubbly, generous and loving person. She was a devoted daughter to my parents, a devoted sister to me, and a much-loved aunt to her niece and nephew. She was loved by both her friends and her work colleagues. She'd never have willingly hurt anyone in her life. As her family, we're at a loss to try to understand why anyone would have done this to her. My parents will never get over what's happened,' he said, his voice breaking. 'We ask anyone, anyone at all, who has any information about whoever did this to come forward as soon as they can and to allow our family some sense of justice.'

The policeman spoke again.

'The person who did this would have sustained some injuries during the attack. There's evidence that Ms Taylor tried to defend herself. It's probable that the person responsible would have had Ms Taylor's blood both on his or her clothes and on their person following the killing. Police believe that Ms Taylor was brought to Coney Road by car and she sustained her fatal injuries at the roadside. The car this person was driving would also likely be spattered with Ms Taylor's blood and would require a significant deep clean.

'If you're protecting someone, the time to come forward is now. Police can be contacted by calling 101 and asking to speak to the inquiry team at Strand Road. Alternatively, members of the public can call the Crimestoppers anonymous line on 0800 555 111. Given the nature of this murder, we believe the person responsible to be a highly dangerous individual. The sooner we can have this person in police custody, the better.'

CCTV images of Clare were flashed on the screen. She was standing at a checkout, a bottle of wine in one hand. She was seen pushing a strand of hair behind her ear and smiling at the cashier.

'The footage we've shown you was taken on the evening before Ms Taylor's death at around 7 p.m. These images are from

Chill Off Licence at the DaVinci's Complex on the lower Culmore Road. We know that Ms Taylor didn't return to her apartment that evening. We believe that her killer may have been known to her and that on the evening preceding her death, she may have willingly gone to meet with this person.

'Police are examining a number of lines of inquiry at this stage, but we're extremely keen to speak to a man Ms Taylor was believed to be in a romantic relationship with. We'd ask that man to make himself known to police to help with our ongoing investigation.'

'So you believe the perpetrator to be a man, then?' a reporter asked from the scrum.

'As I said, at this stage of the inquiry we're examining a number of lines of inquiry and haven't ruled out the possibility the killer was a female. However, given the extent and nature of Ms Taylor's injuries, we do know the killer would have had significant body strength. We also know that she'd recently begun a relationship with an unidentified male who has yet to make himself known to us.'

The policeman continued speaking, but my eyes were transfixed on the now still image of my friend, smiling at the camera, not knowing what had been lying in front of her. It took me back to the last time I'd spoken to her and just how happy she'd sounded. She couldn't have had any idea of what kind of a man he'd turn out to be. What he'd do to her. The death he'd give her.

I shuddered, thankful in that moment for a safe and boring life. Paul and I may not be madly in love with each other any more – truth was, I wasn't even sure we were in love with each other at all any more – but we knew we were safe together. We had our girls to hold on to. We had our perfectly nice life in our perfectly nice house with our perfectly nice jobs. Surely there was something to be said for that?

I glanced at my phone again. Still no reply from Michael. He was probably hurt at my reaction. I doubt it was what he'd have expected. I chewed on my thumbnail, looked at the flowers on the table. I thought of how I'd felt with him on Wednesday night – the delicious thrill that came with breaking the rules. The eroticism of touching someone new for the first time. Of hearing how he moaned and sighed as we'd had sex. How he sounded different to Paul. How he'd felt different to Paul. How the newness of him was an all-encompassing assault on my senses.

But it was more than that, surely. It wasn't just sex – after all, we'd only just, after two months of meeting in secret, gone to bed together. It was the newness of the relationship. The friendship. It was how he looked at me and didn't see, above all else, a mother and a wife and a tired housekeeper. He didn't see me and remember the figure I used to have, or that my breasts used to be firmer, my hips neater. He saw me as the person I was – and without any of the ties of time and duty, he still wanted me.

But it hadn't been real, had it? False names in my phone. Stolen moments. A fantasy that could only hurt other people. I needed to decide to be happy with Paul and work on that. Stop looking for what I didn't have and make what I did have work again.

I picked up my phone and my finger hovered over the 'block' button as I looked at Michael's number. With one touch I could erase him from my life. I could make my excuses and pass my evening class responsibilities to someone else. It wasn't as if we needed the money. I could use those nights to spend more time with my husband. Encourage him to come home more during the week, do things with me. Be a couple again.

We'd been in love with each other once, after all.

Chapter Fourteen

Rachel

The girls were in bed. I was halfway through my third glass of wine. Everything was a little hazy. Paul was sitting on the opposite end of the sofa to me, a glass of whisky in his hand. He swirled the crystal tumbler, the ice cubes knocking together while he looked deep into the amber liquid. He didn't take a sip, just went back to looking at the TV.

There was a chat show on, but I don't think either of us was really watching. We were both too lost in our thoughts. I wanted to reach out to him then, selfishly needed the comfort of his familiarity. It felt strange, though. There was a block between us and I couldn't quite bring myself to reach out to him, physically or emotionally.

I heard him sigh. I glanced back to where he was staring again at his drink, as if it might hold the answers to some great mystery.

'I'm not immune to how awful all this is,' he said, looking up and catching my gaze. 'I know you might think I'm being cold about it, but I'm not. If the truth be told, I just can't get my head around it. That she's dead. How she died. She's one of us, you know. One of our gang.'

His voice was choked with emotion and in that moment I saw his vulnerability laid out in front of me.

'I know,' I said, feeling tears prick at my eyes.

'I don't want to think about it too much,' he said. 'I don't want to know what happened. I just keep thinking, it's so close to home. Too close to home. I imagine if it had been you, or Beth . . .'

I watched as a tear slid down his cheek – down that well-worn face I'd loved for almost twenty years. He sniffed, rubbed his eyes roughly, raised his glass to his mouth and knocked back his drink. That was Paul – never one to let his emotions get the better of him.

'This is something we need to face,' I said. 'We can't run from it. You can see Beth. You can see how hard she's taking it and it's only going to get worse, you know. We're only at the start of this. God knows where the next few months will take us.'

He reached over and took my hand. I didn't pull away, didn't shrug him off.

'Remember we used to say we could get through anything if we did it together?'

I nodded.

'I think somewhere along the way we might have forgotten that,' he said.

He looked directly into my eyes with such intensity that I wanted to look away. I wondered, did he know something, about Michael and I? Could he sense it? Had he seen something or overheard something? There was just something in his demeanour that made me feel transparent. Guilty.

And, of course, I *was* guilty.

I kept his gaze for as long as I could and then I dropped my eyes to our two hands, still together. Taking a deep breath, I vowed again that I was going to stop seeing Michael, no matter how it might pain me in the short term; instead, I'd work on what I had with my husband. Starting right at that moment.

'Shall we go to bed?' I asked him, a shake in my voice.

He nodded.

Quietly, in the darkness of our bedroom, we found each other. We didn't need the light on, we knew every curve and contour of each other's bodies. It felt strange, alien even, and I had to push down any feeling that I was betraying Michael by having sex with my husband. That was absurd.

This was how it should be.

We barely spoke. We barely made a sound, if the truth be told. Years of being aware of two children in the house had taught us to be quiet. We were out of practice with each other. Hesitant. I tried to remember the last time we'd had sex. It had been the winter. January, perhaps. Maybe earlier. I closed my eyes and tried to enjoy his touch, to remember the things he liked. How he liked to be touched.

It didn't quite work. We were trying, but it was perfunctory. Like awkward teenagers, not long-term lovers. When we were done, he rolled off me and onto his back, exhaling loudly. I curled up, fought the urge to turn away from him.

'It will get better,' he said. 'If we keep trying.'

I nodded in the darkness first before muttering a yes. Muttering, 'It will,' but wondering why we even had to try. Surely it should be natural between us after all these years.

I got out of bed and walked to the en suite to freshen up, switching on the light. I was just pulling my dressing gown from the back of the door, when I heard him say my name. I turned and looked at him, there in the half-light. He'd rolled onto his side, facing me, his right arm slung over the covers.

'I love you, Rachel,' he said.

I would have answered him, but I couldn't speak. The vivid red scratches on his right upper arm had caught my attention.

I walked into the bathroom and closed the door, stood with my back to it. I felt sick. Those scratches: three red-raw vivid lines from his shoulder down to his bicep looked like the kind of scratches fingernails might make.

I knew I hadn't been responsible for them. There wasn't a whiff of raw passion about what had just happened in our bed. I sat on the toilet, cold despite the heat in the room. Maybe it was ridiculous to feel a pull of betrayal in the pit of my stomach. In fact, I knew it *was* both ridiculous and hypocritical, but I felt it all the same. Those scratches, the way he'd been acting lately. Even the way he'd looked at me earlier. How he'd insisted on spending more and more time in Belfast – staying there during the week instead of doing the daily commute.

'It makes more sense,' he'd said. 'I can work late and when I come home on Thursdays or Fridays, you and the girls'll have me all to yourself all weekend.'

Except it had never quite worked out like that. I'd strayed; it wasn't beyond the realms of possibility that he could have strayed, too. I sat there, wondering if he'd fall asleep if I waited long enough. Knowing the alternative now was either to go back out there and pretend everything was normal, or open a can of worms I wasn't sure either of us wanted open.

I felt it like a punch to my stomach, the thought of him with another woman. The throes of passion so intense that she'd dig her nails into his flesh and mark him as hers.

What other logical explanation could there have been?

I felt something twist inside me. Something about the way he'd always looked at Clare. Something about the whispered conversations they'd had. Something from the pit of my stomach that had wondered if he really had been working late all those nights he said he was. If, indeed, he had been in Belfast. He could have been anywhere.

An echo from earlier:

'The person who did this would have sustained some injuries during the attack. There's evidence that Ms Taylor tried to defend herself . . .'

Saturday, 9 June

Chapter Fifteen

Elizabeth

I woke to the whimper of Izzy looking to get out into the yard. As I followed her down the stairs, I felt the wooden boards creak and bow underfoot. I'd still not had the seventh step from the bottom looked at properly after the fall. I'd just learned how to step around the dip where the wood had cracked under the weight of my body slamming against it. I knew I should probably get all of them looked at − one of a growing number of things I needed to get looked at in this old, rattling farmhouse.

If this house were a dog, it would have been put to sleep long ago on humanitarian grounds. I suppose I was scared of what might be found. Woodworm. Damp. Rot. Evidence of what had happened here. . .

Before she died, Laura had tried to convince me to sell up and move into the spare room of her spacious four-bed new-build in the Waterside. She kept a lovely home and there was no doubt I would have been made most welcome. I knew she hadn't just been saying it out of politeness; but no − this old farmhouse was my home. I'd spent my entire married life here, raised a family here, buried a husband from here. I'd not leave it until I was carried out in a box myself.

I never imagined I'd bury a daughter from here, too. Never imagined that my perfect family could be obliterated in such a short space of time. Paddy first. Then Laura. Then my son, Aaron, upping and leaving for a new life away from all the pain this house reminded him of. The ghosts of his sister and father were too much for him to take.

But on mornings like this one, when thoughts of all the things that were going wrong troubled me, I wondered if Laura had been right all along and I was, as she'd called me, a 'stubborn old goat who'd rather prove a point than be comfortable'.

If I closed my eyes I could still see the way she used to wrinkle her nose and purse her lips when she was angry; not that she ever was really angry. Passionate might be a better way to describe her. Determined. Would things have gone differently if I'd moved in with her like she wanted?

Each day, no matter how it started, seemed to bring my thoughts to her within moments. I liked it that way, even if it hurt. I feared for the day I'd wake up and she wouldn't be there, at the very centre of my existence.

After breakfast, I decided I'd make some more bread. I was still jittery after my visit to DI Bradley and the press conference declaring this unknown suspect to be dangerous hadn't helped. If I made bread, and lost myself for a bit in the kneading and knocking-back process, I could let the physical work of creating something distract me from everything that was running through my head.

Of course, Izzy wouldn't be happy with another day cooped up in the yard. She kept staring at the door and whining, a not-at-all subtle hint that she wanted a walk. I was nervous, though. I didn't want to walk those roads any more, but she caught me in her gaze – her big brown eyes pleading.

'Just a short walk, then,' I eventually conceded.

We wouldn't go far, just down the road a little. Let her have a runabout and then back in time for the dough to have proved. We set out just after ten, when I knew the roads would already have been well travelled and there'd be other people around. Izzy bounced around my heels as we made our way down the yard, past the old barn that no longer housed any animals or machinery, towards the gate.

At first I thought it was an old bin bag, blown by the wind to the gate, clinging onto the rusting metal's jagged edges. As I got closer I saw that it was something else, satin, black, tied to one of the gate's rails. There was something sickeningly familiar about it.

I called Izzy back to me and looked around for any sign that anyone was nearby, but all was silent bar the sound of my footsteps crunching on the gravel. I arrived at the gate and pulled it open towards me, my worst fears confirmed when I could clearly see a black bow – just like the one we'd hung on the gate when we were waking Laura from the farmhouse. At the centre of the bow, a bunch of wild flowers, forget-me-nots, tied with thick twine. My heart lurched. A small card, wrapped in cellophane, was pinned in one of the loops of the bow. I lifted it, read the four words neatly printed on it in black ink:

Laura sends her love.

I stumbled back as if I'd received a physical shock, an electric pulsing that knocked my heartbeat off rhythm. Everything became hazy. There was a buzzing in my ears, a screaming from deep inside me. Izzy jumped around my heels, desperate to walk on, but I wouldn't . . . couldn't.

Who'd done this? Why would someone have done this? I tore at the blasted bow, tried to haul it from the railing. It was tied too tightly. I pulled, tore at the string until it started to cut through the paper-thin skin of my palms, but still I persisted. There was no way I was leaving that horror hanging there at my gate.

Izzy whined and whimpered, and I shouted at her to leave me alone, realising I was crying and struggling to gain control of my breath. Panic was whipping around me, invading me. Was someone watching? Was this someone's idea of a sick joke? I looked at the ground, scuffed footprints in the gravel and dust. Indeterminable to my tired eyes.

I couldn't imagine how anyone could be so unconscionably cruel. Several of my nails broke on the rough iron of the gate as I pulled against the string and the rust until the bow came undone. Drops of my blood coloured the parched ground beneath, seeping into the dust. Even as I held the bow in my hands, I wanted to keep tearing. I wanted to throw it to the ground and stomp on it, to let Izzy toss it around like one of her toys, but I knew that wasn't the right thing to do. I knew I had to hold on to it and what . . . call the police maybe? Did they not have enough on their plate with the murder inquiry without dealing with someone leaving poison-pen letters at my house? But what if this was proof that I was at risk, after all? How was it DI Bradley had put it? If someone knew what Clare had said to me they might have wanted to keep me quiet.

I walked back home in a daze, a dejected Izzy at my heels. My tears still falling. None of this made sense. Laura had been dead for two years. Gone. Buried. I'd wake sometimes after nightmares about how decomposed she'd now be lying in that cold earth. At times, I had to physically restrain myself from clawing at the ground where she lay just to try to do something to save whatever was left of her. This – whoever did this – was monstrous.

As I slammed the back door closed behind me and walked

into the kitchen, throwing the macabre gift on the table, I picked up the phone to call DI Bradley. The flowers, so beautiful but so menacing wrapped in their mourning colours, taunted me.

Whoever had left them knew just how to get to me and just how to hurt me.

Chapter Sixteen

Rachel

I'd dressed in my gym gear early that following morning, whispered to Paul that I was going for a run, and was out of the house before he could wake. I drove to the walkway along the banks of the River Foyle, where the weekly park-run event set off from, but I knew I had no intention whatsoever of taking part.

I was exhausted. I'd barely slept. My body seemed to have been acutely aware of Paul beside me in the bed with his livid red scratches and his tousled hair and his deception. I'd spent the night clinging to the edge of the bed, reticent to touch him.

When I'd finally come out of the bathroom after we'd had sex, he'd put on his boxers and T-shirt, like he did every night before going to bed, and was sound asleep. I couldn't get another glance at the scratches and while a part of me wanted to shake him and ask him to explain himself, I held back. Had I been scared of where the conversation might have led? Perhaps, but I'd also been aware of the three glasses of wine swirling around in my stomach, my fuzzy head and my emotional exhaustion. In the cold light of the following morning I knew I'd been overdramatic, jumping from scratches on his arms to murder. It would be laughable if it weren't so serious.

But jumping from scratches to an affair? That wasn't overly dramatic at all, especially given that I'd slept with another man just two nights before. Given that I wasn't sure if I was falling dangerously in love with another man. A man who I'd told myself I'd push aside so I could work on my ailing marriage.

Just five years ago I'd have very confidently said Paul Walker would never, ever have an affair. But I'd have said the same of myself. Things change. We'd changed.

Sitting in my car, I watched the runners stretch and limber up in preparation for setting off on their race. I didn't envy them given the heat, but it appeared they didn't want to let anything deter them. I sipped from my coffee cup, the air-con on full in the car. I felt a little lost.

I knew I shouldn't, but I took my phone from my bag anyway and scrolled down until I got to Michael's number. I hit the call button and listened as it went straight to his voice-mail. I was surprised at just how disappointed I felt that it had. I scrolled up my phone until I saw Clare's name. I wondered whether the police had uncovered any information from her phone – were they any closer to catching who was responsible? I dialled her number, listened to her voice telling me to leave a message or, better still, to send a text because she never checked her voicemail.

I ached for her, in that moment. Wanted to say all the things I never had because you never think you're going to run out of time. Certainly not so quickly. So violently. You assume the world is good and kind. You assume bad things won't happen to the people you love. You assume these kind of things only happen on late night TV dramas.

A strange notion overcame me, and I put my phone and my coffee down, put the car into first gear and drove off.

★

The road had been reopened on Friday evening. You wouldn't have known driving along it that just three days before something so horrific had happened here. The faint buzzing of bees filled the air and a heat haze sat over the long grass of the fields. The tarmac road was dusty, the potholes long since dried up of their puddles of stagnant water.

I wasn't sure where on the long road she'd been found. I drove slowly, imagining what had been going through her mind as she'd driven down this road last. Had she known what was awaiting her? Did she know what this monster had intended to do? If it was, indeed, the man she'd been in a relationship with, did she know that he didn't love her, after all? That he was going to hurt her? I hoped she hadn't known until the very last minute. I hoped she'd been blissfully unaware: calm, not scared. I couldn't bear to think of her trying to scramble to safety.

I followed a small bend in the road and saw them. The Taylors, walking with their backs to me towards their car. At the side of the road, Ronan stood at a gap in the hedgerow, his head bowed, his eyes closed. I slowed the car, pulled over to the side, and waited for Mr and Mrs Taylor to set off before I switched off my engine and walked up to where Ronan stood.

I said his name softly, reached out and touched his shoulder. He turned to look at me.

'I just came for a drive,' I said. 'Felt the need to come past here. This . . . this is where it happened?'

He nodded, reached his arm out to me and pulled me close to him, and I slinked his arm around my waist as we stood side by side. I looked to the ground. There was nothing there to show that something so unthinkable had happened apart from a few bunches of flowers, some chalk circles not yet washed away. The smallest remnant of yellow police tape attached to a twig. I wondered if I should have brought some flowers myself. Felt foolish for not doing so. It hadn't even crossed my mind.

'My parents wanted to come up here. Wanted to lay flowers. I don't know why, really. I find it mawkish when people leave flowers at the scenes of a tragedy. It's not like the dead person is there. I don't want to think of any part of her here,' he said, his eyes not leaving the ground.

I looked at the flowers, a bouquet of lilies. A couple of supermarket bouquets. A posy of forget-me-nots, tied with thick twine, the stems wrapped in thick black satin, which looked out of place against the delicate light blue petals of the flowers.

Macabre, even. I had a bad feeling and despite the heat, I shuddered.

Chapter Seventeen

Rachel

I reached down and took Ronan's hand. 'Ronan, how did this happen? How did we get to this?'

I could feel him shake beside me.

'You must be running on empty,' I said. 'You know, you need to look after yourself now too, don't you? You'll run yourself into the ground . . .'

I'd no sooner said the words than I realised that they were grossly inappropriate in the circumstances.

Ronan looked at me, his face crumpled, and my heart sank until I realised he wasn't angry or horrified at my tactlessness but laughing. That hysterical, grotesque laugh that comes from grief and exhaustion. It was almost like a madness and I held him in a hug until he gave way to tears.

I held him until the shaking subsided and then I told him he really did need to get home and get a good rest.

'You're right,' he nodded. 'I've barely closed my eyes since this happened. I'm scared to let my mind wander and I want to be there for my parents.'

'You'll be no use to your parents if you burn yourself out. The best thing you can do for you, and them, and for Clare's memory right now is to look after yourself. Can you get some of those sedatives the doctor gave your parents? Take them, sleep away the afternoon?'

He nodded as another car pulled up further down the road and I heard the opening of their car door.

'More ghouls come to gawk,' he said. Is that what he thought of me? That I'd come to 'gawk'?

'Maybe they just want to pay their respects,' I said softly. 'None of us have been prepared to deal with any of this.'

He nodded, hugged me and walked off, a dejected figure, heading back to his car as I stood and watched him while a couple carrying another bunch of supermarket flowers walked towards me. Ronan was right, I thought, looking at the flowers on the dusty ground. Clare wasn't here. She should never have been reduced to this.

I crouched down to read the cards on the flowers. They were full of the usual trite phrases of condolence. There was a plain white card tucked into the ribbon around the forget-me-nots, wrapped in cellophane. I picked it up and read the words written in black ink:

Every action has consequences. Every inaction, too.

I blinked at it, confused. It gave me the creeps. I shuddered just as Ronan had done. What was it supposed to mean?

I heard a cough from the couple who were behind me, fought the urge to tell them to back off and give me space. Was I getting in the way of their rubbernecking? I stood up, wiped the tears from my eyes and walked back to my car, not so much as acknowledging them as I left, just letting the words I'd read play over and over in my head.

Taking a deep breath to settle myself, I picked up my phone and googled the phrase, trying to find some context. It seemed to be a bastardised version of a quote from the philosopher Jean-Paul Sartre, but it still didn't seem to make any sense when it came to Clare.

I pinched the bridge of my nose to fend off a headache. Then noticed a missed call was logged on my phone. I half expected it to be Paul, calling to ask when I'd be back. My stomach lurched when I saw it was from Michael and that he'd left a voicemail. My hands shaking, I put the phone to my ear and listened.

'Rachel, I'm so sorry. I've had all sorts of problems. Please call me back as soon as you can. I need to know you're not angry at me.'

This was the moment in which I could choose where I went from that point, if I'd do everything I'd promised myself just the night before, where I'd focus on my marriage and my family. I could ignore his call. He'd understand, eventually. It was in my power. But those promises had been made before I'd seen the scratches on Paul's arm. That changed everything. And hearing Michael's voice just confirmed that.

I called his number and he picked up within two rings. He didn't give me the chance to speak before he started talking, his words falling over each other.

'Rachel, I'm so sorry. I dropped my phone in the sink on Thursday and I couldn't get it to switch on. I had to stick it in a bowl of rice to dry it out. I didn't have your number to call you from another phone and my laptop's on the blink, so I couldn't even send you an email or a message.

'I got your message about the flowers just before it happened and I'm so sorry. I just wanted to do something. I watched the press conference and it's just beyond belief. I'm so sorry. What must you think of me, especially after Wednesday night? You probably thought I was the worst person in the world.'

He sounded so genuinely upset, I just closed my eyes and

let his voice soothe me. The knowledge that he hadn't been ignoring me, or huffing with me, came with such a sense of relief that I felt the need to see him as quickly as I could.

'Can I come and see you?' I asked.

'Of course you can. Can you come now?'

'I'll be with you in ten minutes,' I told him and we ended the call.

Even though I knew Paul would be expecting me home shortly, even though I knew the girls would be awake and wondering where I was, I selfishly needed to see Michael more than I did them, so I set off for his house.

I parked at the rear of Michael's house, aware that it was daytime and that my car could easily have been spotted by passing traffic. He was waiting for me at the back gate and quickly ushered me inside. I fought the magnetic urge to reach for his hand as we walked up the garden path, knowing we had to be careful. Once inside, I allowed him to pull me into a hug and, to my embarrassment, I started crying. He held me and rocked me as I let go of the tension I'd been carrying with me all morning.

He didn't make promises that it would be okay, only that he'd be here for me when I needed him. When I broke away from his embrace, he led me to his kitchen, where he sat me down and made a cup of tea. He fetched me a glass of water and some paracetamol for the headache that had just kicked in.

He listened as I told him about going to see where it had happened. About the bizarre note. He listened as I told him that I suspected Paul may be cheating on me.

'How would you feel – really feel – if he was?' Michael asked, his green eyes staring intently at me.

'I suppose it would be hypocritical to say I'd be hurt?' I said, knowing that it was.

Michael shrugged. 'I don't think it's hypocritical. You're allowed to be hurt. But would you be devastated? Do you, given everything, envisage yourself staying with him in the long term?'

This was a loaded question, of course – whatever answer I gave would have ramifications for Michael and me.

'I'm not sure what I think,' I told him.

He shifted in his seat as if my answer annoyed him.

'It's like there's so much going on in my brain at the moment – so much that I'm trying to process – that I don't know. . . my brain can't work anything out. I know we're broken,' I said, raising my eyes to his again. 'Paul and me. I know that there's probably no coming back from this, but my brain's too full of what's happened to Clare, wanting the police to catch her killer, wanting to get her body released and her home to her family . . . My brain's just so full of that to know how I truly feel about anything else.'

He sighed, looked downwards, brushing back a curl that had fallen across his forehead. 'I'm sorry. I know I'm expecting too much from you at the moment. I'm being selfish. The last thing I want to do is to cause you any more upset and stress. What we have is good, and it's fun and pure – I don't want it to make your life tougher.'

I reached out and took his hand, turned it over in mine and bent forwards, kissing the heel of his palm gently, breathing in his scent. 'It's not you who makes my life tougher,' I told him. 'You're the good thing. You're the positive.'

He put his hand to my cheek and I revelled in the feeling of it against my skin, closing my eyes to breathe him in. I felt the gentlest touch of his lips on mine and I was lost to him.

'It's been a long time since I've felt this way about anyone,' he said. 'If ever.'

My phone rang, a Nineties dance tune jerking us from the

intimacy of the moment. Julie was calling me. I grimaced at my phone where it sat with my car keys. I didn't want this interruption. Michael looked at it, then at me.

'It's Julie. You should answer. I imagine she needs you a lot right now.'

I knew he was right, so I answered to hear her, almost hysterical, on the other end of the line.

'Rachel, have you seen the news? Brendan showed me. It's in the paper . . . It says that someone slit Clare's throat so deep they almost cut her head off . . .'

At that I could hear her start to hyperventilate.

'Rachel . . .' she gulped. 'Is . . . that . . . true? Did someone do that? Is that what . . . happened? Rachel!'

I listened as my friend retched and vomited on the other end of the phone. The taste of bile was in my own mouth. Instinctively, I put my hand to my throat. I didn't even have to try to imagine the horror – an image was there in my head. Clare gasping for breath. A knife. Jesus Christ! This man was an animal.

'I'll be with you in ten minutes,' I stuttered, hanging up. 'I have to go,' I told Michael. 'Some newspaper has printed horrific details of what happened to Clare. I've no idea if it's true. Jesus! I hope it's not true. Julie's beside herself.'

'I understand,' Michael said, standing up. 'You have to go. This has to come first for now. Look, maybe we should just take a break. I don't mean stop altogether, but just put it all on pause until this settles. I need you, but others need you more.'

I blinked at him, trying to comprehend what was happening. Was he calling a halt to whatever this was because I was going to help my hysterical friend? Because I was choosing her need over his? He looked away from me and I asked myself had he just been lying to me all along – broken phones and battered laptops, and never feeling like this about anyone else, but *let's just hit the pause button*? I didn't need this game-playing. Or whatever it was.

I didn't trust myself to respond, so I simply grabbed my keys and walked out of the back door, leaving it swinging behind me.

If he called after me, I didn't hear him. All I could hear was my blood rushing through my body and the echoes of Julie's hysteria as she relayed to me what she'd read.

Chapter Eighteen

Elizabeth

It was Constable King and a male colleague who arrived at my door and not DI Bradley as I'd hoped.

'Mrs O'Loughlin,' she said, taking off her hat to reveal a short pixie haircut before reaching out to shake my hand. 'I hear you've had a bit of trouble. This is my colleague, Constable Mark Black. Can we come in?'

I nodded and led them through to the kitchen, where the funereal bow and flowers were sitting on the kitchen table, mocking me. The card that stated that my deceased daughter sent her love was beside them.

Both officers looked at the items before Constable Black produced an evidence bag in which to take them away.

'This must be very distressing for you,' Constable King said. 'And you noticed this first thing this morning?'

'When I was taking the dog for a walk, yes,' I said. 'It was tied to the gate down at the road's edge.'

'And you hadn't been aware of anyone around the house at all during the night? Had you had any visitors at all?'

I shook my head. 'No. I heard nothing and saw nothing. That bloody security light is out. I keep meaning to get it fixed.

But, no, I saw nothing. Not until this morning. I thought it was just a black plastic bag blown onto the railings.'

'And do you have any idea who might have done this, or why?' she asked, her pen poised above her notebook ready to write.

I shook my head again. My arm ached. My right hand was still throbbing after pulling the flowers from the gate. I'd cleaned it up the best I could, dressed the cuts. I must have looked a right sight – two dodgy arms? That was all I needed. I was more useless than ever before.

'No. I don't understand why anyone would be so cruel.'

'When you called this in, you told our dispatcher the items had special significance. That you believe the Laura mentioned in the note is your late daughter. What of the other items?'

'The arrangement is identical to the one we hung on the gate at Laura's wake,' I said, trying to push memories of that awful week out of my head.

I didn't have the mental energy to allow my brain to go there – to relive those horrors – just then.

'Forget-me-nots were Laura's favourite flowers. Her eyes were the same colour . . .'

Constable King nodded sympathetically while Constable Black sat at the table and looked on. I wondered what they made of me – this lonely older woman, living out here on my own. I wanted to tell them that it wasn't always that way. This used to be a happy home. I'd had a husband who loved me until the day and hour a heart attack took him from me. A daughter . . . a son . . .

A mobile phone rang and Constable Black lifted his from his pocket, said he had to answer it and walked out of the back door into the yard.

'Has anything of this nature happened before? At any time following Laura's death?'

I shook my head. 'Do you think it has something to do with that poor girl's murder?' I asked. 'DI Bradley said I wasn't in any danger, that no one knew I was with her when she died and that I'd heard her last words.'

'We've no reason to believe that at the moment,' Constable King said, 'but it's one of the lines of inquiry we'll be looking at.'

I felt uneasy. Vulnerable.

'Try not to worry too much,' Constable King said. 'It could be someone with a very warped sense of humour, but rest assured that we're taking this very seriously and we'll act accordingly, putting on extra patrols in this area. I'll talk to the DI, see what he thinks.'

Constable Black walked back in, his tall frame almost filling the doorway. He looked at me first before walking to his colleague.

'The boss wants us to check out the crime scene again,' he said. 'They've had reports of an unusual floral arrangement left on the ground.'

He looked nervous, as if there was something he was holding back, but I wasn't stupid. I didn't even need to ask about the unusual floral arrangement, especially when his eyes darted to the evidence bag on the table and then back to Constable King.

'I wonder, Mrs O'Loughlin, do you have anyone who could come and stay with you, or is there somewhere you'd feel comfortable going to stay just until all this blows over? It might make you feel a little more secure,' Constable King said.

'You think it's someone connected to that poor woman's death, don't you?' I asked, my chest feeling tighter.

'We can't say that at the moment,' she said. 'But it certainly won't hurt to be more vigilant until we rule that out entirely. And maybe get that security light fixed.'

I didn't want to feel scared in my home any more. I didn't

want to step away from the quiet and easy routine I had for myself here. It was far from perfect and I'd had to work hard to get used to living alone, but it was my home and for all its faults, I loved it. It held a lot of difficult memories, of course, but also so many happy ones.

Pictures hung on the walls of more innocent, happier times. They reminded me that I hadn't always got it so wrong. We'd been happy. Our family unit had been untouchable back then. I couldn't imagine walking away from this place, but nor could I deny I was scared or that I'd feel better if I wasn't alone. The problem was, I didn't exactly have a queue of people waiting to come and stay with me. Selling it to them on the basis that a killer might have left me a creepy note, never mind the fact that the house was in growing need of repair, would be a hard task.

Constable King must have seen the look on my face.

'I'm going to speak to DI Bradley about this as soon as I get back to base and we'll see what we can do to offer you all the support you need.'

I smiled, grateful for her kindness.

'How long ago did your daughter pass away?' she asked.

'Two years ago,' I said. 'Still feels like yesterday in some ways and in others it feels like it's been decades since I saw her.'

'I'm very sorry. It must be terribly hard. It's true what they say that no parent should have to bury a child. May I ask, had she been ill?'

I shook my head. 'I'm surprised you aren't aware of her case, or you weren't made aware. No, it wasn't an illness as such. She took her own life.'

Constable King couldn't quite hide the look of shock from her face.

'Oh,' she said. 'I'm very sorry to hear that. That must be very difficult.'

'It is,' I said, knowing that 'very difficult' was a massive understatement.

It came out of nowhere. Or at least I think it seemed to. There were none of the signs. She hadn't sat down and told me she was feeling particularly depressed or that she wanted to harm herself. She didn't seem demotivated. She hadn't given away possessions. It had never felt like she was saying goodbye. She'd had her problems over the years, of course. We'd worked hard – supported her through CBT and NLP and group therapy. I thought she was okay. I thought she'd beaten it. Finally.

She'd appeared to be stable when it happened. I'd actually thought she was finally beating it all, that she'd put her demons to rest once and for all, and that she was moving onwards and upwards. It had been months, if not more, since she'd spoken to me about low moods. She'd seemed happier than she'd ever been.

Of course, I was told afterwards that I'd been blind to her moods. That it was easier for me to think she was okay. Those words hurt. They were so unforgivable that they took what was left of my family and tore it utterly asunder.

As far as I was aware, one day I'd had my daughter, sitting with her two children in my kitchen, talking about any old nonsense – Christmas, school shoes, what we'd watched on TV the night before – and the following night she was gone.

Her husband had come home to find the two children sitting in front of the TV. There was no sign of Laura. The children, Ava and Max, were only seven and nine. She wouldn't have left them on their own. She never did before. They told their daddy that Mummy had gone to the shops and she'd left him a note in the kitchen.

He'd imagined she'd be home soon. The shop was a five-minute drive. Even given heavy traffic and queues at the checkout, he'd figured she'd be back any minute. So he busied himself fixing his dinner and looking after the kids, and all but forgot about Laura's note.

But the minutes ticked on.

'How long ago did Mummy go?' he asked the kids.

They shrugged. Her eldest, my granddaughter, Ava, told her daddy it was 'just after we finished homework', adding, 'she's been gone a long time, Daddy, hasn't she?'

That's when he went into the kitchen and opened the note. He admitted to me after that he thought it might have been a Dear John. Although she hadn't said anything to me, he'd said they'd been having a few problems. She'd seemed cold and distant. He'd wondered if she was having an affair.

My Laura would never have had an affair.

He couldn't take in the words he was reading at first, he told me. They didn't make any sense. The writing didn't even look like hers. There was something off about it. 'Too jaggy,' he'd said. 'There were rips across the paper, as if she'd scrawled really heavily,' he'd said. His brain couldn't process what he was reading. She was sorry. She'd had no choice. She didn't want to hurt the children any more. She didn't want to risk them growing up to become how she was. Weak. Stupid. Ugly.

My Laura was none of those things.

She'd never been any of those things.

She'd wished she'd had the courage to do this a long time ago, but she'd been too cowardly. And she'd wanted to see if she could change. If she could fix things. Become likeable and loveable.

How that broke me. My darling, darling Laura was always likeable and she was the most loveable creature who'd ever roamed the Earth. My life had been completed the day she was first placed in my arms – the love I felt for her was the purest, most powerful force in the world. I thought I'd known love with Aaron, had worried through my pregnancy that I wouldn't find enough extra love for a new baby, but when she was here, it was almost as if my heart grew. I had love enough for both of them. But she was the icing on the cake and I adored her, perhaps even more than I had Aaron. As he'd grown, connected with his father, I'd been left out of their games. But Laura, she was my girl. My best friend. My everything.

But it hadn't been enough to save her.

'Tell my mum that I love her and she's not to blame herself. There's nothing she could have done to fix me,' the letter had read, and I was angry then. She should have given me the chance. She should have let me try to fix her. Not that I ever thought she needed fixing. To me, she was perfection.

She'd left instructions. Told him to call the police. Told him not to go after her himself. She'd told him where she'd be. She'd asked him to forgive her. She'd asked him to tell the children she'd got sick and died. 'It's the truth, after all,' she'd written. 'A part of me has always been sick.'

He'd called the police. He did go after her. He'd bundled the kids into the neighbour's house and he drove as fast as traffic would allow until he'd reached the place she said she'd be. He drove his car as far as he could, not overly familiar with the site, and then he'd run in the dark and the rain, the torch on his phone guiding the way, trying to find her. He could hear the sirens of the police and ambulance approach, but on he ran.

Until he found her. But she was gone.

It was too late. There was nothing anyone could have done to fix her then.

I try not to think about what he saw, but it haunts me in the night. Just as the image of her in the morgue haunts me. She'd taken no chances. She'd hung herself from some old railings and she'd also slashed her wrists. She'd taken some time to die, the pathologist believed. Strangled. No quick break of her neck.

Her husband had tried to lift her, even though he knew it was too late. Police arrived to him covered in his wife's blood, holding her up by the legs, screaming at her to come back.

I'd learned very quickly that it didn't matter how much anyone screamed, Laura wasn't coming back. I'd never see her again and I'd never really understand why my beautiful girl believed that she was so broken she no longer deserved a place in this world.

Chapter Nineteen

Rachel

I was still in some sort of shock about what had just happened with Michael when I arrived at Julie's. At least, I thought with a grimace, it distracted in some small way from what Julie had told me on the phone. I noticed Brendan's car wasn't outside and the front door was ajar.

When I walked in she was sitting on the sofa, smoking. She looked as if she hadn't slept since we'd left the Taylors. She was still in pyjamas, despite it having gone eleven, and her hair was tangled and knotted at the top of her head. There was a mug of tea sitting on the coffee table in front of her, but there was also a quarter bottle of vodka, with its distinctive red lid unscrewed, sitting beside a glass with ice.

Julie must have noticed me looking at it.

'You don't need to worry. I'm not turning into an alcoholic. The sweet tea just wasn't working for the shock and I'm not sleeping. Are you sleeping? I just can't and then this . . .'

The front pages of several newspapers were scattered all over the sofa, all open at different pages about the murder. On top was a tabloid paper, *The Chronicle*, splashed with pictures from Clare's Facebook page with the headline 'Police hunt "ripper" killer' in red, the only slightly smaller subheading declaring 'Woman "almost decapitated" in brutal Derry slaying'.

Julie jabbed at the page; I noticed her nail varnish was chipped, her hand shaking. She took a long drag on her cigarette and looked back at me.

'Is it true? They wouldn't have printed it if it wasn't true, would they? I can't. . . I can't even think. She was alive for a while after the attack. So it can't be true. Oh, God, what if she wasn't unconscious? What if she knew?'

Julie was almost manic, her words falling over each other. Her thoughts forming quicker than her words and rushing to get out.

'Why would they say that? The police didn't say that to us. Ronan didn't say it. Who told the newspaper? It says "a source close to the investigation",' she read, her fingers still jabbing at the newsprint. 'I always thought that meant it was a lie, but this is too serious. Why would they make her death so salacious? That same "source" said there was evidence she'd had sex on the night she was killed. Why would they print that? That's nobody's business. What'll her parents think? Why won't they leave her alone? Maybe I'll ring this journalist and ask her. This Ingrid Devlin,' she said, looking at the picture byline, 'she might tell me.'

I realised I hadn't spoken a single word, just listened to Julie rant and rave, crying as she recounted what she'd read and how she felt about it. I suppose the truth of it was that our friend didn't just belong to us any more. She was a headline. A story. A victim. Would she always be looked at that way? Would how she died now define her more than everything she'd been to everyone in her life? Now, she'd be remembered as a victim first and foremost.

I glanced at the gaudy headline, the pictures of Clare, drink in hand and grinning at the camera. Painting her as some sort of party girl. Without even thinking about it, I swept the papers to the floor and trampled on them.

'This is just shit to sell papers,' I said to Julie. 'It's just shit.'

I sat down beside her, realising I was crying, too. Not hysterically like Julie but, nonetheless, my face was wet and I felt as if a knot of tension or grief or anger wanted to escape from my body in shuddering sobs.

'Give me one of your cigarettes,' I said to Julie.

It was enough to make her take a breath and look at me, her eyes narrowing.

'You've not smoked since we were sixteen.'

'I don't care. It's either a cigarette or the vodka and I've got to drive home to the kids, so the cigarette's safer. Give me one.'

She fumbled with the white-and-blue packet in front of her and handed me a cigarette. Gingerly, my own hand shaking, I lifted it to my lips and inhaled as Julie helped me light. The hot smoke caught at the back of my throat, making me cough and shudder.

'Jesus! this is vile,' I said to Julie as I tried, and failed once again, to inhale the smoke deeply.

She looked at me, I looked at her. Then I put my cigarette down in the ashtray and pulled her into a hug.

'What are we going to do without her?' I cried.

'I don't know,' Julie mumbled. 'I don't even know where to start.'

'I think we start by throwing these papers in the bin where they belong,' I said, reaching down and lifting them before folding them and carrying them out to the recycling bin.

It was only as I walked back in that I noticed the bouquets of flowers in vases on the kitchen table. All still wrapped in their cellophane. Among them, stems wrapped in black ribbon, was a posy of forget-me-nots, a familiar-looking small white card pinned to the ribbon. That uneasy feeling was back, but this time it was stronger.

'Who are the flowers from?' I asked, trying to keep my voice steady as I walked back into the living room.

Julie was staring at the bottom of her mug. She didn't look up.

'People from work. My sister . . . I don't know really, Brendan's been taking care of them. I've not even had the energy to look. I just told Brendan to put them in water. They're not going to do much good, are they? They're not going to bring her back.'

I lifted the posy of forget-me-nots, the satin-wrapped arrangement.

'This one's unusual,' I said. 'Do you know who sent it?'

'No . . . I didn't look. Why do you ask?'

'Well, it's just quite unusual and there was something similar left up at the spot in the road where Clare died. It stood out from the other tributes.'

Julie shrugged her shoulders. 'Read the card if you want.'

She put her mug back down and lit another cigarette.

I unpinned the card from the flowers and read it. Again, a message was written in blue ink. Again, something cryptic.

'Let me see,' Julie said, looking at the card and reading from it. 'Three green bottles, hanging on a wall. And if one green bottle should accidentally fall . . .' Julie looked at me, eyes narrowed in confusion. 'What the hell's that supposed to mean?'

I looked around, saw the chaos where we were sitting – in what was usually a pristinely kept home – and I saw how manic and near the edge Julie was. She'd spiral further if I told her what the note had said at the roadside, but I knew I couldn't ignore it. This was something dark. I didn't know why, but I was sure it was no coincidence that Julie had received an identical arrangement to the one left where Clare had died.

'Who brought these?' I asked, without answering her question.

My heart was thudding. I looked out of the window as if there was a chance I'd spot someone waiting in the distance. The glare of the midday sun caught my eyes and made them water.

'I've no idea. Sorry. I've not exactly been coping,' Julie said, 'as you can see.' She gestured around the room, to the chaos evident on every surface. 'Brendan took the kids out because he said he needed a break from it all. I promised him I'd try and do something . . . but that was before I saw the papers.'

She leant forwards and poured a generous measure of vodka into her glass.

'I don't like this,' I mumbled.

The sense of unease I'd been feeling had started to slip into panic. The words of that stupid rhyme playing over and over again in my head. Counting down until there were no green bottles left.

'I'm old enough to drink if I want to,' Julie bit back.

For a second I was pulled from my thoughts. Confused.

'I'm not talking about your drinking, Julie. I'm talking about these flowers. That note.'

She started to sing the words, swaying her vodka glass. She was more drunk than I'd thought.

'Some silly nonsense,' she added. 'God, do you remember when people used to sing that to us when we were at school?' she laughed, a hollow laugh. 'God, we thought things were so hard then. Little did we know. To be a wee "green bottle" again . . .'

It was a nonsensical nickname, based solely on the green of our uniform. Our green pinafores. The heavy gabardine of our school coats that covered us from the knee up in voluminous bottle green. Sometimes it came with a gentle shove from the singer, just to see what would happen if we did 'accidentally fall'.

It was harmless.

It had been harmless.

But now one of my very solid group of three friends had become just two. One of us was gone. . .

I felt my stomach contract, a wave of sickness not just from the stale cigarette smoke wash over me. I drew in a breath.

'Julie, there was an identical arrangement left at the side of the road where Clare died.'

'So someone got a job lot,' she said.

'No,' I told her. 'No. Those words, Julie. Don't you get it?' My hands were shaking now. I wanted to shake Julie from her drunkenness and get her to understand. 'Someone's trying to frighten us. That note, the one left at the side of the road. That's not what you write to offer condolences. That's there to scare us. The other note said something about consequences . . .'

I glanced out of the window, saw a lone figure, jeans and a hoodie, hood pulled up to cover his face – clothes that were much too heavy for this weather. I fought the urge to pull the curtains. Or shout at him. I relaxed only when he walked past, not so much as casting a glance at Julie's house.

'I'm phoning the police,' I said.

Chapter Twenty

Rachel

There was something about the way the young policewoman looked at the flowers then nodded to her tall colleague that told me I'd been right to call them. This was no simple coincidence, or someone trying to wind us up.

'And when did these arrive?' Constable King asked.

Julie, who'd pulled on some yoga pants and a loose sweater, and who'd thankfully pulled a comb through her hair, wrung her hands. 'I phoned my husband. He thinks it arrived this morning. I was in bed. I didn't even look at it until Rachel arrived.'

She lifted her glass and drank some more. The ice clinked and clattered as her hand shook. She was just as spooked as I was.

'And, Rachel,' the policewoman, turning to look at me, said, 'what drew you to these flowers and the cards?'

'I was up at Coney Road this morning. I'd seen an identical arrangement where Clare was found. The card with it was bizarre. The wording, I mean. I was sure I was just being overly dramatic, given what's happened, but when I saw the flowers here, too . . .'

'We *are* just being overcautious, aren't we?' Julie asked, her eyes wide.

She, and I, needed the police to tell us that yes, of course we were being completely overcautious and there was nothing to worry about.

'That's possible,' Constable King replied unconvincingly. 'But I think we should take these and the card for examination all the same. And perhaps you can get your husband to call us. Just to see if he can fill us in on any details about the delivery.'

'Is that really necessary?' Julie asked.

'At the moment we're looking at a number of lines of inquiry,' Constable King said, which of course told us nothing that we didn't already know. She turned to me. 'Have you received anything like this?'

I shook my head. 'No, nothing like that all.'

'But you've been out all morning, you said,' Julie interjected. 'Maybe something's been delivered and you just don't know about it.'

She was right, of course, so I agreed to call home and ask Paul. I hoped he'd tell me no. I felt as if I couldn't breathe while I waited for the phone to be answered. I wasn't expecting Molly's baby voice to pick up.

'Mammy! When will you be home? I miss you a hundred and a million and can we go swimming or to the library?'

The sound of her voice didn't soothe me as it normally did – everything about her was pure and innocent and I couldn't help but feel it was all under threat.

'Hi, baby,' I said, trying my very best to keep my voice normal. 'I'll be home in a bit and sure, we can make some plans then. Is Daddy there?'

She didn't answer. I could just hear the sound of her feet running across the wooden flooring in the hall down to the kitchen and her calling 'Daadddeee, Mammy's on the phone.'

'Paul, this might sound a little strange,' I said as soon as he picked up, 'but have any flowers arrived for me this morning?'

'As it happens, yes,' he said and my heart sank.

I nodded at Constable King and saw Julie put her head in her hands from the corner of my eyes.

'A bunch of blue flowers; they look like wild flowers. Is there something you want to tell me?' he said with a false-sounding laugh. 'Have you a bit on the side or a secret admirer?'

'Are they tied with ribbon?' I asked, ignoring his question.

'No. Well, sort of. They're tied with twine and then some black ribbon. I'd say whoever paid for these hasn't the best taste in florists.'

I sat down, my legs shaky beneath me. I asked him if there was a card attached and if he could read it to me. I waited until he spoke.

'Well, this is a nonsense,' he said.

'What does it say?'

'It's some stupid rhyme or something . . .'

'What does it say, Paul?'

'Everything is a source of fun. Nobody's safe, we care for none.'

I lifted a pen from the coffee table and scribbled the words on the back of an envelope.

'Rachel, what's going on?' Paul asked. 'What's all this about?'

'It's to do with Clare. I don't know exactly what it means, but, look, I've to talk to the police. I'll talk to you when I get home.'

When I hung up, I looked at the expectant faces of Julie, Constable King and her colleague.

'There was a rhyme in mine, too, but it's not green bottles. I don't know what it is.'

I repeated the words Paul had read down the phone to me. Julie and Constable King looked at me blankly. Her colleague,

Constable Black, a sturdily built man at least six feet in height, cleared his throat and spoke.

'It's *The Mikado*. The opera? Gilbert and Sullivan. You know, the one that goes "Three little maids from school are we"?' He sang the words to the song in a falsetto voice that seemed at extreme odds with his appearance.

On any other occasion it would have made me laugh – the sight of this tall, well-built man in uniform singing about being a schoolgirl. But this didn't make me laugh. Julie and I had received these flowers. Another bunch had been left where Clare died. And two of the messages made vague references to our schooldays – our group of three. I felt tears prick at my eyes. Heard Julie mutter: 'Oh, God. . .'

'I think we need to bring this to the immediate attention of the DI,' Constable King said.

'Is whoever did this coming for us?' Julie asked, her eyes wide.

Constable King shook her head, but I could tell she wasn't convinced.

'It's important that we all try to keep calm now,' she said. 'Things like this, they bring all sorts of weirdos out of the woodwork. There's nothing to say it was the killer who left these – it could just be someone's idea of a sick joke, someone with a grudge.'

She looked at me and I tried to think who, if anyone, might have a grudge against us. We weren't the kind of people to make enemies. We lived our lives. We'd spent most of the last couple of years just trying to hold on against the trauma of Clare's marriage breaking up, my mother dying. . . I shook my head. Julie just looked at me, as if she needed me to tell her it was all going to be okay. But I couldn't. Could I? The knot in the pit of my stomach grew tighter, heavier. I thought I might be sick.

Constable King left the room to call her superior officer while Constable Black perched uncomfortably on the edge of an armchair.

Julie spoke first.

'I need to call Brendan. Get him to take the kids to his mum's. Should I go to his mum's, too? Or what if that puts us all in danger?'

She was spiralling again. I didn't blame her. I may have held onto the appearance of being calm on the outside, but inside my heart was thudding and I was asking myself the same questions she was. I told her I didn't know, because I didn't. Should I be on the phone to Paul just now to ask him to take the girls away from the house? The thought of someone harming them made me feel physically sick.

It wasn't ideal, but maybe he could take them to his flat in Belfast. There were two bedrooms, so the girls could share. Beth wouldn't be happy sharing her space with a three-year-old, but surely they'd be safe there? If I spoke to Beth's school, I'm sure they'd understand. Maybe I could get her to attend classes in Belfast for a while. Just until this all blew over. Was I over-reacting? I didn't care if I was, because I didn't want to take a chance – not with my girls. Not after reading those details in the paper.

'Is it true?' I asked Constable Black.

'Is what true?' he replied.

'The reports in the papers today. In *The Chronicle*. The report about how Clare died. The horrific injuries. A "source close to the investigation" told that Ingrid Devlin woman all those horrible details.'

Constable Black shifted uncomfortably in his seat. A thin layer of sweat had formed at his hairline. I felt sorry for him in this heat – in full uniform, the only concession to the weather being a short-sleeved shirt.

'I'm not in a position to comment on that,' he said, his face blazing a little.

'Maybe I'll call her and ask,' I said just as Constable King walked back into the room.

'Call who and ask?'

'Ingrid Devlin at *The Chronicle*. Ask her if it's true about how Clare died. That she was almost decapitated.'

'I wouldn't advise that you speak to the press at the moment,' Constable King said. 'I'm sure you understand that the investigation team want to make sure that the release of information to the press is handled sensitively and in a way that benefits our work.'

'Then you should tell your sources to keep their mouths shut,' Julie said, wringing her hands. 'I don't know what to think, or what to do. And I don't know why we're receiving these notes. Or why they're mentioning our schooldays. It's more than twenty years ago, for God's sake.'

'And no one from then would be holding on to a grudge?'

I shook my head, noticed that Julie, too, was shaking hers. The very notion was absurd. Who carries a grudge around for more than twenty years? It made no sense, but regardless of that, our schooldays weren't particularly noteworthy.

'We weren't anything special in school. We weren't trendy enough to be in the popular cliques and we weren't moody enough to hang out with the cool girls – the goths and the rockers,' I said.

'We just did our thing. Hung out together. Nothing to report at all,' Julie added.

Constable King nodded. 'Okay. Look, ladies, we're going to get forensics to look at these flowers. I've spoken to DI Bradley and we'll be putting an extra police presence in your areas. We'd like you to contact us immediately should anything out of the ordinary happen. Even if it seems inconsequential. I'll give you both a direct line through to the incident room, which'll guarantee you won't have to wait to speak to someone. I know this must all seem a bit overwhelming just now, but we remain hopeful that we'll catch whoever is responsible.'

I can't say that either Julie or I felt comforted at all by her words.

Paul was on edge by the time I got home. He was standing in the kitchen chopping vegetables to make a stew, but the manner in which he wielded the knife was very much like those poor vegetables had personally offended him. The loud thud of the blade as it hit the wooden chopping board over and over made my head hurt.

'You've had an eventful morning, then,' he said. It wasn't a question.

'Paul, we need to talk,' I said.

'Talk away,' he said, turning his back to me to start throwing some of the vegetables into the pot bubbling on the stove.

'Paul, this is really serious. I need your attention,' I said.

He turned and glared at me for a moment. 'What is it now, Rachel? You know, I thought we were getting somewhere last night. Then you sneak out at first light this morning, gallivant around the place and wander back in here now with a face like thunder on you, demanding I stop what I'm doing because you need to talk to me now. Well, maybe it doesn't suit me right now.'

He lifted the knife and started chopping a carrot. The repetitive thump of the blade made me jump. I closed my eyes, tried to squeeze away the headache that had been building over the last few hours.

'This isn't about whether it suits you or not. This is about our girls. About us.'

He stopped chopping and sighed. 'One of those big, serious conversations, then. God, Rachel, do we have to start pulling everything apart again?'

He was right that any time we'd been in a room together recently we'd ended up having a serious conversation, which inevitably seemed to turn into a row, but this was different, which was just what I told him.

'The police will be here shortly to pick up those flowers,' I said. He raised an eyebrow.

'For forensic examination. Julie got a similar display and one was left at Coney Road. All had weird messages.'

'And?' He shrugged, lifted the knife and started cutting again.

I wanted to scream at him to stop. How could he not see how serious this was?

'They can't rule out a link between the flowers and Clare's murder. They can't rule out, yet, that her killer sent them – that he might have some grudge against us, too.'

He put the knife down, looked straight at me as if waiting for a punchline. 'Are you actually serious?' he said.

'Of course I'm serious!' I snapped. 'I'd hardly joke about something like this, would I? The police are putting on extra patrols. They've given me a direct line to the incident room in case anything happens.'

He visibly blanched. 'Why would anyone have anything against you three? Come on,' he said with a hollow laugh.

He was trying to lighten the mood, detract from the fear he was feeling, but it just angered me more.

'I don't bloody know!' I said. 'I wish I did. No, I wish none of this was happening, but it is. And I'm scared. Julie's barely holding it together. Ronan's like a broken man – it's devastating. We don't know what to do.'

'When did you see Ronan?' he asked as if that was the most important part of what I'd just told him.

'I drove up Coney Road and he was at the site of Clare's death. That's where I saw the flowers that had been left there.'

'Did he ask you to meet him there?'

'Of course not. He just happened to be there. He'd taken his parents up. But that's not important, Paul. It's important that we do what we have to, to make sure we're all safe, the girls in particular.'

He shook his head. 'I've no idea why you'd want to put yourself through going up there, Rachel. It's like you're revelling in the horror of it.'

He lifted the knife and started chopping again. I wanted to snatch it from his hand.

'We're in the middle of the horror of it!' I shouted. 'We could be at risk, Paul. How many times do I have to say it before it sinks into your head? And I'm sorry if all this is taking over our lives at the moment – Clare was one of my best friends, I've known her longer than I've known you. She's been a part of my life for thirty years. Do you think I should just get over that? Did you even see the paper today? The horrific details Ingrid Devlin printed in *The Chronicle*? That whoever did it cut her throat so deeply that they almost decapitated her? Do you think it's okay to subject the girls to that kind of risk? And what about me? Are you happy knowing it could be your wife that's next?' I was shouting now to drown out the repetitive slam of the knife blade against the block.

I was shouting so loud that I hadn't heard Beth come down the stairs and walk into the room. It was only when I heard her wail 'Mu-um!' that I looked around to see her pale face, her eyes open wide in shock. 'That's not true, is it? Mum?'

'For Christ's sake!' I heard from Paul behind me.

I turned to look at him, saw the sharp end of the knife pointing directly at me.

'Just look what you've done now!' he yelled.

I stared at him, the silence stretching between us. I didn't know how to react or what to say. The phone rang. We both looked at each other for a moment before I turned and picked it up. It was Ronan.

'Rachel,' he said. 'The police have been on to us asking about any unusual floral arrangements. They said some of Clare's friends had received something strange. Have you?'

I turned my back to Paul and walked out of the room, cradling the phone to my ear. 'Yes. Julie and I both have.'

'Like the ones left at the roadside? The forget-me-nots?'

'Yes, with a strange note.'

'We received some, too,' he said. 'Some garbled eye-for-an-eye type message on it.'

I sat down on the sofa. How was it possible that this nightmare kept getting worse?

Chapter Twenty-One

Elizabeth

The rattle of the door-knocker just after 8 p.m. made me jump and sent Izzy into a barking frenzy. Normally I'd have laughed and told her to calm down, but I was on edge, too. People didn't routinely call to my door without letting me know they were coming to visit.

Nonetheless, I managed to quiet Izzy down and walked to the front of the house, to the formal front door – which was really more ornamental than anything, as most people came in through the kitchen door.

I put my eye to the peephole and saw a glamorous-looking woman – her no-doubt designer sunglasses pushed to the top of her smooth blonde bob. She fumbled through her green leather handbag and pulled out a notebook and pen.

When I opened the door, she thrust one hand out to shake mine.

'I'm so very sorry to bother you, especially given the hour,' she said, her face tilted to one side, her tone abjectly apologetic. 'I'm Ingrid Devlin, from *The Chronicle*.'

'Can I see ID?' I asked.

She looked a little shocked to be asked but reached into her bag and took out her purse, pulling out a blue National Union of Journalists membership card, which confirmed her credentials.

I eyed her suspiciously. 'What can I do for you, Ms Devlin?'

'Look, my sources have led me to believe you may have been with Clare Taylor when she died. That you may have been the woman who called for help.'

'Your sources?' I asked. 'And who might they be?'

I'd been assured my details hadn't left the incident room at Strand Road and wouldn't go beyond the four walls of the Taylor house.

'I'm not at liberty to say,' she said, 'but I do know you visited the Taylor household on Friday.'

'And? Is a woman not allowed to pass on her condolences any more?' I was on edge; Ingrid Devlin's presence on my doorstep wasn't a welcome one.

'Of course,' she said sweetly. 'And it's very kind of you to do so. I'm sure the entire experience has been exceptionally traumatic for you.'

I wanted to say something but feared that if I did, I'd say too much. I'd let slip something that would confirm what her 'sources' had told her.

'I think the Taylor family are the people experiencing trauma here – and I'm just as sure reporters knocking on doors asking questions probably doesn't help them, either.'

'Oh, goodness, absolutely. And I certainly wouldn't pressurise that poor family into talking. But you must know, Mrs O'Loughlin, that people are scared out there. This is a particularly nasty murder.'

The sun was shining in my eyes and I put my hand up to shield my face.

'I can see you're getting blinded by the light there, Mrs O'Loughlin. Maybe if I came in we could talk inside over a cup of tea or a glass of cold water. I'm roasting today in this heat. And, of course, our chat could be off the record, if you want. You don't have to tell me anything you don't want to.'

She was so saccharine sweet that my teeth hurt just listening to her. I'd seen her type before. Many times. Never trusted any of them.

'You're absolutely right,' I said and she moved to take a step inwards. I put my arm out to stop her. 'You're absolutely right. I don't have to tell you, or anyone else, anything I don't want to. As for it being a nasty murder, I don't think you'll find any murders anywhere that aren't nasty. That kind of goes with the territory of murder, don't you think?'

'But. . . but. . .' she stammered. 'That's not what I meant. I just meant that we all have to work together to try to get this monster caught as soon as possible. It seems to me that he's very dangerous. I just wondered if you would help us with that. You know, tell us what you saw. Anything she might have said. . .'

'I think you've got the wrong person for that,' I told her.

It wasn't too much of a lie. I wasn't the right person to talk to a journalist. I certainly wasn't the right person to divulge any information about the case. The police had asked me specifically not to and that was before the nastiness of the funeral bow on my gate that morning. I had no desire to draw any more attention to myself.

'And we don't know for definite it was a man. Even the police won't say that,' I added.

Ingrid tilted her head to one side. 'Ah! now come on. I think we all know it was a man. This mystery boyfriend. Did she mention him at all to you? Give a name? Blame anyone?'

There was something about this woman that made me feel deeply uneasy. I couldn't put my finger on it, but there was a falseness to her that gave me the creeps. I shivered, even though it was still so very warm. I wanted her as far away from me as possible, so that she couldn't wheedle any information out of me that I didn't want to give.

I tried to push the door closed.

'Thanks, Ms Devlin, for your interest, but I really don't think we have anything more to say to each other.'

To my shock, she put her foot out to stop the door from closing.

'Please, Mrs O'Loughlin. I'd ask you to reconsider. This is very much in the public interest. If we could just chat for a bit. I can explain what I need from you – what could help us to get the story out there. We want to make sure no other family has to go through what the Taylors are going through. No other person has to see what you saw.'

'I've told you already that I'm not the person you need to talk to. Now, please can you remove yourself from my property or I'll call *my* sources at the police station and have them remove you.'

Ingrid cast her eyes downwards then looked back at me. I could see tears glistening in her eyes as she chewed on her bottom lip.

'Please, it's very important that I get this story. Can I level with you? Woman to woman. My editor has told me that I can't come back to the office without a story. My job depends on it.'

'I'm very sorry for you, Ms Devlin. But if I were you, I'd question whether or not I really wanted a job that made me act in such an unscrupulous fashion. I wish you a good evening.'

She had the good grace to look defeated then. She fished around in her bag and pulled out a business card, which she handed to me.

'Mrs O'Loughlin, I'm going to park my car on the main road. Outside your property. I'm going to wait there and give you time to think about things. If you decide to talk to me, and I really, truly hope that you do, my number's on that card. Just call me and I'll come up to the yard. I can assure you I'm not unscrupulous, at all. I just want to do a good job and get the real story out.'

'Good evening, Ms Devlin,' I said and closed the door firmly.

I peered through the peephole again until I saw her turn and walk back down the yard to the road, which is when I allowed myself to have a cry.

All I wanted to do was to turn the clock back and not have gone for that blasted walk at all. Or, better still, turn the clock back two years and save my daughter. I was struggling to cope; I could feel anxiety building up inside me. Why couldn't people just leave me the hell alone? I just wanted to live my life out here in peace and quiet.

The stress was causing my body to react, my muscles to stiffen, my head to hurt. My bad arm ached and I rubbed it, hoping it would ease some of the pain.

Even though it was still early, I locked every door in the house and climbed the stairs. From my bedroom window I could see Ingrid Devlin's car parked on the road. She could wait there till Christmas for all I cared. There was no way on earth I was going to talk to her about what horrors I'd seen.

I pulled the curtains across, barely making an impact on the streaming evening light, climbed into bed then hoped against hope that I'd fall asleep and that it would be dreamless.

I slept until the small hours, my body clearly having been in desperate need of it. Waking just before five, needing to use the bathroom, I decided it was as good a time as any to get up. Glancing out of the window, I could see that Ingrid Devlin had clearly given up waiting – hopefully some hours ago – and her car was gone.

131

I breathed a sigh of relief and hoped she wouldn't be back. I'd tear up that stupid card of hers and call either Constable King or DI Bradley as soon as was reasonable to let them know that she'd been sniffing round. No, more than that, it seemed very likely there was a mole in the investigation who was leaking information to the press. Information that could put me in direct danger.

I decided to go downstairs and make myself a cup of tea and some toast. Maybe I'd watch some TV, something light to distract myself from everything that was happening around me. When I got to the bottom of the stairs, I saw a lined page from a reporter's notebook that had been folded over lying on the floor by the door. My name was scrawled on the cover. I had to give Ingrid Devlin something: she was persistent if nothing else. I picked it up and carried it through to the kitchen, where I switched on the light and put on my glasses before reading her looping, swirling scrawl:

Mrs O'Loughlin,

I'm sorry you didn't feel you could talk to me earlier. I assure you I have your best interests and the best interests of the story at heart.

I've heard you received a nasty surprise this morning, one that may have referenced the very tragic death of your daughter, Laura, and that police believe may also be linked to the murder of Clare Taylor.

Mrs O'Loughlin, I've spoken to my editor and we fully intend to run a piece in the paper showcasing this new information. We believe it will ultimately help the police to catch the person responsible for Ms Taylor's death.

As a courtesy, I'm letting you know about the article, which will be running in Monday's edition, so that you can decide whether you want to add anything, or speak about your relationship with your daughter and how you feel in the wake of being so close to yet another terrible tragedy.

You can reach me on the numbers on my business card, either my office number or my mobile.

Best wishes,

Ingrid

In my anger, I kicked the leg of the kitchen table so hard that I made Izzy yelp in fright and I was pretty sure I'd also broken at least one of my toes. That horrible woman was going to make a salacious headline of my daughter's death – as if we all hadn't suffered enough. That time – and the months that had followed – had been the darkest of my life. I'd been left emotionally, mentally and physically broken, and it had taken me a long time to piece myself back together again. I wasn't sure I could relive any of it.

Chapter Twenty-Two

Rachel

I'd pulled Beth into a hug and rocked gently back and forth while I told her that no one knew all the facts yet. Sure, the media were in the business of selling papers and getting Internet hits, but you couldn't always believe what you read. I advised her it might be better for her if she kept her distance from social media for a bit. Rumours can very easily get out of hand. However, telling a fifteen-year-old to stay off social media seemed like a cruel and unusual punishment in her eyes.

'I can't do that. I won't be able to talk to all my friends,' she said.

'Can you not, you know, just phone each other and have actual conversations instead?' I asked.

The roll of her eyes was enough to let me know that wasn't a viable option.

'This is hard enough,' she said. 'All of this is hard enough without being banned from going online or talking to my friends, too. They're the only things keeping me sane now. They understand in a way you and Dad never could understand.'

Part of me wanted to argue back with her, but that same part of me remembered what it had been like to be fifteen myself. When it was Julie, Clare and me against the world. We thought no one could ever be friends like us. No friendship was as strong as ours. No matter the drama, the only people I was sure who could understand me were my friends. If my parents had tried to block contact between us, I would have been utterly bereft. The thought of not seeing them . . .

The reality that I wouldn't see Clare again came at me like a wave. I choked back my emotions and pulled Beth into another hug.

'You're right, darling. Of course you are. I'm just trying to protect you from the world and all this horrible information about Clare's death. What happened was wrong and cruel and brutal, and I'm afraid you're going to hear things over the next few days and weeks that are going to be hugely upsetting. Not all of it's going to be true, either.'

'Why did they do it, Mum?' she asked. 'I don't understand.'

I shook my head. 'I don't understand, either. I can't think of anyone who had a bad word to say about Clare. But the police are working morning, noon and night to track whoever it is down and get the animal who did this behind bars.'

She rested her head against my shoulder and I kissed her hair, angry and upset that my child had been robbed of her innocence in such a violent manner.

'Do you really think they might hurt someone else?' she asked.

My heart lurched. How much should I tell her? She was fifteen. A bright kid. If I was to suggest her going to Belfast for a bit, we'd more than likely have to tell her the truth – but the thought of her being scared horrified me.

'One of the boys in the youth club said it was like those shows on TV, you know, like *Criminal Minds* or something. Like what if it's a serial killer? I told him to wise up, we don't get serial killers in Derry.' She looked up at me, chewed her lip a little. 'I heard Dad on the phone to you earlier about those flowers and I probably shouldn't have, but I looked at the card after. It gave me the creeps. I heard you talking to Dad about what if you're next and now I'm wondering if that boy in youth club was right?'

I was sure she must have been able to hear the persistent thudding of my heart in my chest. I wasn't equipped for this. This wasn't supposed to happen.

I took a deep breath. 'Darling girl, we all need to be brave now and we have to remember that the police are on our side. They're aware of everything that's happened and they're going to put extra patrols on in this area. They've assured me they're watching out for us, but I'm not going to lie, darling. You're an intelligent young woman. This is a scary time. I'm scared and I'm sure Dad is, too. But we're doing everything we can to keep you and Molly extra safe.'

'How can you do that if we don't know who we're watching out for?' she asked and I felt her squeeze my hand tighter.

She didn't look so much like a young woman as she did a scared child and I wanted to run away from all this with both her and with Molly, the two most important people in my life.

'We have the police on our side,' I repeated with a confidence I certainly didn't feel. 'But we may have to make some tougher decisions in the short term to be extra sure.'

'Like what?' she said.

I shook my head. 'I'm not sure yet, sweetheart. I need to talk to your dad. But please believe me, neither he nor I are going to let any harm come to you. I promise you that.'

She nodded but I could tell she didn't quite believe me. The worst part of it all was that I wasn't sure if I believed me, either.

I got straight to the point with Paul. Told him I thought we should consider the girls going to Belfast to stay with him in the flat until the police were in control of the situation. He looked at me as if I'd grown an extra head.

'Surely that's going a bit far?' he said. 'What exactly have the police said? Remind me.'

I sighed. 'They're going to put on extra patrols. They're taking these flowers seriously enough to get both them and the cards forensically analysed. They've given me a direct line if I need them.'

I was exasperated. I'd told him all this before but he didn't seem concerned in the way I was. Was I overreacting? Was I losing it?

'And Julie got something similar?' he asked.

'Yes, but a different lyric. A couple of lines from "Ten Green Bottles".'

He stifled a laugh. 'You do know how ridiculous this sounds?'

'Of course I do. And if it wasn't for the fact my friend has been murdered I'd probably be a dismissive asshole just like you.'

He blinked at my words. Looked as if I'd hit him with them. I knew I'd snapped at him and I immediately felt shame pile in on top of me.

'I'm sorry,' I said. 'It's just hard and I'm scared. I'm really scared.'

I willed him to cross the room and take me in his arms to comfort me. It's what Michael would have done. He'd have made me feel better. Feel protected. He wouldn't have laughed at me. Despite my feminist principles and belief that women can rescue themselves, I wanted an alpha male in that moment. I needed Paul to show he felt protective of me, of the girls. Of what we had.

'So you've told me,' he said, not moving from his spot. 'But don't you think it's a gross overreaction to take the girls away from their home environments, their friends, what they know

– to ship them to another city when the most the police think it merits is some extra patrols in the area? Surely if you, if they, were in real danger the police would do more than that? I think we risk doing more harm than good.'

'But wouldn't you sleep better just knowing they're out of harm's way?' I asked.

'Rachel, you're being completely impractical,' he said. 'I can't take them to Belfast. I've work to do. I'll be out at the office and who'll mind Molly? I'm pretty sure you're not planning on running out on work and coming with us?'

'You know I can't. Not with exams coming up. My pupils are relying on me to get them through. Maybe I could travel up and down every evening . . . I don't know. Let me think about it.'

'So you're putting your kids at school ahead of our children? You know it'll unsettle them and Molly wouldn't even see you. She'd be sleeping when you left and back in bed by the time you reached Belfast. But yeah, tell yourself it's in the best interests of the children if you need to,' he said, rolling his eyes.

'That's not it at all. I just want them to be safe.'

I was shouting then, crying. I couldn't understand why he was making it so difficult, except to think that he really didn't care about us. He liked his alone time. He didn't need the girls cramping his style. The scratches – and they were unmistakably scratches – didn't get there on their own. Had he someone he was aching to see in Belfast? Was this murder just a massive inconvenience to his extra-curricular love life?

I knew I was a hypocrite. I'd lost the right to be suspicious and angry the first day I'd agreed to go for coffee with Michael after class. Or the day I'd stored his name as 'Michelle' in my phone. If I'd been planning to keep things platonic, if it was no threat to our marriage, then why would I have done that? Maybe it was my fault Paul had been seeing someone else. My fault that he was angry and hard to reach. Had I pushed him away as I'd pulled Michael closer? Was it my coldness that made him talk to me as if my very existence annoyed him? The scratches on his arm, the angry pointing of the knife, the laughing away of my genuine concerns.

'Please,' I asked him. 'Just think about it.'

'I have thought about it and no. There has to be a better solution.'

Chapter Twenty-Three

Rachel

Evening arrived and we sat together in the living room, but even though we were in the same space we might as well have been miles apart.

I looked to where Paul sat. He'd been glued to his iPhone for the last half-hour. We'd barely spoken since our argument earlier. There'd been no discussion on further options. He'd even left the room when the police arrived to pick up the flowers. Molly had looked on open-mouthed from the top of the stairs as the two uniformed officers came into our house.

'Is someone going to jail, Mammy?' she'd asked, sliding down the stairs one at a time on her bottom and looking at me with trembling lips.

'No, pet. No one's going to jail. These lovely police officers are just taking these flowers to give them to someone who doesn't have any. Sure, look at us, we've two bunches.'

She might only have been three, but she was a smart kid and the look she gave me screamed 'I don't believe a word you're saying, Mum.'

'They need to be careful not to squish them,' she'd said solemnly as they were slid inside an evidence bag. 'Nobody wants squished flowers. You always have to be careful 'cos the petals can fall off and the flowers get broken. You can't fix flowers with glue, Mammy. You told me that before.'

I nodded, lifted her up into my arms. 'That's right. You smart cookie.'

She was in bed now. Beth sat at the other end of the sofa to me. She'd been clingy; not disappearing to her room as she normally did or asking to meet her friends in the park. Instead, she was lost in the world of Snapchat. I was staring aimlessly at the TV but nothing was going in.

I looked at them both, my family. I'd die for Beth, I knew that. For Molly, too. I'd do whatever I needed to protect them. At one stage I'd been sure I'd die for Paul as well, and him for me. Would I still? Would he want me to? Would he care if I'd been the one found lying on the side of the road and not Clare?

I chided myself. Of course he'd care. He wasn't a bad man. I'm sure it would hurt him; but would he be driven mad with grief for me? I doubted it. That made me so incredibly sad. Could I pinpoint where it had started to go wrong? I wasn't sure there was one event, one cataclysmic explosion of something that broke us. I think we'd just been chipped away at over the years.

We were very good at pretending, though – we could act the part. We could act the part so well that sometimes I wondered if I was acting at all. Sometimes I believed my own hype and a surge of hope that we could save what had resurfaced, but it was never long before old patterns re-emerged.

Until we found ourselves, once again, on opposite sides of the sofa and opposite sides of the relationship spectrum. Maybe that was why I'd been drawn to Michael – to that promise of passion and desire. To someone who listened to me intently, who looked at me as if I were the most fascinating creature who ever walked the planet. When he kissed me I felt alive. My body tingled and I'd been so completely numb for such a long time that I welcomed it. Even though I knew it was dangerous.

There was a big part of me that didn't care about the danger. Life was for living and who knew what was ahead of me, anyway? An early death like my mother's? Years of battling cancer to leave the world in my sixties? That didn't seem so far away now that I was in my forties and the years seemed to speed by at an increasing pace.

And then there was Clare – gone, too. All those years she'd wasted her energy on trying to save her marriage with James, all the times she'd let him hurt her. If she'd known she only had a few years left, would she have tried so hard? When he didn't make her happy anyway. When he didn't make her feel alive.

But then, Michael had the power to hurt me, too. He'd told me he'd never felt this way about anyone before and then, almost in the next breath, he'd told me we needed to cool things. The same old 'It's not you, it's me' trope jilted lovers have been listening to for so long. He wanted to give me space to grieve. To be there for my family. Or maybe he'd just got what he wanted. The sex we'd had wasn't worth the drama my life had become.

Looking around the living room – Paul still on his mobile, Beth, too – I wondered when they'd be there for me. I needed someone to be there for me, to care about how I was feeling.

I could feel something rise up inside me. I needed to get out of this house.

'I think I'll go for a run,' I said.

Two heads looked up at me simultaneously.

'You can't do that!' Beth cried.

'I don't think that's a sensible idea,' Paul said.

'Why not? I need to get out and clear my head and burn

off some of this nervous energy. It's still light. A few kilometres and I'll feel better for it.'

'But, Mum, it's not safe,' Beth said, shuffling closer to me, wrapping her arms around my waist.

'Beth's right,' Paul said. 'You've spent the afternoon telling me the police are putting extra measures in place because there might be a crazy person on the loose and you want to go out running on your own?' He raised an eyebrow.

'I'll take the car and drive to the riverside. There'll still be loads of people around. I'll stick to the walk along the quay. It'll be jammed with the weather being so nice. Safety in numbers,' I said, although even as I spoke I felt my own nerves resurface.

The thought of a crowd of people may well provide a safety of sorts, but I didn't know who this was. I didn't know who was trying to scare me. I could brush past them in a sea of people and not know. At the same time, I didn't want whoever this was to make me a prisoner. I needed room to breathe, and in that house – the air thick with heat, and tension, I couldn't relax.

'I suppose,' Paul conceded. 'And if it stops you sitting there like a cat on a hot tin roof all night, it might be a good thing.'

'I don't like it, Mum,' Beth said.

'Your mum'll be fine,' Paul said. 'And sure, she'll have her phone with her at all times, won't you, Rachel?'

'I will,' I said.

'Besides, when she's out, we can watch some more of the TV series *Stranger Things*, since she refuses to watch it with us.'

Beth smiled nervously but seemed reassured by Paul's words and his promise of some quality time together.

I went to get changed back into my running gear, no longer convinced it was a good idea but too stubborn to back down. As I tied the laces on my trainers, my phone beeped. Picking it up, I saw a message from Michael. I immediately felt a swirling in the pit of my stomach:

> Rachel, we need to talk. I'm so sorry about this morning. This just all felt out of control. Is there any chance at all you can get away, even for half an hour?

I didn't think twice before responding. I simply asked him when and where.

Michael and I had met when he'd registered for a three-month creative writing class I taught at the local technical college. It was something I'd fallen into, but I found that actually I quite enjoyed it. My students were older than the truculent teenagers I stood in front of every day in my day job and they had a genuine enthusiasm for what they were doing.

Michael caught my eye as soon as he walked into the class-room. He was tall, his hair messy, his hands pushed into the pockets of his baggy jeans. He looked mean and moody. Dark and brooding. As I'd have imagined a Heathcliff to look, perhaps. He looked nervous despite his cool appearance and he took a seat near the back of the classroom before pulling a battered notebook and pen from his satchel.

He barely lifted his head as I spoke, taking notes furiously, his brow furrowed in concentration. At least half an hour of the class session had passed before I saw him look up for the first time and he looked intently at me.

I was struck by the vivid green of his eyes, so bright against the weatherworn tan of his skin. I found myself lost for words just momentarily, having to work at remembering what I'd been talking about.

But I'd put him out of my head that night, as soon as I got

home and into the familiar routine of keeping the house running while Paul was in Belfast. It was only when I heard the words he'd written for his homework the following week, and the week after that, that I found my mind starting to wander to him more and more.

There was a rawness to his writing. An honesty to it. A grief behind it that made me want to hear more. That made me long for his turn to read, so I could hear the soft, deep lilt of his voice. When, three weeks in, he'd asked me for some feedback on a one-to-one basis, I found myself agreeing to coffee with him after class. A part of me knew I shouldn't. Even though he was an adult, and even though this was just an evening class for fun, he was still my student. It was still against the rules. But a bigger part of me couldn't resist.

I drove to the lay-by on Foyle Bridge at the top of the walkway down to Bay Road Park. Michael's car was already there and I felt my heart quicken.

When I climbed into the passenger seat beside him, he reached out his hand to mine, tanned, strong. I hesitated just a moment before I responded. I didn't know why he wanted me here when this morning he'd been so sure we should give each other some space.

'I know what happened this morning, but I just got scared, Rachel. All this – it's intense,' he said, looking straight ahead at the trees in front of us.

He seemed nervous. Jittery. I wasn't sure how to respond to him. If he was already freaked out by what was going on, what would he make of the flowers, the strange notes, the concerned police . . .?

He turned to look at me and on feeling his gaze I felt tears prick at my eyes.

'It is intense and I'm scared too, Michael. About everything. I shouldn't even be here. My family think I'm out having a run, but I'm here because you make sense when not a lot does at the moment. I could easily just run away from it all and not look back. Ever since my mother died, that's all I've wanted to do. But I can't and things just keep getting worse. And now Clare . . .'

'Don't run away,' he said intently, reaching across and cradling the side of my face in his hand, tilting my head so that he was looking directly into my eyes. 'Don't ever do that. Not without me.'

It was magnetic, the pull he had on me, and I let him kiss me and take my mind away from all of my worries and all the horror in my life. He was what I needed to get through this.

'Can't you stay with me tonight?' he asked, his voice strained with desire as his lips brushed against my neck. 'I guess I know the answer, but I have to ask.'

I threaded my hands through his. 'I wish I could . . . but things are even worse now than they were before. Michael, the police suspect, or are at least looking into the possibility that someone's trying to spook me, and Julie, too.'

'What? Why?' He shifted in his seat. Looked alarmed, held my hand a little tighter.

I explained to him about the flowers, about the notes and the rhymes – the possible link to our friendship.

'And they think the killer might be behind all that?'

'I suppose. I don't know. I mean, they haven't ruled it out and they've put on extra patrols.'

'So they're taking it seriously by the sounds of it,' he said. 'Rachel, you know, we could do it. Run away. Get away from all this. You don't have to stay.'

How I wished it were that simple.

'If only,' I told him. 'Where would we run, Michael? I have

146

daughters, a job. A mortgage. You've a house, a job. We can't just walk away from everything, not really. It's nice in theory, but. . .'

'Bring the girls. We can all make a new start.'

I shook my head. How simple he made it all sound. The girls had school. Beth was getting ready to sit her GCSEs.

He ran his fingers through his hair and then slammed them on the steering wheel. 'This is bullshit!' he said and I shrank back from him. He shook his head. 'I can't protect you. I can't be with you. You might be in danger – real danger, Rachel, and there's nothing I can do about it.'

'The police are doing all they can,' I assured him. 'I'm sure it's probably just someone trying to get a rise out of us. The police officer who came to speak to us, she says these kinds of things bring all sorts of weirdos out of the woodwork. Some people just see it as a game.'

'It's only a game if no one gets hurt,' he said, staring ahead of him. 'This doesn't feel like a game. You're not a chesspiece, Rachel. You're someone I need to be okay. I need you in my life. In whatever way I can. Be it five minutes at a time, or half an hour here or there. I just want to take care of you.'

He leaned across and kissed me then, his lips soft, breath warm. I could have lost myself there, in those moments, but for the sound of the engine from another car as it pulled into the lay-by and parked a short distance from us. We pulled apart, my heart thudding. We shouldn't have been so careless. Cars came and went here at all hours, people parking while they walked their dogs or went for a run. I looked over at the car. There was something familiar about it. Blue, dusty. I couldn't place it but I was sure I'd seen it somewhere recently. I tried to glimpse the figure behind the wheel, but whoever it was had concealed themselves well. A hoodie pulled up over their head. Totally unnecessary in the current weather. I felt uneasy.

'I think I'd better go home,' I said to Michael. 'They'll be starting to wonder where I am. And we really have to be careful.' I nodded my head in the direction of the blue car.

Michael glanced at it.

'Probably some pervert trying to see if he can watch some couple getting lucky,' he said.

'Still, I'd better go home,' I told him, squeezing his hand.

He looked dejected but told me he understood. Told me to take care and to stay in touch. He added that he'd always be there for me, whenever I needed him. I just had to call.

I got out of his car and crossed to my own, glancing back at the blue car, which still had its engine running, the driver sitting in the front seat, watching.

Sunday, 10 June

Chapter Twenty-Four

Elizabeth

The police couldn't do much about Ingrid Devlin's threats to publish details of how Laura had died. They could get their press officer to appeal to her better nature, but DI Bradley said he wasn't sure Ingrid Devlin *had* a better nature.

'I've had dealings with her before,' he'd told me, his face stony. 'She'll do anything – and step over anyone – to get a byline. We can ask, and we can definitely investigate who in our team is leaking information, but beyond that . . .'

He was apologetic, which was something, even if that something was woefully inadequate. The thought of Laura's last moments, her death being spilled all over the papers, was incredibly painful. We'd managed to escape it at the time – the papers very sensitively reporting that a woman had died in tragic circumstances without revealing the gory details. I'd been so very grateful to them for that – not that I believed in covering up suicides, more that I wanted to protect her children from knowing just how horrific it had been.

I knew in time, when they were older, that they'd want to know more about their mother. But I wouldn't always be around to explain, or to protect them. I didn't want a Google search to lead them to a salacious report that didn't reference the wonderful, caring person she was, or just how very much she'd loved them.

I supposed I should phone my son-in-law and warn him. I felt guilty that it was me who'd be bringing this trauma on them after all this time. Maybe if I did talk to Ingrid Devlin, maybe if she allowed me to talk off the record, it might stop her. But what would DI Bradley say to that? Would it hinder their investigation more?

When DI Bradley called me back to break the news that Ingrid and her editor were still planning to run with their story, I broke — told him I had to protect my family and that I'd talk to her.

'We'd really prefer it if you didn't. I know this is a lot to ask of you, but at this stage it could really make things difficult for us. If the information gets out about her last words, for example, or about the flowers you've all been sent, it could cause panic.'

'The flowers we've all been sent?' I asked. 'Who are "we"?'

He went silent, clearly aware he'd said too much — spoken out of turn. I could hear him sigh. Imagined how exhausted he was, the public clamouring for progress on this case and nothing forthcoming.

'A number of people have received similar arrangements to you, with cryptic notes attached. I can't reveal any more information than that,' he said dejectedly.

'A number of people? Who are they? Do I know them?'

'For operational reasons, that isn't information I can reveal to you at this time,' he parroted.

'Are these people connected to my Laura? Those were her favourite flowers. Are they connected to Clare Taylor?'

'Please, Mrs O'Loughlin, you know that I'd reveal information to you if I could. We'll keep you informed of any developments as they occur and when they have relevance to you.'

I ended the call frustrated and angry. Who were these other people who'd received floral arrangements? What had their notes said? They were enough to give the police cause for concern. I didn't like that.

It dawned on me that there was someone who seemed to have an inside source who was on the ball when it came to what was happening in the investigation. It was entirely possible Ingrid Devlin could tell me what DI Bradley wouldn't, or couldn't.

I had nothing to lose and my daughter's reputation to protect, so I pulled the business card Ingrid had thrust at me out of the bin and looked at her phone number. I was going to call her.

I'd like to say she didn't have a look of smugness about her when she sat down, but she did. It was subtle; something in the way she tilted her head and said: 'I'm so glad you called.' It was as if she'd never had even a moment's doubt that I would, indeed, call. She spoke slowly, as if my age made me stupid.

Maybe it did. A sharper me would have called her out. I would have said: 'Well, it's not like you left me much choice, is it?' But I wanted to keep her on side. If she had any information about any of this, from who'd sent the flowers and who else they'd been sent to, then I very much needed her to be on my side.

'I think maybe we can help each other,' I said, offering her a cup of tea.

She accepted and took out a notebook and pen, as well as her phone.

'Do you mind if I record this interview as well? I always feel more comfortable when I can record. It means I can make eye contact with you more and I don't have to have my head down over a notebook all the time.' She smiled.

I agreed. 'I'm only talking to you on the condition you leave my daughter out of this,' I said. 'We've been through enough. Her children don't need to have what happened splashed.all over the papers.'

Ingrid blinked her clear blue eyes at me and chewed on the end of her pen. 'Well, the thing is, I wanted to talk to you about that.'

'I'm sure you do, but it's a no-go area for me.'

'What if I told you that you weren't the only person to receive flowers on Saturday? That they were all similar – all posies of forget-me-nots, all decorated with black ribbon. Cryptic messages.'

'I'd tell you I already knew about that and it doesn't change anything.'

'I think it does,' she said. 'And, Mrs O'Loughlin, while I appreciate this is very difficult for you and you have my abject sympathy, I think the police are letting the investigation down by keeping the information they have silent. People need to know what they're dealing with. You've a right to know what's really going on.'

I couldn't deny it – she'd piqued my curiosity. I felt the weight of anxiety that had been hanging over me these last few days grow even heavier. Whatever she was going to tell me, it wasn't going to be pleasant, but I felt I needed to know it all the same.

'And you know, do you? All that's really going on?'

'I have sources,' she said, her expression serious. 'I'm not at liberty to reveal who they are, of course, but they're reliable and I have no reason to doubt them. But if you really do doubt me, I can show you that at least some of what I'm about to tell you is very easily accessible online.'

I raised an eyebrow. Ingrid put down her pen and sat back in her seat.

'Four other arrangements similar to yours were delivered on Saturday morning,' she said. 'One was left at the roadside, at the spot where you found Clare Taylor.'

I felt a shiver run up my spine.

'Two others were delivered to friends of Clare Taylor. The fourth to the Taylor family at their home address. My source hasn't been able to tell me the exact contents of the messages they received, but they were suspect enough in nature that the police seized both the arrangements and the cards and have been running forensic tests on them – trying to find fingerprints, et cetera.

'They believe these might be messages from the person responsible for Clare's death. They've not ruled out that this monster may strike again, Elizabeth, which is why I think it's unconscionable that the police aren't warning people about them'

Clare's last words ran through my head again: 'Warn them'. I shivered. What Ingrid was telling me was ringing true and that scared me, but not all of it made sense. Why involve my daughter? Unless that was intended as a threat towards me? Was I in danger, too? I felt myself tense.

'It makes no sense, though, to involve Laura in this. Is that supposed to be a threat to me? I don't understand.'

'It could be that it's some sort of muted threat to you, but I think that's overlooking a more obvious link to Laura.'

'Which is?'

'Well, how about you tell me Clare's last words first?' she said, raising her eyebrow again and brushing her hair behind her ear.

This was a game to her and she had me in a position where I couldn't back out. I needed to know.

She started to speak before I did.

'Look, I know you think I'm the enemy here, but I'm not. Really, I'm on your side, and the side of getting the truth out there. I can help you to control what information does get out about Laura and her tragic death, and you must believe me when I tell you that this information is going to come out, one way or another; whether or not you speak to me. And that's not meant as a threat – not at all. You do know that Clare Taylor knew your daughter, don't you? And the other two women who received flowers yesterday? They went to school together. I went to the same school, but a few years after, of course.'

I blinked. I didn't know. Yes, Laura had mentioned a Clare, but there were so many of them in her year group. There was no way I could have made that link.

'I knew there were Clares in her year. It was a very popular name at the time,' I said. 'But I don't think Laura had any friends by that name.'

'They were in the same class,' Ingrid said. 'As were the other two girls who received flowers yesterday. Rachel McCay and Julie Diver, as they were then. Clare, Rachel and Julie were best friends – they still are, or were.'

I remembered, vaguely, those names when grouped together. Laura had never really been one to talk about her school friends. She was quiet, shy. Had preferred to stay at home with her family than to go into town with friends each weekend. Occasionally she brought a friend home for tea, but I was pretty sure she'd never brought a Clare, or a Rachel or a Julie home. I was pretty sure they hadn't been in her peer group – not that she'd kept much of a peer group. She'd always been happier lost in a book or trailing around after her father down in the fields, before Paddy had to admit farming was no longer profitable for us.

I'd always been proud of her that she never felt the need to conform to what the other girls were doing. She didn't show much of an interest in make-up. Wasn't one for wanting to go to discos. I never had to worry about her being found drunk on the city walls or outside The Venue on a Saturday night. It had made my life so much easier. Maybe I should have worried more, but she was my 'easy' child. And it was easy for me to let her slip through the net – my attentions being dominated by her infinitely more gregarious brother.

'Elizabeth,' Ingrid said, bringing me back to myself. 'Do you remember Clare from then? Or the other girls?'

'I can't say that I do.'

'My source in the police seems to think there may be some link between Laura's death and Clare Taylor's murder,' Ingrid said.

'That's ridiculous,' I replied. I could feel my anxiety growing. My sense of claustrophobia at where this conversation was going. I don't think I'd ever heard anything quite so absurd in my life before. 'Laura died two years ago. She wasn't murdered. She took her own life, you know that, Ingrid. What link could there be?'

'That was the part of the puzzle I was hoping you could help me fill in on,' Ingrid said. 'You didn't recognise Clare as she lay on the roadside? She didn't say anything that might give us a clue?'

'I doubt her own mother would have recognised her how she lay on the roadside!' I snapped. 'The poor creature barely looked human, all bloodied and covered in mud. Those horrific wounds . . .'

I trailed off, aware of the flashing light on Ingrid's phone, which indicated she was recording every word I'd said. Aware that those words, words that could break whatever was left of Clare Taylor's mother, could appear in print. While she tried to keep her expression neutral, I could see the glint in Ingrid's eyes. I was no journalist, but I'd spent enough time in their company to know what made for story gold.

I took a breath and started again. 'No. I didn't recognise her. I'm not sure I ever met Clare when she was at school with Laura. I may perhaps have seen her at a school event, a Mass or something, but it was a long time ago. She wasn't one of my Laura's friends. Nor were those other girls, Rachel and whatever you said the other girl was called.'

'Julie. Julie Diver. She's married now, of course. As is Rachel. Both mothers now, too.'

'My Laura was a mother,' I said sadly just as Clare's last words chimed again in my head.

Was it Rachel and Julie she wanted to warn? Given the flowers, it was possible. I could feel a headache nip at my temples.

Ingrid just looked at me, waited for me to talk. I had to give her her dues, she was good at her job. She knew how to tease a story out of someone. She'd given me information the police hadn't. She'd told me more than that kindly-faced DI Bradley with his 'operational reasons' for keeping me in the dark had done.

'She told me to "warn them",' I muttered.

'Sorry?'

Ingrid looked at me. I noticed her eyes widen just that little bit.

'That's what she said. Before she died. Those two words: "Warn them". That was all. She was barely alive when I got to her. It was just too late. Her injuries. . .'

My mind drifted back to that roadside and the horrific sight that had greeted me that day. All that blood. So much blood.

I wondered if that was what it had been like when they found Laura. Two girls, from the same class in school. Gone. Brutally taken. One by her own mind and one by someone deeply twisted.

I didn't care then what Ingrid thought of me. I didn't care about trying to play her at her own game. I simply broke down and cried, now fearing for the safety of those other two women and their children.

Chapter Twenty-Five

Rachel

My back ached and my head was pounding when I woke. I remembered that I'd drunk the best part of a bottle of wine the previous night and my tolerance for alcohol was no longer anywhere near what it had been in my twenties. Or my thirties, for that matter.

I stretched and looked around. Felt the figure in the bed beside me move, turn over and flop one arm over my stomach. I revelled in the moment. The closeness. The sheer uncomplicated nature of how I felt for this person. My beautiful Molly. My innocent baby girl.

I remembered climbing in beside her the previous night – unable to face getting into bed beside Paul. I didn't want him to touch me. I didn't want to talk to him. I needed space to breathe. That space had ended up being about six inches on the edge of Molly's bed as she starfished her way through the night, but the wine had ensured that I'd dropped off to sleep with little effort.

I replayed my conversation with Michael over and over in my head when I went home. His plea to run away. I thought of the figure in the blue car, cursed my stupidity for not writing down the registration number, then cursed myself again for being paranoid. Any number of cars could park there. It didn't have to mean anything.

I'd poured myself a large glass of wine. The registration number had started with PFZ, the same as Paul's, but I couldn't remember the numbers. My head throbbed. I'd sat in the living room as Beth and Paul watched their programme about a curious place called the 'The Upside Down' on *Stranger Things* and part of me wondered if I'd passed through some sort of portal myself. My life was more upside down than the poor child on the screen.

Wouldn't it be so simple if I could just run away? If I could forget I had a family, if I could stop my heart loving my children. I could get away from this madness; from the disintegration of a relationship that had once been everything to me. From the dread every time my phone rang, or a message landed, or there was a knock on the door. More bad news. More horrific revelations.

Things would never be normal again. This wasn't a short period of upheaval and upset after which we'd all slip back into our old routines. This was raw and pain-filled, and there was no escape for any of us.

Crying into my glass of wine, I thought about the Taylors. About Ronan and Jenny and how their marriage was struggling to cope with this unthinkable tragedy. I thought about Julie and how she seemed to be disappearing bit by bit in front of my eyes. I thought of Paul – of the Paul I once knew – of whom I'd been so very certain. It had been a long time since we'd laughed together, I realised.

I couldn't pin all the blame on him. I was no innocent party. I'd allowed myself to start falling for another man. I'd allowed myself to *sleep* with another man. And I'd enjoyed every touch, every sensation, as I'd felt desired and wanted for the first time in years. Lying on the edge of Molly's bed that Sunday morning, feeling her soft breath on my face, her mass of blonde curls tickling my cheek, I wondered what on earth would become of us all.

It felt as though Paul was watching me like a hawk all through that morning. No matter where I went, I felt his eyes on me. As I loaded the dishwasher and sorted through piles of washing, he took a seat at the kitchen island, poured himself a cup of coffee and continued his vigil.

He wasn't reading the paper or even going through his phone, he was just sitting there, watching me as I separated the dark-coloured clothes from the lights. My head was still thumping. My stomach wasn't feeling the best, either. I didn't have the energy to engage him in conversation, so I just continued about my work.

'What do you want me to do this week?' he eventually asked.

'What do you mean?'

'You said last night you wanted me to take the girls to Belfast. I said that wasn't a good idea for a hundred different reasons, but we never actually decided what would happen. Did you speak to that policeman again? Get his advice?'

'On what? We know what we know, Paul. My friend has been murdered. Julie and I have received cryptic notes. Some people might find that threatening. I was just thinking of the girls. Thinking how to protect them.'

He rolled his eyes. 'I think the best thing we can do for them both now is to try to keep things as normal as possible. That means keeping them here.'

'And you will come home each night?' I asked.

'Well, I have a few late meetings, but if it means that much to you . . .'

He let it trail off as if my friend's murder was some massive inconvenience to him. As if I was being unreasonable to ask him to commute back and forth while this hung over our heads. I suddenly felt so very tired of it all.

'Paul, it's not that it means so much to me. It's that I need help. I'm grieving and I'm scared, and I don't know how to be there for the girls and hold myself up at the same time.' My voice broke and even though I'd been determined that I wouldn't cry, I felt tears prick at my eyes. 'And I know we're broken, by the way. Whatever this is between us.'

He didn't speak for a moment. He just looked at me, his mouth open just a little as if trying to find something to say that would prove I was wrong. As if he was trying to find the right words of reassurance, but we both knew it had gone beyond that now.

'You're being overly dramatic,' he eventually said, dropping his eye contact for just a second too long.

'My friend has been *murdered* and I'm being overly dramatic?' I struggled to keep the incredulity from my voice.

'Well no, not about that, but about us being broken. That's ridiculous.'

I couldn't hold it in any longer. I knew starting this conversation would take us down a very dangerous road, but how could I not ask?

'Is it? Is it really? Because I feel it. Every day. We've become so distant with each other. You've become so distant. So much so . . . I've started to wonder . . .' I paused for a moment. 'Paul, are you having an affair?' I asked.

He stood up and looked at me, shaking his head. 'You think what you want to think, Rachel. You always do anyway.'

At that he stormed out, lifting his keys and slamming the front door behind him.

Monday, 11 June

Chapter Twenty-Six

'Warn them'

**Murder victim's chilling last
words provoke fear killer will
strike again**

The woman who held murder victim Clare Taylor's hand as she died has revealed the 41-year-old's chilling last words.

Retired nurse, Elizabeth O'Loughlin, who came across the fatally injured Civil Servant while walking her dog, has exclusively revealed to *The Chronicle* that just before she died, Clare Taylor pleaded with Elizabeth to 'Warn them'.

Meanwhile, a source close to the investigation has told *The Chronicle* that a number of people have received floral arrangements with sinister notes attached, which police believe may be some sort of calling card from the murderer.

'There is no doubt in my mind that more people may be at risk and that whoever is behind this killing is an extremely organised and sick individual. Police are worried and have been trying to stop this information from getting out, fearing it could provoke panic. But people need to know how serious this is,' the source said.

Mrs O'Loughlin spoke of the 'horrific' scene she came across as she was walking her dog in the early hours of last Wednesday: 'We were walking early in the morning as we usually do, when my dog, Izzy, ran to the side of the road and started yelping. I could see the colour of her jumper first. I did what I could to help her [Ms Taylor], but she was too far gone.

'I called an ambulance and was trying to reassure her that help was on the way, but she was so badly injured. I tried to keep her warm and was holding her hand when she muttered those words to me.

'She was gone the next minute. I haven't been able to get her out of my mind since.'

Mrs O'Loughlin, who worked as a theatre nurse at Altnagelvin Area Hospital during the height of the Troubles, said Ms Taylor's injuries were 'as horrific as anything she'd seen before'.

'I've seen a lot, especially working in theatre during the Seventies and Eighties, but this was something else. I don't know how that poor girl survived for any time at all. Whoever did this is nothing short of evil.

'I don't understand why the police have kept her final words a secret. People should know they're in danger. The look on that poor girl's face. It'll live with me until the day I die.'

In a cruel twist of fate, sixty-seven-year-old Mrs O'Loughlin didn't realise as she sat with Ms Taylor that the fatally injured woman had been a class mate of her own daughter, Laura O'Neill, who died unexpectedly in tragic circumstances two years ago.

Laura left behind two young children and a husband.

'I didn't make the connection,' Mrs O'Loughlin said. 'But it would appear they were in the same year group in St Catherine's College in the late Eighties and early Nineties. The thought of two women, still so young, losing their lives is awful. I know how Clare's parents will be feeling right now and I wouldn't wish that on anyone.

'A mother can never get over the loss of a child — and to lose a child in such a violent way is just horrendous.

'I just want whoever did this to be

behind bars where they belong. Until that happens, I can't see me getting a moment's peace.'

Of the police investigation, she said: 'It's been almost a week and I don't think they're any further forward. People are at risk and that's what worries me. How many more families will have to go through the hell the Taylors are going through?'

A spokesperson for the Police Service of Northern Ireland said the investigation was continuing, with all available resources at the disposal of the inquiry team.

'This was a brutal murder and one which, rightly, has aroused a deep feeling of revulsion within the community. Police are doing everything in their power to bring the person or persons responsible to justice.

'Again, we would ask anyone with any information that may lead to the arrest of those responsible to come forward.

'Police are particularly interested in speaking to the man Ms Taylor was believed to be dating at the time of her death.'

They refused to comment on the delivery of sinister notes and gifts to several parties in the city.

Chapter Twenty-Seven

Rachel

It was Monday morning and I was strapping Molly into her car seat. Paul had left for Belfast an hour early. We hadn't spoken to each other since the day before and I'd been glad to see him leave. The tension had been almost suffocating.

I shouted through the open front door of the house to Beth to get a move on before climbing into the driver's seat to wait for her.

'Your sister'll be late for school and Mammy'll be late for work if she doesn't get a wriggle on,' I said to Molly, who'd started wriggling furiously in her seat.

'I'm wriggling on, Mammy,' she said. 'So we can go superfast.'

I smiled at her innocence and how she took me at my word about everything. It used to be like that with Beth, before we had these morning shouting sessions to get her in the car in time. I was just about to get out of the car and walk back to the house to call her again, when I saw Constable King accompanied by DI Bradley walking up the driveway towards the house. They had serious expressions on their faces and my heart sank.

'Mammy, that police lady's here again,' Molly called. 'Do we have more flowers to give away?'

'Mrs Walker,' DI Bradley said, 'would you mind if we went inside and had a word?'

'Is everything okay?' I asked, which seemed like a bit of a stupid question.

'We really should talk about this inside,' he said and I nodded.

My heart was thumping as I took Molly from the car just as Beth was walking out of the front door.

'What's going on?' she asked, her face ashen.

'We're just here to speak to your mum,' Constable King said. 'Why don't you help me take your little sister in and we can have a chat?'

Beth looked between Constable King and me and then to DI Bradley as if she didn't know who or what to trust.

'Want to stay with Mammy,' Molly said, her bottom lip wobbling.

'Your mummy'll be right here,' Constable King said, getting down to Molly's level and smiling at her. 'We're just going to have a little chat, is that okay? Maybe you could show me your toys?'

At the thought of showing off her My Little Pony collection, Molly flipped from wanting to be at my side to proudly leading Constable King in through the door. Beth was altogether more reticent.

'Can I stay with you, Mum?' she asked.

I looked to DI Bradley for guidance.

'If you don't mind, I'd really like to talk to your mum alone first. Just for a little bit and then you can come in.'

'How about you make a pot of tea?' I said, trying to calm my thumping heart and look in control for Beth.

The truth was, of course, that I didn't feel in control at all. DI Bradley wouldn't be coming to my house unless something had happened.

'What about school?' Beth asked.

'We'll talk about that in a bit,' I said, adding to DI Bradley that I'd really need to phone my work if I was going to be late.

As Beth reluctantly headed in the direction of the kitchen, DI Bradley told me that it might be better to tell them I'd need the day off.

My stomach lurched so far that I was sure I'd throw up the tea and toast I'd had for breakfast just half an hour before. I felt myself start to shake and I stumbled as I tried to sit down.

'Has something else happened?' I asked. 'Has someone else been hurt? Have you caught him?'

'I'll assume you've not seen *The Chronicle* this morning?' he said.

I shook my head. I didn't routinely buy it and to be honest, after what had been printed on Saturday – all those gory details – I'd decided that I'd make a point of never buying it again.

'I'm afraid some information sensitive to the investigation has got into the public arena,' he said. 'This information is relevant to you and also to your friend, Julie Cosgrove.'

'Is it about the flowers?' I asked.

He shifted uncomfortably in his seat. 'It is related to that, but there's more. Does the name Laura O'Loughlin mean anything to you?'

It rang a bell, but I couldn't place her immediately.

'It's familiar, but I'm not sure I know her and I definitely don't know her well.'

'Well, it would have been a long time ago. When you were at school.'

An image of a skinny, tall girl with long dark hair, which she always wore hung around her face as if she were trying to hide herself, came to mind. She kept herself to herself. She never really showed an interest in joining in with the rest of us, always happier to have her head stuck in a book.

Bookworm – that's what we called her. If she was who I was thinking of.

'She wouldn't have been in my friendship group, but I think we shared a few classes,' I said. 'I haven't seen her since school. Is she okay? Has something happened to her?'

DI Bradley coughed just as Beth walked in with a tray laden with mugs, milk, sugar and a plate of chocolate biscuits. Constable King followed her in, nodding to her colleague.

'Beth, would you mind keeping your sister occupied for a bit? Just while I speak to your mum,' she said.

I saw the reluctance to leave in my daughter's eyes but she turned and left anyway. Constable King sat down opposite me. I thought about lifting a mug, my mouth had gone dry, but I was afraid my hands would shake too much and I'd spill it.

'Laura died two years ago,' DI Bradley said. 'She was married, called Laura O'Neill then, and she left two young children. A son and a daughter.'

Although she meant very little to me, my heart sank at the news. She was too young, just like Clare. And those poor children, left without a mother. But I still didn't see what relevance it had to Clare's case. Surely if she'd been murdered, it would have made the headlines back then? I'd have heard about it.

'What happened to her?' I asked. 'Was she ill? I don't understand what this has to do with anything.'

He shook his head, rubbed the stubble on his chin. He looked tired; I imagined the investigation was taking its toll on him.

'Laura took her own life. She was a troubled individual, it seems.'

I was still confused. Tried to cast my mind back more than twenty years to remember her. Had she left after fifth form? Gone on elsewhere? I couldn't think straight.

'Five deliveries were made of the forget-me-nots wrapped in black ribbon on Saturday. As you know, one was left at the roadside where Clare was found. You received one, as did Julie Cosgrove and the Taylors. Both yours and Julie's had rhymes, which we can link back to your schooldays. Two others, those left at the roadside and those received by the Taylor family, contained cryptic messages, too.' He took a breath. 'The fifth delivery was made to a Mrs Elizabeth O'Loughlin, Laura's mother. It contained a note referencing her daughter.'

'I don't know Mrs O'Loughlin,' I said. 'I mean, this seems strange, but I don't know where you're going with this.'

'Mrs O'Loughlin lives on Coney Road. It was she who found Clare last week and was with her in her last minutes.'

My blood ran cold.

'Couldn't this all be a coincidence?' I asked, grasping at straws that were well beyond my reach.

He shook his head. 'We don't think so, unfortunately. We had asked Mrs O'Loughlin not to reveal her conversation with Clare for operational reasons. Details of that exchange have now, sadly, been printed in this morning's *Chronicle*. Given the delivery of the flowers and other information we've been able to gather about Clare's last days and weeks, we believe we have a duty to advise you that we believe her last words may have referred to you and Mrs Cosgrove.'

He paused, giving me a moment to take in what he was saying.

'We understand this'll be extremely distressing for you, so we're here this morning to speak to you about increased security measures. At this time, some of my fellow officers are also with Mrs Cosgrove and she's being given the same information. We'll be doing all we can to ensure that you and your family remain safe while we work to get this individual into police custody once and for all.'

'But what's changed, between Saturday and today? You presumably had all the information that's just been published anyway. You didn't think we were targets then, did you?' I asked, pressing my fingernails into the palms of my hands to try to distract myself from the panic building inside me.

I watched as Constable King glanced at the ground. DI Bradley cleared his throat.

'It's more that we fear the coverage will now embolden whoever did this. They may feel we're on to them and that may make them panicky, or braver. Neither is good. Given what was written in each of the cards on Saturday, and the information we now have about the shared link between Clare, Julie, Laura O'Neill and you, we don't think it wise to take any chances with your safety.'

I felt a cold sweat break on the back of my neck, reached up to rub it, to try to ease the tension in my muscles.

'Why? What did Mrs O'Loughlin's card say?'

'I'm not at liberty to reveal that at the moment,' he said, blushing. 'But we really do need you to think about any links, any interactions you may have had with Laura; especially in later years.'

'But I don't think I saw her at all after we left school. I don't think I'd have recognised her anyway if I did. There were two hundred girls in our year group. I don't mean to sound dismissive, but she meant nothing to me. We weren't friends. We weren't really anything. I barely remember her.'

My head hurt as I tried to bring an image of her into focus. It was so long ago. A different lifetime and certainly a different me.

DI Bradley nodded. I wasn't sure he believed me and that left me feeling uneasy.

'What were Clare's last words?' I asked him. 'Seeing as they're out in the public domain anyway, you might as well tell me.'

'"Warn them",' he replied and I felt my desire to run away grow stronger.

Chapter Twenty-Eight

Elizabeth

The paper sat in front of me. My words, stark, in black and white. A picture of my beautiful daughter. Ingrid Devlin had at least been true to her word. She hadn't gone into any salacious detail about Laura's death – just that she'd died unexpectedly at a tragically young age.

I knew it was journalist code for 'killed herself' – everyone reading would know that – but at least it wasn't spelled out. My fears that there'd be lurid details of how she'd done it were assuaged, for now at least.

Had I made DI Bradley angry with me? I didn't know, and part of me felt guilty for talking to the press, but what choice had I been given? I'd done this to protect my grandchildren. To protect my son-in-law. To protect me, if I was honest. Not that I felt ashamed of how she died. Ashamed maybe that I hadn't seen how bad she was feeling. That I hadn't seen how much she needed me.

No, that wasn't shame. That was guilt. People would judge me for letting her slip through the net. They'd blame me. It had already happened before.

I wasn't surprised when the police knocked at my door later.

Nor was I surprised that my phone wouldn't stop ringing, and that journalist after journalist walked up through the farmyard and knocked on my door.

'I have nothing more to say on the matter,' I told them all. Each eager reporter with their phone set to record. 'Any statement from now on will be issued through Ingrid Devlin at *The Chronicle* and you can contact her if you have any further queries.'

They looked disappointed. As did the police. Constable King arrived and sat opposite me at my kitchen table, barely touching the coffee I'd made for her.

'I'm sorry,' I muttered. 'She didn't give me much choice and I was just so frustrated by it all. If anyone else had been hurt, I'd never have forgiven myself.'

Constable King was as pleasant as she could be about it, I suppose.

'The difficulty now is that our investigation lines have been rammed with calls from people wondering if they're at risk, or what measures they should take, or just trying to find out all the insider information. The team is flat out trying to sift through all that.' She rubbed her neck, the tension obvious in her face. 'We fear the attention might make the killer bolder. They might thrive on it, take risks.'

I felt wretched. Had I inadvertently made things worse?

'They're very clever,' Constable King continued. 'They've left us no clues. We still haven't been able to locate Clare Taylor's phone or laptop, and nothing of use showed up on the records from her phone company.'

'I've done this all wrong,' I said and I could feel my composure slip.

I was just a stupid old woman. It wasn't the first time I'd been called that, but it was the first time I truly believed it.

'You've been manipulated by a very clever journalist,' Constable King soothed. 'Try not to feel bad about it.'

178

Her facial expression didn't match the comforting nature of her words, however. She was clearly annoyed. DI Bradley was probably fuming.

I was angry with myself. I never seemed to be able to do anything right any more. I deserved everything my life had become.

'So, where do we go from here?' I asked, hoping she wouldn't suggest I leave the house.

I wanted to cling to it even more now. It felt like the only constant in a world that wasn't making much sense.

She took a breath and told me patrols would be increased further. Police would look into fitting panic alarms to the house and I'd be given a panic mobile phone for when outside the house.

'I know this must sound scary, Elizabeth, but we'd rather be overly cautious than sorry. Normally, these measures are reserved for when a direct threat has been made to someone's life. I want to stress, we don't feel this is the case for you, but given that the suspect still hasn't been identified and is therefore still at large, we don't want to take any chances. Extra resources are being drafted in to work on this investigation. I want you to understand that we're doing everything within our power to get this person apprehended. We'd ask, again, if there's someone you could stay with or who could come and stay with you? Being here must feel quite isolated at times.'

'It never has before,' I said, and it was true.

I was able to cope with the isolation before – I'd spent too many years caught up in noise and trauma and constant activity. I didn't know if I could take it any more. I cursed Paddy for being dead. Laura for leaving me. Aaron, too, for running away and not working through his grief properly here.

'Okay,' Constable King nodded. 'Now, Elizabeth, you're aware that it seems to be the opinion of Ms Devlin that there's a direct link between this murder and your daughter. What do you think?'

I shook my head. 'I can't see how that could be the case,' I said. 'And I told Ingrid as much. I think it's just some twisted coincidence. Laura was never friends with Clare.'

'Can you give me any names of any of Laura's friends from school who'd have any information about the girls from back then?'

'I don't see how it's relevant,' I bristled. 'It was more than twenty years ago. They left school in the mid-Nineties. Built their lives.'

'Mrs O'Loughlin, the notes the other ladies received seemed to make reference to their schooldays. I know this is difficult for you, but any information, any names you can give us, may really help to close the net on who did this.'

I didn't want to tell Constable King. It felt wrong. It felt as though I was betraying Laura. It felt as if I was telling the world she was anything less than perfect and worthy of love, which was nonsense. She'd always been perfect to me. She'd always been worthy of love. She'd been the sunshine in my life.

'I can't tell you the names of her school friends,' I said, my heart cracking a little. 'Because she didn't have any.'

A couple of friends had come and gone, but Laura had struggled to maintain friendships. She'd tell me that people would like her for a few months but then grow bored. She wasn't cool enough. She didn't have the same interests. She preferred to stay at home on the farm. She didn't wear her hair in a perm, or follow Bros or Take That or any of the bands her classmates did.

I reassured her as often as I could that it was okay to be her own person. That I was exceptionally proud of her for being so steady in her beliefs, in walking her own path. But I knew she was lonely at times. I thought things would get better – in that way mothers do. I thought she needed some time to settle in. To find her tribe. There was bound to be someone she could bond with . . .

Every time she brought a friend home it was almost as if we welcomed the prodigal son to the house. I made sure we had the best spread in for tea. I knew I was stupid playing a game to fit in when Laura had been happy enough to be her own person, but I didn't want to give any of them even half a chance to cast aspersions about her.

We had branded treats – Coca-Cola, Tayto crisps, McVitie's biscuits – even though times were tough and we normally stayed with supermarket own-brand goods or value-pack treats. I'd hire movies from the video shop, make big bowls of popcorn. I'd encourage them to listen to music as loudly as they wanted, but every time I heard some pop tune I knew that Laura didn't like blast through the house my heart would sink.

Every now and again she'd try to fit in. She'd mould herself. And although I'd always been proud of her individuality, a part of me hoped that these changes would make the difference.

After a while she stopped bringing people home for tea. When I asked her about friends, she'd tell me that she had a few people she chatted to in class and at breaktime. She'd smile and then we'd go back to talking about our usual subjects. She seemed content.

It was only when my friend at work took me aside one day to ask if Laura was okay that I realised I'd been kidding myself all along. Even as I smiled and said my daughter was happy and settled with friends, I knew it didn't ring true.

'It's just my Fiona says she wanders around the hockey pitch alone at breaktime. In all weathers. She looks a bit lost.'

Of course 'her Fiona' didn't think to reach out a hand of friendship.

When I asked Laura about it, her face had burned red. Tears

pooled in her eyes and then she'd stomped off defiantly, shouting that it was none of my business and I should 'just keep my bloody nose out of things'.

I wanted to go to the school – see what they could do to help her – but she'd refused to allow me. 'I don't want people being friends with me out of pity,' she said. 'Besides, I'm happy enough on my own.'

She'd smiled so brightly when she'd said it that I'd believed her. I liked my own company; it stood to good reason that my daughter would, too. And there was always someone to talk to in the farmhouse, so it wasn't like she was totally isolated. She'd smile and tell me that as she helped me cook the dinner. It was only after she died that I came to realise that Laura had been incredibly good at faking smiles.

Tuesday, 12 June

Chapter Twenty-Nine

Rachel

In three weeks it would be the end of term. If they hadn't been caught by then we'd all move to Belfast until they were, or rent a house in Donegal, or do something to get away from the oppressive nature of what was our home.

But going away would mean leaving Michael. It would mean spending more time with Paul and I wasn't sure how I was supposed to feel about that. I could barely look at Paul, let alone try to play happy families in front of the girls for intense periods of time.

The girls.

I was trying my best to protect them, but it wasn't enough. Beth jumped every time a car drove past or there was a knock on the door. Molly, although not quite aware of what was going on, sensed something was very wrong in her universe, and had become increasingly clingy and tearful as the day had gone on. For the first time in over a year she'd wet herself during the night and sobbed into her daddy's chest while I stripped her sodden bed sheets and put them in the washing machine.

'I want to sleep with you,' she'd sobbed as I told her

I'd fixed her bed and put her favourite My Little Pony blanket on it.

I was too tired to argue, so I lay down beside her and stroked her hair until her eyes fluttered and she drifted back off to sleep.

'This isn't good for them,' Paul said.

A part of me wanted to bite back that of course it wasn't good for them. It wasn't good for any of us. I couldn't switch my brain off, not even for five minutes. No matter how heavy my eyes felt. Everything just ran over and over through my head.

Laura O'Loughlin – it was a name that didn't mean much to me. Had she been the girl who'd spent every lunchtime reading Jane Austen or the Brontë sisters and hadn't been interested in reading *Just 17* or *More* magazine? A little odd in her demeanour.

Not like us.

Was that her?

At around 3 a.m., I got up and slipped downstairs. At least it was a little cooler there. I sat and watched as the first strobes of light started to break through the night sky then I made myself a coffee and pulled out a dusty cardboard box from the cupboard under the stairs. It had been a long time since I'd looked in it, but I knew exactly what it contained. Photo albums, everything from my teenage years until my late twenties when digital cameras took over. Yearbooks from school. I knew exactly which album I was looking for – one that had two Forever Friends teddy bears on the front – and I pulled it out before sitting back on the sofa. The memories contained in those pages – they'd been such innocent times.

I flicked through the album. Bad haircuts, unkempt eyebrows, teenage skin and thickly applied make-up. The three of us pulling poses and laughing at the camera, together, individually, in pairs. At birthday parties, or on the beach, at concerts. Dressed up for Halloween. Pictures from school – faded now. The colours muted as if they'd always been that way. Slightly out of focus. Just like my memories of that time.

A group of our classmates, pulling poses and grinning outside the school canteen. Set on hills that rolled down to the River Foyle, our school site – now closed, just a collection of decaying buildings and overgrown grass. On warm days – days just like the day that was dawning – the all-girl school population would lay our coats down on the grass banks then sit and soak in the sun at lunchtime. Hundreds of milk bottle-white legs, our regulation grey socks pushed down to our ankles trying to catch a bit of colour. Girls rubbing cooking oil into their white skin in the hope of getting a tan, long before SPFs were thought of.

Innocent times. There were pictures of us making daisy chains. Heads bowed in concentration. Pictures of us messing about in the science lab – an old, dark room with high ceilings and a permanent musty smell. No doubt we should never have been messing around in there or taking pictures. But it was harmless, our harmless rebellion.

I looked at the picture closely, at Clare's smile. The braces on her teeth still evident then. She only really bloomed into herself when they were gone. Her hair was tied back in a ponytail, her skin shiny. She was so young. We all were.

It was only then I saw another face, at the bench behind. Long hair, greasy strands, hanging around her face. No silly smile. No friends posing beside her, just a head bent forwards. Doing her best to avoid eye contact with the camera and the person behind it. There was a paleness and a sadness there; or maybe the lack of sleep was causing my brain to play tricks on me.

I blinked and I swore, even though I knew it was impossible,

I saw her lift her head and stare directly at the camera, directly at me, with such hurt in her eyes that I wanted to look away but couldn't.

It was the flash of a memory, maybe. I was the person who'd taken the picture after all, back then. It pinched at me. Her face. That expression. In the background of my schooldays. I'd paid no notice then. Had looked away. Had continued in my selfish teenage bubble.

I flicked through more photos and again and again I saw that lonely figure in the background. The person not laughing. The person not posing. The person we were happy to ignore, but not out of badness. The person looking at me occasionally in those pictures with something akin to sadness on her face – or was it disgust?

Laura O'Loughlin. Seeing her face, I remembered her in a way I hadn't at the mention of her name. I felt my stomach sink. I recognised her. Remembered her. Remembered the things we'd said and done. Or hadn't said or done. We'd been so silly then. Immature. Bitchy at times, but no more than other teenage girls.

I blushed at the memory of it now. Ashamed. I remembered Clare snatching Laura's beloved book from her, mocking her by reading the passages out in an exaggerated posh voice. Everyone had laughed. Even Laura had cracked a smile. Hadn't she?

She'd been less happy when Clare had declared the book rubbish and threw it in the bin. But Clare hadn't damaged it. Laura had been able to retrieve it just fine. She'd stuffed it into the bottom of her bag and laughed along. I remembered that, sitting in my living room that morning. I remembered her laugh and I remembered that I'd thought it was a bit cruel of Clare. Out of character for her, too. I remembered that I wanted to say something to her about it, but for the life of me, I couldn't remember if I had.

Jane Eyre . . . that was the book. I think. Or *Wuthering Heights*, maybe. Something suitably gothic and brooding. No Judy Blume or battered copy of *Flowers in the Attic*.

I don't think I'd given her a second thought in years. I probably hadn't given her much thought while at school, but now our lives were linked. Our fates linked too, maybe.

I lifted my phone and typed her name into Facebook; even though she was dead, I wondered would her Facebook account, if she had one, still be there? Maybe I'd see her as she looked now, maybe it would ring some more bells. I scrolled through a number of accounts until I found a Laura O'Neill from Derry.

Her profile picture was of two children, a boy and girl, dressed in school uniform and smiling at the camera. It was the same school uniform that Beth had worn when she was at primary school. The same that Molly would wear the following year. Was it possible I'd seen Laura at the school gates when Beth was still a pupil there? I tried to count backwards, guess the age of her children.

If I had seen her at the school, I hadn't paid attention. I was fairly sure we hadn't spoken. Or if we had, it had been small talk, the way anyone would talk to a stranger.

I clicked into the profile, dormant since 2016. There wasn't much to see, except that it appeared that she'd sent me a friend request, to which I still hadn't responded. I didn't even remember seeing it. But there it was, with an option to accept it, or not.

My finger hovered over the button. It would be wrong to accept now. What good would it do? But would I see more of her profile? Get more of an idea of who she'd been?

I shivered. I didn't want to dig deeper, so I closed the Facebook app and slipped the photo album into my bag. What I'd do with it, I didn't know. But there was a part of me thinking of the look on her face when Clare had tossed her book into the bin. There was a part of me that wondered whether I'd sensed her vulnerability then, or had the knowledge of what had happened since coloured my faded memories? Was there more in our past that I'd filed away to the deep recesses of my brain? Was I an unknowing guilty party in whatever had driven Laura to take her own life all these years later?

It seemed absurd, and yet the police believed there was a link between us all now. That whatever had happened to Laura may well be linked to what had happened to Clare. Where did that leave Julie and me?

I was still on edge when I woke the girls; caffeine was surging through my veins to try to keep me focused on what I needed to do. We'd decided they still needed to go about their daily routine but that Paul would drop Beth at school and I'd pick her up. We wouldn't leave her to walk on her own.

Beth had rebelled against it, of course. I couldn't blame her, but I didn't want her to be home when the police came to fit the panic alarms. If I could get just one more day of normality out of this madness, I would.

I'd leave Molly at daycare. She'd be safe there. Distracted. Keeping things as normal as possible for her was key. I'd hung her washed sheets out on the line first thing, tried to reassure myself that her accident was just one of those things and didn't mean she was being damaged by the atmosphere that hung all around us.

Paul had agreed to cut his hours in Belfast. Only be there when necessary. I'd have preferred it if he'd worked at home, but he said he couldn't let his clients down. He wouldn't be drawn further on it.

But at least if he was away for a few hours I might get a chance to see Michael. I hadn't been able to get him out of my head since we'd last seen each other. His plea for me to run away with him. Maybe if he wanted the girls to come too, we could?

My head hurt. I took a couple of paracetamol. I knew this was a flight of fancy – even to think I could run away to be with him – but it provided some comfort.

I was making the breakfast, plastering on my biggest, fakest smile, when my phone rang. The number was listed as private and my heart hammered as I answered. What if it was Clare's killer? They knew where I lived, who was to say they wouldn't get my phone number?

I was relieved, at first, to hear Constable King's voice on the line. The familiarity of it soothed me.

'Rachel,' she said, 'we were wondering if you could call into the station, maybe this morning?'

'What's happened?' I asked, immediately suspicious.

I saw Beth look at me, saw the fear in her eyes.

'Don't worry. There have just been some developments on the case overnight and we'd like to talk to you, and to Julie, about them.'

'What developments?' I asked, wanting to ask why Julie and I needed to come in.

'I'd rather not talk about it over the phone. Look, I know you have things to do first thing. So maybe you could call in after ten? We can send a car to get you, if you'd prefer?'

I tried to keep my voice light, aware that Molly and Beth were both within earshot.

'I'm fine to drive, honest. But you're making me a little nervous here,' I said with a false laugh.

'Look, we'll talk about it when we see you. If you ask for me when you arrive, I'll come down and get you.'

With that she was gone and I looked to see Beth staring at me wide-eyed.

'What is it now, Mum? Where do you have to drive to?'

'The police just want to update me on what's happening. Routine, don't worry.'

There was no chance that she wouldn't worry. Paul looked at me, one eyebrow raised.

'They said they'll fill me in when I get there. They said not to worry.'

'Well then,' Paul said, 'if the police say not to worry, there's no point in wasting any energy on worrying now, is there?' he said before urging Beth to hurry up getting ready.

'But I really don't feel very well,' she said, clutching her stomach.

She knew he'd not ask too many questions if he thought there was any chance it was her period that was ailing her.

'Rachel, are you sure she's fit for school?' he asked me.

'I'm pretty sure she's absolutely fine and isn't it better to have the school look after her than to leave her alone?' I said, nodding towards Beth while I spoke.

'But, Mum, I really, really don't feel great. I've awful cramps and I'm afraid I'll just start crying every five minutes.'

Paul shrugged his shoulders, absolving himself of any further parental responsibility with a smooth: 'Your call, Rachel.'

'But I've got to go to the police station; I can't bring you with me,' I told her.

'I'll lock all the doors and windows and go straight to bed. I'll only answer the door when I know it's you or the police.'

'She's a sensible girl, Rachel,' Paul said, already filling his briefcase and getting ready to leave. 'Besides, the police have said this is all just precautionary. We can't change the course of our entire lives because of this. We can't live in fear.'

I was so tired, my brain so fuzzy. I could have argued with him, but what would it have achieved except to upset Molly, and me into the bargain?

'Okay then, Beth. You stay in bed.' I glared at Paul as I spoke. 'I'll be back from the police station as quickly as I can and you must promise me not to open the door to anyone. Not a single soul! And keep your phone at your side. If anyone even remotely suspicious comes to the door, you call the police, okay? Don't hesitate.'

She looked at me, solemn with just a hint of fear in her eyes as if she'd bitten off more than she could chew.

'Okay, Mum, I will. I promise I'm not faking.'

I didn't have the patience to console her, so I just turned my attention to getting Molly ready.

'What does sausagepuss mean, Mammy?'

'Sorry?'

'Sausagepuss! You just said it to Beth. Anyone sausagepuss comes to the door?'

I wanted to pull that child to me and keep her this innocent forever.

'It's like a sausage dog, only a cat instead,' I said with a giggle and she ran off to grab one of her soft toys, a well-loved cat, from the sofa.

I felt a wave of emotion rise up in me and I let out a shuddering breath.

'Rachel, you need to try to keep calm or this is going to destroy you,' Paul said.

But he didn't stop to offer a hug. He didn't offer to stay with Beth while I went to the police station. He just lifted his travel coffee cup and briefcase, called goodbye to the girls and left.

Chapter Thirty

Rachel

I phoned Julie as soon as I'd dropped Molly at daycare and asked her if she needed a lift to the police station. If I wasn't mistaken, her voice was slurred as she told me that would probably be a good idea. She was at her mother's house, had gone there after the police visit yesterday.

I arrived just after nine thirty to pick her up and saw she was waiting for me at the garden wall. From a distance she had looked well enough presented, but once I got closer the cracks were more obvious. The T-shirt she wore was crumpled, as were the loose linen trousers she was wearing. I noticed what I took to be a coffee stain on them. Strands of her hair had escaped from her ponytail and it was clear she hadn't washed it in a few days. Her skin was dull and dry. She wore no make-up, which wasn't like her at all, and as she climbed into the car and buckled her seat belt I could see her hands were shaking and I could smell alcohol on her breath.

When she looked at me I noticed that her eyes were bloodshot, tired.

'You okay?' I asked, even though it seemed obvious she was anything but.

She shrugged. 'Not sleeping well,' she said, looking out of the car window. 'Brendan's taken the kids to his parents for a few days.'

'Maybe you should have gone too, cleared your head a bit?' I said.

Brendan hailed from County Down on the East Coast of Ireland and a few days away might have done Julie the world of good.

She gave a strangled laugh. 'I wasn't exactly asked.'

I was shocked. Brendan and Julie were a great couple, always holding each other up.

'Don't worry, it isn't that serious,' she said, looking at me with tears forming in her eyes. 'He just didn't think the kids needed to see me getting so upset all the time. It was upsetting them. And I can hardly leave now – sure, we have the police looking to see us this morning . . .'

She looked back out the window, wrung her hands together. I could see she was on edge.

'Can we go?' she asked. 'I just want to get this over and done with and get back home.'

I nodded, gave her knee a squeeze and we set off, neither of us speaking during the short drive. I felt aware of the photo album in my bag, which was thrown on the back seat, but now wasn't the time to mention it. She was already worried about going to the police station. Or maybe I was just trying to hide it from myself. I still couldn't shake the feeling that there was some level of responsibility on my shoulders. The weight of it threatened to crush me.

Once parked, I took Julie's hand and we crossed Strand Road heading towards the police station.

We asked for Constable King and took our seats in the soulless reception area while we waited for her.

'I've never been in a police station before,' Julie said, jiggling her legs up and down, clearly nervous. 'I wonder what they're going to tell us. I mean, it's not been good news whenever they've come near us; in fact, it's been more bad news.'

'Maybe they have a lead,' I offered.

'They wouldn't call us in for that,' Julie said, her eyes darting around the room at the tired posters on the walls offering advice on legal aid or how to beat drug and alcohol addiction. She stood up and walked to the Perspex screen at the reception desk. 'Would I have time for a smoke, do you think? Before we go in?'

The portly officer on duty looked her up and down; Julie was already rummaging in her bag for a packet of cigarettes.

'There's no smoking here,' he said.

'I know,' she replied, 'but outside? There has to be a place outside.'

She was sounding increasingly agitated and I got up, encouraged her to sit down, told her that Constable King wouldn't be long.

'I just want a smoke, Rachel!' she snapped, twisting away from me and heading for the exit.

Just at that moment, Constable King walked through the door to our left and called our names. Swearing under her breath, Julie put her cigarettes and lighter back in her bag and followed Constable King through the door while I trailed behind, offering a weak apology of a smile to the officer behind the desk.

It wasn't like Julie to be so short with anyone. Not even on her bad days. Then again, everything had been turned on its axis and nothing made sense any more, so it wasn't really a surprise that Julie no longer seemed to be the Julie she normally was.

'We appreciate you ladies coming in,' Constable King said, 'especially at such short notice. DI Bradley will be joining us and we hope you can help us to go through some information that might be of assistance to the investigation.'

'Anything that can help,' I said, while Julie stayed quiet.

We were led to a small room, devoid of any character or redeeming features. A white MDF table sat in the middle, surrounded by eight office chairs, some of which had clearly seen better days. Strip lights overhead buzzed to life as we took our seats; the only natural light in the room came from several small windows high on the walls on the right-hand side of where we were sat. None of them big enough to make any real difference to the dank feel of the place, no matter how hot and bright it was outside.

'Can I get you a tea or coffee?' Constable King asked.

'No vodka on offer?' Julie asked with a nervous laugh, but the way she was behaving I'd say she'd quite happily accept one if it were.

'Sadly not,' Constable King said. 'Just tea or coffee. And if I'm honest, the coffee here is pretty disgusting. I'd stick with the tea, if I were you.'

We agreed we would and she went to fetch it, leaving Julie and I alone in the room.

'What information do you think she has?' Julie asked.

I shrugged. God only knew. All we'd been told before was that they were examining a number of lines of inquiry. It could be anything.

Julie drummed her fingers on the table. 'Have you thought about it much, Rachel? Not just Clare, but those flowers? Laura? Do you think. . .'

Before she could finish her sentence, the door opened and DI Bradley walked in, carrying a folder and looking very much like a man on a mission.

He sat down opposite us and smiled. It should have been reassuring, but I didn't feel especially reassured. Constable King followed just after carrying two Styrofoam cups filled with tea so strong you could stand a spoon up in them. I sat mine on the table in front of me. I was too nervous to drink.

'Thanks for coming in. I hope we haven't put you to any trouble,' DI Bradley said. 'I'm sure you appreciate that we're all trying to get this man behind bars as soon as possible.'

'You said you wanted us to go through some information or something?' Julie said, fidgeting with a thread hanging loose from the hem of her T-shirt.

'Well, you know we've been having difficulties tracing Ms Taylor's digital footprint. We didn't find her phone, her laptop or any tablet in her flat, or in her car. We were able to trace her phone records, but they didn't throw up anything out of the ordinary. There weren't any numbers she called or messaged repeatedly, apart from both of yours. This sounds like a strange thing to ask, but do either of you know if there was any possibility she may have had a second phone?'

I shook my head. 'I wouldn't think so, certainly not one that I knew of.'

'I only knew about the one you've been searching for,' Julie said. 'Although . . . we were issued work phones at one stage. Don't know why. No one ever used them. Mine's still lying in my drawer.'

'That's interesting,' DI Bradley said. 'No one at your work mentioned that to us.'

'It was a while back. And as I said, no one really used them. They weren't great handsets and managing two phones was a pain. I imagine most people wouldn't have given them a second thought.'

'It's a lead we'll look into, anyway,' he said.

'But I don't understand why she'd have started using it after all this time,' Julie said, shaking her head.

DI Bradley looked to Constable King. 'I know it seems a

little out of character for Clare from what you've told us, but we can't rule out that she was deliberately trying to keep secret who she was seeing and that she'd taken steps to ensure her privacy.'

'But we knew she wanted to keep it quiet anyway, she didn't want to jinx it. We've already told you that,' Julie said.

'Do either of you have cause to think it might have been more complicated than that? That perhaps this is a man who has a lot to lose if his personal affairs are revealed?' DI Bradley said. 'He might be married, for example.'

'I really don't think Clare would date a married man. Not knowingly,' Julie said. 'It wouldn't be like her.'

I stayed quiet. We all did things outside our character from time to time.

'We've run searches on various dating websites and apps. You'd said this was where Clare met the man she was dating. We've only found one account linked to her known email addresses and that's been dormant for the last seven months. Even before then, she didn't appear to have responded to any messages she received.'

That was definitely strange. I was absolutely sure Clare had told me she'd met this mystery man on Perfect Partners. I told DI Bradley as much and he checked his files.

'We definitely checked that company and there was no record of any account attached to Clare's name or any of the email addresses she was known to use.'

Julie started jiggling her legs again, her nerves showing.

'I still don't see why we've been brought here,' she said. 'You could have told us any of this, asked us any of these questions, over the phone.'

'We've more to go through,' he said as I placed my hand gently on Julie's knee to still it.

She brushed it away.

'Have you more aspersions you want to cast on her character? Is that it?' she barked. 'Because I don't want to hear lies about my friend, having affairs, sneaking around or lying to us. There has to be a more reasonable explanation. Either that or you've overlooked something. God knows, it's been almost a week. She's still lying cold up there on her own and you're no further forward.'

'I know this is very difficult,' DI Bradley said.

'No, you don't. You've no idea of just how difficult this is.'

'Julie, please,' I urged. 'They're trying to help. They're not the enemy,' I soothed, even if I did wonder why we were here.

She threw her hands in the air, muttered something under her breath then folded her arms and sat back in her chair.

'Okay, okay, then. Let's get on with things.'

DI Bradley pulled some grainy images from the folder and turned them in our direction.

'We did a sweep of CCTV on nights when Clare's bank records showed she'd stopped at Chill Off Licence, as we know she did on the night of her death. Just on the off-chance they might have showed her with someone we'd be able to identify. We did find someone with her on 24 May. I wondered if you'd have a look? We've already shown these images to Mr and Mrs Taylor, and to Ronan.'

Julie looked at me as DI Bradley pushed two pictures in our direction. Was it possible we were about to see our friend's killer for the first time? I felt the claustrophobia of the small room start to swoop in around me. I braced myself and then looked at a picture of the back of Clare's head as she walked into the off-licence.

Her head was tilted to the side as if she was chatting to the person who was with her. There wasn't much to guess from. He was tall. Looked to be wearing suit trousers and a short-sleeved shirt. His face wasn't picked up with the angle of the

200

camera, but I could see his hair was on the longer side. Curled. In need of a trim. There was a familiarity about him, but before I could place him, Julie spoke.

'That's Liam Connolly. He works with us.'

Constable King wrote the name down.

'And he and Clare got along well?'

'Well, he's worked there as long as we have. They got on grand. Had a bit of a laugh, you know. He's more senior than us, so they'd have worked together on a few projects, but I don't think . . . No . . . there was nothing like that going on. He's married. A few kids, too – one only a few months old.'

I saw the two police officers exchange glances again, as if this could confirm their theory that Clare had been having an affair.

'There's no way Liam Connolly would hurt, or could hurt anyone,' Julie added. 'He's a good person.'

'This is just one in a number of lines of inquiry,' DI Bradley said. 'We have a second picture for you to look at, as well. This one was captured outside Primrose on Strand Road, on the evening of 9 May. Clare's bank records showed that she paid for a meal there that evening, most likely a dinner for two from the receipt amount. This was captured by the City Centre Initiative outside.'

He pushed two more pictures towards us. Julie noticed it first, or at least it sank in with her first. Her hand went to her mouth.

'This doesn't mean anything,' she said. 'They're friends. Have been for a long time.'

I just looked at the picture, taking in the shape of my husband, his arm protectively around my friend's shoulders as they walked out of the restaurant.

I heard Constable King speak.

'So you know who this man is?'

I felt the room start to swim around me. I looked up to the

windows high on the wall, partially open but not a breath of air breaking through them. I wanted to climb the walls, stick my head through the narrow opening, past the safety glass. Breathe.

The scratches on his arms.

His coldness.

How broken we'd become.

Did I know him at all?

'That's Rachel's husband, Paul,' I heard Julie say in a small voice.

Maybe it wasn't so small. It was hard to tell over the sound of my blood rushing through my veins.

Chapter Thirty-One

Elizabeth

I'd called my son-in-law and asked him to bring the grand-children around to see me a day early. Ever since I'd spoken to the police, told them more about Laura, I'd felt as if I'd betrayed her in some way. A part of me thought I'd be able to assuage some of that guilt if I spent time with Max and Ava.

She'd been a great wife and a loving mother. She'd doted on the children from the day and hour they were born and seemed to take to motherhood like a duck to water. She'd said having the children made her feel less lonely – she'd always have company, even when her husband was at work. As a family unit they were a joy to watch. He made her happy. The children made her complete.

She was never one to complain about them waking in the night or teething or any of those things that can break the spirit of the most devoted parent. I admired her for it. Growing older had robbed me of some of my patience and while I, too, doted on those children and loved to see them coming round, there were times when I was happier to see them leave.

They were whirlwinds of activity – and they'd rush into our home, pull it apart bit by bit, eat all my food and then leave later, tummies full and hearts fuller. I'd survey the spilled buckets of building blocks and the scattered crayons, rescue a half-chewed pencil from Izzy that had left a trail of splinters in the hall, and restack the sofa cushions, dismantling their forts and picking up crushed biscuits from the floor.

The moment of peace and quiet when they'd left – the first time I'd sit on my chair and listen to the silence around me – was always blissful. Paddy and I used to smile at each other, revel in the quiet, but we were always so grateful to have them in our lives. After he died, Laura spent more and more time with me. The children became my refuge. Their silliness and innocence had pulled me through the darkest of days.

Of course, Laura had been at the centre of most of that silliness and mayhem when she'd been here. She'd played with a lack of self-consciousness and a joy that she hadn't been so free with in her own childhood. It fed both my heart and my soul to see them together. God knows I tried, once she died, to keep some of the fun, some of that adventure going with the children, but their lives were never going to be the same. They simply couldn't be.

They didn't want to play any more at building forts, or towers, or having picnics in the barn. Those were 'mummy things'. Doing them without her was too painful, no matter how I tried. They'd arrive at my house like little grey shadows of the children they once were. Smaller, quieter, haunted. Afraid to step into the shadows of the farmhouse as if every nook and cranny held a dark secret. Slowly, gently, I coaxed them not exactly out of their grief, but just a little further from the centre of it, and we made our own routines. They helped me to heal, too. Those innocent interactions.

We baked. We found programmes to watch together. Ava enjoyed rifling through the books on her mother's old bookcase in her childhood bedroom, then curling up on the bed and reading. Max, well, he enjoyed taking Izzy out for long walks, when he'd talk to her like only a boy could talk to his dog. I imagined Izzy heard a lot of secrets.

We'd play in the yard after, Max and I. Throwing balls for Izzy to chase. Getting the hose out in the warmer weather and watching Izzy run through the cold spray. Slowly, tentatively at first, Ava started to join in. Eventually, we started to hear little bursts of laughter again.

I needed to hear it that day, of all days. I suppose I also needed to see my daughter's own eyes, her mannerisms, her reflection in their faces. That kept her alive for me.

I'd baked banana bread, wiped the sweat from my brow after I set the bread to cool on the windowsill. I'd prepared a 'party tea', as the children would call it. Crisps and sandwiches, biscuits and chopped fruit. Fizzy drinks to wash it down with. I'd filled the small paddling pool with water. The kids were too big to sit in it now, but they could play with Izzy.

I'd even gone out and bought the largest tub of ice cream I could find and had it waiting in the freezer. There would be jelly and chocolate sauce to go with it.

It was overcompensating. I knew that. But I needed to do something to make myself feel better. This would help, a little.

I'd been on edge all day waiting for them. For once, time to myself didn't seem to be a good thing. It gave me too much time to think. As soon as the clock turned three and I knew they'd be finished at school, I felt my mood start to improve. They'd be with me soon. I looked at the photograph of Laura on the mantlepiece and I apologised for letting her down. Again.

The ticking of the clock and the occasional whimper from Izzy as she dreamed of chasing a ball or a rabbit were the only noises that interrupted the silence, so I jumped when the phone rang. It was too loud, or my head was too full, or something just wasn't right, and I wanted the noise to stop.

The name flashing on the screen was Ingrid Devlin's. I wondered whether or not to answer. I didn't feel I had anything else to say to her, even though she'd stuck to her word and not reported anything overly salacious about Laura. I didn't want to get any further on the wrong side of the police and they clearly didn't want me talking to her, but I couldn't resist answering.

'Elizabeth,' Ingrid began. 'Look, I promised I'd keep you in the loop if I heard anything at all and I just wanted to fill you in on something my source has told me.'

I wanted to know, but at the same time was afraid of what she might tell me.

'Do I need to sit down to hear this?' I asked.

'I don't think so,' she said. 'It's not bad news as such.'

Those words 'as such' came with so much portent.

'I'll come right to the point,' she said, her voice low, almost a whisper. 'The police are going to talk to two different men who had a connection to Clare. I think one was a work colleague and another the husband of one of Clare's friends. They're describing it as significant.'

'And Laura? Is there a connection to Laura?'

'Not that police are aware of at the moment. Between ourselves, my source seems to think that the husband of the friend might offer some clues to what happened.'

I wanted to know more. I wanted to know which friend. I wanted to know what had happened that had turned police attention towards these two men. I wanted to know why Laura had been brought into it all, but Ingrid didn't have any more answers for me.

'Elizabeth, I just wanted you to know that there are other angles being looked at. Important angles. I know it doesn't answer any questions as to who was behind the flowers and the notes, but it's something.'

I thanked her for telling me, hung up and sat down feeling a little easier, my heart lifting further at the sound of a car driving into the yard, followed by the excited shouting of Max and Ava. They ran in through the door I'd left open for them and directly at me, almost knocking me off my feet with the impact of their hugs, before they both got down on the floor to play with Izzy.

Watching my family, the smiles on their faces, the way the sun had kissed their skin over the last few weeks, bringing with it a new crop of freckles, I felt a sense of peace wash over me that I'd been struggling to find for a long time. Maybe it was selfish of me to hope that the moving of the investigation away from Laura was a good thing, but we'd all had our own suffering. More than enough of it.

Their father followed them in, looking tired.

'Are you staying for tea?' I asked. 'I've more than enough prepared.'

He shook his head. 'I thought I'd use the time to run to the supermarket. Run a few errands, if that's okay?'

'Of course it is,' I said. 'But at least get a cup of tea or a cold drink or something first. You look done in.'

'I feel done in,' he said, sitting down.

He looked to the children and then back to me. The strain of Laura's death being brought up again had clearly been getting to him. A wave of guilt swept back in.

'I know this week has been tough,' I said. 'I'm sorry for that.'

'Every week's tough, Elizabeth,' he said quietly. 'I thought it would be getting easier by now, but it's not.'

'I know,' I told him, but my words felt inadequate. 'We just have to focus on the kids. For her.'

He nodded. 'We do. Which is why I need to go and get some food or they'll be living on cereal for the next week.'

He gave me a lopsided smile – a smile that lied and said everything was normal when it wasn't.

'You're a great dad,' I told him. 'And a good friend to me. I'm not sure I'd have got through this last two years and everything that's happened without you. Don't ever be afraid to ask me to help more if you need it.'

'I won't,' he said and he stood up, hugged me awkwardly. 'Thanks, Elizabeth. Right, kids, I'll be back in a couple of hours. Be good for your granny.'

'We will!' the children chorused, and he left.

I wished, again, that I could take his pain away. I felt such guilt for letting him down, too. The man who'd promised to love her. Who did love her. He'd made her smile from the moment they'd met. She hadn't long turned thirty and even though thirty is no age at all these days, she'd been convinced she would end up on the shelf. Resigned herself to it. But then she came home from after work drinks one night with that special kind of a smile on her face – one I'd recognised from my own face when I'd met Paddy, and her life had changed.

She finally found happiness.

Or so I thought. Even his love and faith in her wasn't enough to save her.

If I'd been a better mother, maybe he'd still have his wife by his side. Maybe he wouldn't look so tired all the time. I vowed to insist on having the children more and to visit them more. Anything to lift the burden from him. I didn't want them to lose someone else. I vowed to be extra cautious.

Chapter Thirty-Two

Rachel

'You don't really think my husband could have anything to do with this?' I stuttered, knowing what their answer was before I asked.

'We're not saying anything like that,' DI Bradley said. 'But we will need to ask him a few questions, just to clear up a few things. I'm assuming by your reaction that you didn't know that he'd met with Clare on that evening?'

I shook my head. I hadn't been aware of him spending any time with Clare outside the time we all spent together. He was in Belfast on week nights and we'd spent every weekend for as long as I could remember sat on either end of our sofa playing at some sort of normal family life.

'What night of the week was that?' I asked.

DI Bradley looked down at his file. 'A Wednesday,' he said.

'Well, then, it can't be him, because he's always in Belfast on a Wednesday night. Let me see the picture again.'

Julie pushed it towards me, but there was no mistaking that my husband was in the photo. The image was grainy but clear enough to leave no doubt at all in my mind. I could see his hair, his profile. I could even see the wedding ring on his left hand, which he'd draped casually over my best friend's shoulder.

'There has to be some innocent explanation,' Julie said. 'And it doesn't mean he hurt her.'

'Of course it doesn't,' DI Bradley said. 'Nonetheless, we do need to speak to him, preferably as soon as possible. Can you also give us his mobile phone number, Rachel? So we can check it against our records.'

I rhymed it off robotically. I felt Julie, Julie who'd been falling apart just minutes before, reach over and take my hand. She was trying to act like the strong one for me now. I resented it. I pulled my hand away.

'Is he at home today?' DI Bradley asked.

'No. He's in Belfast. Or he should be in Belfast,' I said with a hollow laugh. 'He'll be home tonight.'

I thought of the scratches. I should tell the police. I knew that. But I was scared. Scared to say anything that would make this worse. I thought of my daughters. How they hero-worshipped him. How I had once, too. This would break them. Did I want to protect him? A part of me thought that maybe I did. And I didn't want to say it in front of Julie. I know that was bizarre. She knew everything about me. But I didn't want to see pity in her eyes.

It didn't mean anything, did it? The scratches, and the mystery dinner with Clare, and the lies . . .

But I was kidding myself. I had to say something. Even if it made me feel sick to do so. I couldn't be complicit in protecting him if, and it was a big if, he had done something.

'He had scratches on his arm,' I blurted.

Three sets of eyes were on me.

'When?' DI Bradley asked.

'Last week. Thursday. Friday. I can't remember exactly.'

'Did he say what caused them?' Constable King asked.

'I didn't ask. I couldn't bring myself to ask. But they looked like, you know, fingernails had caused them. Things just haven't been great between us.'

I could feel my skin start to burn. I was flushed with embarrassment. I should have asked him. I should have told the police. I should have admitted before now that things were terribly wrong in our relationship. But I thought it was just that – a marriage in free fall, not a possible sign of something worse.

And Clare? With her head leaning towards his in the picture . . . My friend, for whom I was grieving, had she betrayed me in the worst way? So much ran through my head. Had my husband been her mystery man? The man she wouldn't, or couldn't tell us about. The police thought whoever it was had been trying to keep their liaison secret. They might be married. Could it be Paul?

Was he really capable of killing someone? I felt my stomach start to turn.

'I don't feel well,' I managed to mutter, wanting to run from the room to be sick, but I didn't know where the toilets were.

My head was spinning as the questions I asked of myself came thick and fast and memories flooded in. Clare and Paul sitting together in a corner after a dinner party, deep in conversation. Their heads bowed close together. Them taking Beth to the panto together the year Molly was born and I was too pregnant to sit through a few hours in the theatre. Clare had jumped at the idea. The pinging messages late at night on Paul's phone. Work stuff, he said. Clare being coy about her new man. It was more than just the fear of jinxing it, wasn't it?

I felt the heat rise at the back of my neck. A cold sweat broke out. I was going to be sick, I knew it, and I glanced around the room until I spotted a wastepaper basket, into which I emptied my stomach in great heaving sobs.

Constable King was sitting beside me, encouraging me to sip from a cold glass of water that she'd brought into the room.

211

She'd dampened some paper towels and was using them to cool my forehead and the back of my neck.

Her voice was gentle and calm. Soft. I let it wash over me. She was a nice woman, I thought, although she didn't look much older than Beth. No wrinkles, I thought as I focused on her face. Clear skin, minimal make-up. That wouldn't last past her mid-thirties. She had one of those pixie haircuts, cropped, that anyone with anything less than perfectly sculpted cheek-bones couldn't get away with, but she carried it well.

'What age are you?' I asked, my tongue feeling thick and heavy in my mouth.

'Twenty-nine,' she said. 'Big birthday next year.'

I envied her youth. Wanted to tell her to appreciate it while she had it.

'I don't know if you ever told me your first name,' I said.

'Eve,' she replied.

I nodded.

Julie sat silently at my other side while DI Bradley talked to someone outside the room – some poor unfortunate who'd been tasked with removing the wastepaper bin and cleaning it. I wondered if DI Bradley was telling that poor officer to go and find my husband.

I pulled my gaze from Constable King's youthful face and looked down at my wedding ring. My solitaire engage-ment ring nestled on top of it. A strange tradition. Pieces of metal we put on our fingers to claim ownership of someone else.

'He didn't hurt her,' I said, for myself as much as anyone else. 'I know that. He might have been seeing her. He might have lied to me about where he was, but I know he wouldn't have done that to her. He's a good man. A good father. A good friend. He wouldn't . . .'

Constable King took my hand. 'Please try not to worry. We'll just be asking a few questions. It'll be informal, but it is important that we talk to him. I understand this is very distressing for you.'

I nodded, because there was nothing else I could say.

'If we give you a few minutes to gather yourself, do you think we could continue? We've a few more questions that you ladies may be able to answer for us.'

I heard Julie say, 'Of course.' Felt Constable King pat my hand and get up to go and talk to her colleague.

'Did Clare ever mention Paul to you?' I asked Julie.

'No, Rachel. I swear. Not outside any conversation we had about you guys. Just boring stuff. There might be a rational explanation.'

It may well be rational but it wasn't pleasant.

My phone rang then, Molly's daycare.

'Mrs Walker,' her teacher said in the voice she reserved only for the most serious of occasions. 'I think you'd better come to the nursery. There's been an incident and Molly's very upset.'

'An incident?' I asked. 'Has she had an accident or something?'

I thought of how she'd wet the bed. Had been extra clingy.

'No. I'm afraid it's more serious than that. We've had to inform the police, too. A man was seen walking around the periphery of the outdoor play area. He called Molly over to him; I'm afraid our assistants didn't see her walk over at first.'

I held my breath, gripping Julie's hand as she looked at me, eyes wide with concern.

'As you know, the area's secure, so he wasn't able to take her, but he did talk to her through the railings. One of our assistants saw what was happening and ran over, but the man made off. Molly's become very distressed. She won't tell us what he said, but she's been crying for you since. We've tried to calm her down . . .'

'I'll be there as soon as I can,' I said, hanging up and lifting my bag.

My baby . . . Not my baby!

Chapter Thirty-Three

Rachel

Constable King agreed to drive me to the crèche. She'd been made aware of the call from the nursery staff and was also only too aware of the state I was in. If I thought running there would have got me there quicker, I'd have run. I'd have done anything to get to my daughter as soon as was humanly possible.

Who had been at her daycare? Why had they called her over? Did they know her name? All these thoughts, all these questions ran through my head and I didn't know the answers. I just wanted to get to her, to soothe her and to make her safe. To keep her safe. Anyone who wanted could come after me, but to come after my child? My innocent little girl. Was it the person behind the flowers? The person who'd killed Clare? Was it not bad enough that they were coming after me? Why did they have to come after my baby, too?

'Try to stay calm,' Constable King said. 'I know that's very hard right now, but the main thing is that she's safe and we'll be with her soon.'

I nodded, a tear sliding down my cheek. My heart was beating so fast I was sure I'd be sick again.

My mind jumped to Beth, at home alone. Panicked, I told

214

Constable King, who said she'd send a car around there to be sure everything was okay. I called Beth's number, listened as it rang out. I swore. She'd been told to keep her phone with her at all times. She knew I was worried. I called her number again and listened to it ring out, go to voicemail.

'Beth, where are you?' I shouted into the phone. 'Call me as soon as you get this. Straight away! The police are on their way round to the house now. Let them in. Beth, please, call me back.'

I hung up, stared at my phone, felt my worry rise. My girls. I called Beth's number again and again, until I could feel tears falling down my cheeks. I tried the landline, but she didn't answer that either. My family was being ripped apart. My husband had been lying. My eldest child wouldn't answer her phone and my baby was terrified. And me? I could hardly breathe.

'Why won't she answer?' I wailed.

'Take a deep breath, Rachel. Constable Black will be at your house any minute now and he'll be able to check on Beth.'

'Just let her be okay,' I said.

We pulled into the car park of the daycare centre where Molly was and I don't think Constable King had even put the handbrake on before I'd jumped out of the car and was running towards the entrance.

'Rachel!' she called to me. 'You don't want to run in there like that. You need to be calm for her. If she sees you upset, you'll only scare her more.'

That stopped me in my tracks. She was right, of course. I had to act the part of being calm and in control and hope that Molly wouldn't hear how hard my heart was beating or hear the tremor in my voice.

Constable King put her hand on my arm, her touch soothing me. 'Steady yourself. Take a deep breath,' she urged and I did.

She reached out and pressed the buzzer to gain entry to the centre.

My daughter's caregiver, a softly spoken woman called Marie, who seemed to exist in floaty skirts, voluminous tunics and chunky necklaces, answered within seconds.

'She's through in the quiet area,' she said. 'We've managed to calm her a little and she's reading a story now with Catherine. I'm so sorry that we didn't see her toddle off to the fencing. She can't have been there long. She'd been playing in the sandpit just minutes before.'

'Did your staff get a good look at him? Or do you have CCTV that might have captured his image?' Constable King asked.

'He was wearing a jacket, a hoodie, with the hood pulled up. Shorts, white trainers. His face was obscured. There's CCTV capturing the front of the building but none on that side. We can have a look and see,' Marie said.

'But can I please just see Molly now?' I asked.

Surely there would be time for all this after I'd seen my daughter? She was my priority. And Beth. I looked at my phone. She hadn't called back. Constable Black would be there now, but he hadn't called yet, either. Hadn't radioed to say she was fine. But I knew Molly was just metres away, and I needed to see her and hold her.

'We've tried to keep what happened from the other children,' Marie said, 'so we've moved them into the art room so they don't get upset. We'll go through this way.'

She led me through the playroom – toys scattered on the floor, abandoned doll's prams and trucks – until we reached the small reading room, softly lit, with beanbags and cushions all over the floor. Molly was sitting there cuddled into the nursery assistant, her eyes transfixed on the book that was being read to her, her thumb in her mouth. She looked so small.

'Molly?' I said softly.

She blinked and looked up at me, her bottom lip starting to tremble.

'Mammy!' she said. 'The bad man said he was going to take you away.'

'No one's going to take me away, darling,' I said, walking towards her and pulling her into a big hug.

She sobbed into my shoulder.

'He said I wouldn't ever, ever, ever see you again, Mammy.'

'I'm here, baby,' I soothed. 'I'm here and no one's ever going to take me away from you.'

'Molly?' I heard a voice behind me. 'Did the man call you by your name?'

Molly raised her head and looked up to see Constable King standing in the doorway. At the sight of the police officer, she curled her body into mine.

'Mammy, why's the police here?'

'They're going to help catch the bad man and stop him from scaring any more children,' I said. 'You remember this lady, don't you? She played My Little Ponies with you. Her name's Eve.'

Molly eyed her suspiciously, but Constable King got down on her knees close to us so that she was on Molly's level.

'You can help me to catch the bad man and you'll be a real hero,' she said. 'Like Wonder Woman.'

'He called me Molly!' she said, mimicking how he'd called her. 'He said he knewed my mammy was called Rachel and he said she was a bad lady.' Molly looked at me, her gaze low as if she was scared I'd be cross at what the man had said. 'He said to tell my mammy she was in big trouble and he was going to take her away.'

'Well, we're not going to let him do that,' Constable King said.

Her phone rang and I jumped. She nodded at me when

she looked at the screen and then made her way outside to answer it. I felt torn between being there for Molly, who so clearly, desperately needed me, and also wanting to know if Beth was safe.

I was so angry with myself for leaving her alone in the first place. I shouldn't have. How stupid could I be? But then again, I'd thought Molly was perfectly safe at daycare. Molly was clinging onto me for dear life.

'He knewed my name, Mammy. I told him that I wasn't aposed to speak to strangers, but he said he wasn't a stranger. I even asked him for the secret special password.'

Her voice was shaking. Her little hands clinging tightly to my top. She was only three, for goodness' sake. Still a month away from her fourth birthday. I'd given her the password, never thinking we'd need to use it. It was only supposed to be a precaution in case anyone told her that Paul or I had sent them to get her. It was a silly word. Jellybean. One that made us laugh.

'He got it wrong, Mammy.'

'What did he say, sweetheart?' I asked, smoothing her hair and hugging her close.

'Forget me not,' she said and started to cry. 'I want to forget him. He's a scary man.'

I pulled Molly as close to me as I could. This wasn't someone playing some sort of silly game. This was someone trying to scare me. This was someone who'd scared my child. My poor, innocent baby. This was someone twisted and I didn't know what I'd done to bring it all on us. What had Clare done? What had Julie done? My husband? And that woman who'd found Clare?

It all raced through my mind as I rocked my child in my arms and looked at the door, anxiously waiting for Constable King to let me know if Beth was okay. I felt so disorientated by it all. Then there was Paul and his secret meetings. The scratches. But it clearly wasn't Paul who'd visited Molly's nursery. There was someone else. A scary man.

The door opened and Constable King walked back in. I tried to read her face for some clue. She crouched down beside Molly and me and started to speak.

'First of all, Beth's fine. Constable Black's with her now and he'll stay with her until we get back. Perhaps if Molly can sit with her teacher for just a moment, we can have a chat outside.'

Molly held onto me tighter. I don't think she had any desire to let go.

'Sweetheart, if you sit with Catherine she'll read you more of your story and I'll just be outside the door. You can see me through the little window.'

'But what if you don't come back like the scary man said?'

'Molly, all my friends in the police are going to be looking for the silly, scary man right now. He's not going to get anywhere near you or your mum again. If he even tries, we'll take him straight to jail,' Constable King said.

Molly blinked, the blue of her eyes even brighter as her tears fell.

'Is that true, Mammy?'

'It is, pet.'

She sniffed and toddled over to Catherine, who started reading the book again.

I got to my feet, my legs shaky and my head spinning, and followed Constable King out of the room.

'The man, he told Molly "forget me not" – he's linked to those flowers,' I told her.

'If you don't mind, we'll get one of our team experienced in working with children to have a good talk to Molly about it. Try and get as many details as possible.'

'Of course,' I said. 'And Beth?'

'As I said, she's okay, but she did have a scare. Someone tried to break into your house, it seems. She heard someone rattling the back door and then the front. She was so scared she hid in the bathroom. When our team arrived to fit the alarms, whoever it was ran off, but not before he'd managed to smash a hole in your French doors.'

I didn't think I could take any more panic, any more worry. Everything was so completely out of control. I was dizzy trying to think about it all.

'I don't understand any of this,' I said, feeling my legs give way.

I sat on one of the small chairs in the playroom and tried to steady my breathing.

'We're doing our best to get to the bottom of it,' Constable King said, but she looked as confused as I was.

Chapter Thirty-Four

Rachel

We were travelling back home in the police car with Constable King when my phone rang and I saw Paul's name flash up on screen. I didn't want to answer. I didn't know what I could possibly say to him at that time. How I could be civil to him.

I was tempted to let the call go to voicemail, but I knew, for all his faults, he would worry if he couldn't get a hold of us. I was angry, but I wasn't cruel.

He had a right to know that his daughters had been in danger and that the threat I had warned him about was real.

I answered the call, could hear that he was driving – the hum of traffic in the background giving it away. I spoke first, trying my best to keep my voice steady. I didn't want to alarm Molly more than necessary.

'Paul, some things have happened here today. I don't want you to hear it from someone else.'

'I'm driving home now. I've had a call from the police. They want to see me. Is that what you're talking about, because I swear Rachel, I've no idea what's going on or what they would want to speak to me about.'

I bit my tongue. I wouldn't tell him where I had been, or

about the images I'd seen of him with Clare. That was not a conversation I'd have within earshot of our daughter, never mind a police officer. 'There was an incident at Molly's daycare,' I said. 'A man approached her. She was behind the railings and he didn't touch her but he gave her a real fright.'

I heard a deep intake of breath. 'What did he do? Who was he?'

Paul sounded angry, scared, protective.

'She's here with me now,' I said, 'in a police car. The police are going to help catch him.' I spoke in my best sing-song, child-friendly voice, hoping Paul would realise I wasn't free to tell him all the details. 'There was an incident at home, too, with Beth.'

'I knew you shouldn't have left her alone,' he said before swearing. 'Is she okay?'

I ignored the dig, fought the urge to scream at him that he had left her too. It wasn't all on my shoulders, and from what I had seen earlier there was every chance he was more involved in all of this than I ever thought possible. I took a deep breath.

'I'm on my way home now. The police are with her and she's fine, but she got a bit of a fright, too.'

'I'll be home myself in about an hour. I'll come and see you all before I go to any police station. Whatever the police want, it can't be that urgent. I think they just like to mess people around.'

I felt myself tremble. Emotion itching to burst out of me. Fear and love. Betrayal and guilt. From what I knew, it was Paul who had been messing people around.

'Give the girls a big hug from me,' he said, cutting through my thoughts, his own voice thick with emotion. 'Tell them I love them.'

I couldn't speak. I just nodded at the phone, as if that were any good to him, and hung up.

'Is Daddy coming home?' Molly asked, her eyes bright.

'He is, darling. And the first thing he wants is a giant hug from you.'

If Constable King thought anything of my husband not going straight to the police station, she said nothing and simply kept her eyes on the road ahead.

Beth sat cowed on the sofa, cradling a mug of tea. Her eyes were red from crying. It was the first thing I noticed. She looked up at me when I walked into the room and her face crumpled.

'I'm sorry, Mum,' she said. 'I just ran into the bathroom and locked the door when I heard someone at the back of the house. I didn't lift my phone. I could hear it ringing, but I was too afraid to go and get it.'

'You've nothing to be sorry for,' I said, sitting down beside her.

'I was so scared,' she said, sobbing into my shoulder.

'Was the bad man here, too?' I heard Molly ask, her eyes wide.

Beth looked at her sister and then at me.

'What does she mean?'

Molly pulled herself up on the armchair and grabbed her favourite pony, which she hugged close to her.

'A bad man came to my school and said he was going to hurt Mammy and take her away.'

'Mum?' Beth said, her lip wobbling again. 'Is that true?'

I nodded. 'But, Beth, the police are looking into it all. Look at how many officers are here now. And they're putting in alarms for us. They're going to make sure I'm safe – that we're all safe.'

I saw the doubt in her eyes and it almost broke me. It was

my job to make my children's world safe and this wasn't even close.

'Rachel, could we have a chat with you in the kitchen?' Constable King asked. 'The girls'll be fine here with Constable Black, won't you, girls?'

Both nodded but neither looked convinced.

'I won't be long,' I said to them.

My head now pounding, I walked into the kitchen. The sight of the French doors, one smashed at handle-height, broken glass lying on the tiled floor, made my heart sink.

'They clearly got scared away,' Constable King said. 'But whoever it was left something. You might want to sit down, Rachel. You're very pale as it is.'

'What is it?' I asked, placing one hand on the back of a kitchen chair to steady myself. What other bombshells could possibly be dropped today? 'Just show me.'

She handed me a photograph, old and faded. Not unlike the ones I'd been looking at in my photo album just the night before. The uniforms we were wearing weren't the first things I noticed, though, nor the background of the school we'd attended. What was most notable was that there were four of us in the photo, not three. The fourth person, standing on the outside of our group, her smile not as bright as ours, was unmistakably Laura.

One of the faces in the picture, Clare's, had been scored out. Scored out so deeply that the pen had broken through the photographic paper, leaving a hole where her face should have been. Red biro circled both my face and Julie's. The words 'Yr Next' were scrawled under my name.

Chapter Thirty-Five

Elizabeth

My heart was full by the time the children went home. I could almost forget all the nastiness of the last few days. When I'd been with them, I'd allowed myself to become immersed fully in their worlds. I'd listened to them talk about their schoolwork. Their hopes for the summer. Their badgering of their poor father to get them a dog just like Izzy to play with. They'd invited me into their lives, sharing every little detail with such enthusiasm that I swear I'd felt so much lighter, both physically and emotionally, just for having seen them.

As we'd played together in the yard, the hot sun beating down on us, their laughter ringing in my ears, I could almost remember what it had been like years before, when the sound of my own children's laughter rang through this old farmhouse in the Seventies and Eighties.

Maybe that was part of the reason the house was falling apart around us now. Just like me, it had been sustained by laughter and love, but there was little of that left in either of us these days.

I'd pushed away those thoughts and concentrated on what I could do and that was to make the rest of the day as pleasant as possible for Max and Ava.

They'd astounded me with their ability to eat so much ice cream and even when I'd warned them they'd end up with a tummy ache, they'd insisted on one more scoop. I didn't have it in me to refuse them, so they'd each got one more, very generous, serving.

By the time their daddy came to pick them up, they were sitting on the sofa in my living room and we were looking through old family photographs. They loved that. Loved seeing their mother when she was a little girl. Seeing me with bad hair and worse glasses. Seeing pictures of their granddad, their uncle; people who were no longer a part of their lives but always a part of their family. Seeing us all in different, easier times.

Ava looked so much like her mother had as a young girl. Sometimes it would catch me unawares. It would almost feel as if Laura were back with me.

'Look, Daddy!' Ava called as he'd walked in. 'Have you seen this picture of Mammy before? When she was my age. She's reading one of the books from her room that I've read.'

'That's lovely, pet,' he'd said, giving little more than a cursory glance at it before urging the kids to pick up their things and get ready to go home.

As he'd sat waiting for them, I couldn't help but notice he still looked as if he had the weight of the world on his shoulders, as if there was something he was trying to tell me but couldn't.

'Is everything okay?' I'd asked.

He'd sighed. 'Just a long day,' he'd said. 'Maybe it's just with it coming to the end of term, I'm almost as worn out as the children. A holiday'll do us the world of good.'

'It will,' I'd said. 'And no one deserves it more.'

He'd lifted the photo album from where Ava had left it on the table and started to flick through it, smiling every time he saw Laura.

'I do miss her, you know,' he'd said. 'I wish she could see how the kids are growing. Ava's coming to an age where she needs a mother's influence, if you know what I mean.'

'I can have those kind of talks with her if you want,' I'd offered.

'That would be good,' he'd said, turning the page.

I remember looking over his shoulder, when I noticed something strange. There were blank spaces in the album. Spaces where pictures had been stuck in but where now only remnants of backing paper were left stuck to the glue. I hadn't taken them out. I hadn't looked at those albums in a long time.

By my reckoning, the missing pictures were the ones Laura had taken herself when we'd loaned her our camera to take into the school fun day. We'd been so excited when she'd shown us pictures of groups of girls. Girls she'd said were her friends. She was in some of them herself. Maybe standing to the side. Not grinning at the camera like the rest of them but offering her small, shy smile instead. She'd insisted we put them in the album and we did as she'd asked.

'That's strange,' I'd said. 'There's some pictures missing. I'm sure I didn't take any out.'

'Do you think maybe Ava did? Or Max? Maybe they wanted a picture of their mum.'

My heart had contracted a little at the thought of the children smuggling pictures of their mother out of the house.

'Sure, all they had to do was ask,' I'd said, my heart too sore at their loss to be cross with them.

They'd run back into the room and I'd watched as their father asked them to sit down, then asked them very solemnly if they'd taken any pictures from my photo album.

Both children shook their heads.

'It's important to tell the truth,' he'd said.

'I didn't take them, Daddy,' Ava had said and Max just shook his head.

'It's okay if you did. I know you love your mum very much. I just need to know,' I'd said.

They'd both looked at me.

'I swear, Granny, I didn't,' Max had said.

'Me neither,' said Ava and I could see her bottom lip wobble a little.

I'd no desire to upset the children over a couple of photos, so I'd told them I believed them. I'd made sure to give them extra hugs and slip a fiver into each of their hands before they left.

It had felt like order was restored in the world and I'd sat down to bask in the memories of a mostly very lovely afternoon.

It still didn't answer the questions about where the photographs were, though, or who'd taken them.

Chapter Thirty-Six

Rachel

We were in a hotel room. I was trying to keep a brave face. Talk it up to Molly, like it was a treat. Beth was a bit more savvy. She knew something was wrong. She wasn't overly comforted by either the suite we had or the access we had to the swimming pool. She was clingy – not that I could blame her.

We could have stayed at home, the police had said. They'd given us the panic phones, put in the alarms and were increasing patrols even more, but Paul and I had decided to get some space from the house. For the night, at least. Until the doors were properly repaired and security lights had been fitted. I'd little desire to spend any time in his company, found it hard to look him in the face but I forced myself to act as if everything was normal. The girls needed some sense of stability.

We'd packed what we needed and drove with Paul to the police station, where I'd picked up my car and he went in to 'help with the inquiry'.

I'd driven us to the hotel, my eyes darting to the rear-view mirror for any signs that we were being followed. I'd parked close to the hotel door, wondering if it was wise that my car was in clear view but not wanting to take the risk of parking in any secluded corners.

The woman at reception had been full of smiles and welcomes.

'Just a wee break, is it?' she'd said while I filled in the paperwork.

I'd nodded, looked back to where the girls were sitting on a sofa in the lobby. Molly hugging her favourite pony as if she'd never let it go and Beth was looking as if she could faint at any moment.

I'd handed over the paperwork and the receptionist had read through the details.

'Oh, you're local,' she'd said, her eyebrow raised a little.

'We are,' I'd said, refusing to be drawn any further, much to the apparent disgust of the receptionist.

'And how long will you be staying?' she'd asked.

'I'm not sure,' I'd told her. 'Tonight, anyway . . . obviously. And tomorrow, maybe. Is it okay to confirm in the morning?'

'I'll have to check with the computer if we have availability,' she'd said and tapped her long acrylic nails on the keyboard in front of her, pulling all sorts of 'I'm thinking' faces before finally looking up. 'Well, yes, at the moment we do have availability for the family suite tomorrow night, but if a confirmed booking comes in . . .'

'We'll deal with that then,' I'd said.

I was tired. I was scared. I needed a shower and something to eat. I hadn't eaten anything since breakfast, which I'd managed to throw up in the police station. I could feel sweat trickle down my back and the air was thicker now than before, as if rain was on the way but not soon enough. My head hurt.

'Of course, madam,' the receptionist had said, handing me three key cards and telling us where our room was.

She'd started to launch into her full spiel about when

breakfast was served and what was available in the gym facilities, but I'd been too tired to listen. I knew it was rude, but I didn't have the energy to care.

'Come on, girls,' I'd said and we'd headed off to our first-floor suite.

Molly was bouncing on one of the two single beds in the living area, claiming the bed nearest the door for her ponies and her, while Beth sat on the sofa and started flicking aimlessly through the TV channels.

'How long'll Dad be?' she asked.

'I don't know, darling,' I told her.

'Why are they talking to him?'

'They're talking to lots of people. Everyone who knew Clare.'

'Will they talk to me?' she asked.

'I don't think so, pet.'

'I wish none of this had happened,' she said.

All I could do was agree.

'I don't think I want to go home ever again.'

'Well, Beth, the police are securing our house. It'll be the safest house in Derry by the time we get back. And I promise you, I'll not leave you alone again.'

'Can I tell my friends what happened?'

To be honest, I was impressed she hadn't done so already. I expected her to be on Snapchat as soon as the police left, filling everyone in.

'Don't look at me like that, Mum. I know this is serious. I'm not going to tell people what happened or where we are.'

I sat down beside her and took her hand.

'You're a very smart young woman, Beth Walker, and I love you very much.'

'Do you love me too, Mammy?' a little voice from the corner of the room piped up.

Molly was sitting cross-legged on her bed now, her eyes

growing tired. She hadn't had a nap all day, so I knew she'd be exhausted.

'Of course I love you, poppet,' I told her. 'You girls are the most important thing in the world to me.'

'And you won't leave or let the bad man take you away?' Molly asked.

'I promise,' I said.

But I kept thinking of the picture, the score marks, the circle drawn around my face. Those words. The truth was, I was as scared as my girls were. I pushed down my emotions, told the children I needed to get a shower and that they could order anything they wanted from room service.

While they discussed what the menu had to offer, I locked myself in the bathroom, stuffed a towel into my mouth then screamed and cried as if my heart were breaking.

Chapter Thirty-Seven

Elizabeth

Maybe the photos had been gone a while. I tried to think of the last time I'd looked through them. It had been months, if not longer, but I knew the last time I'd looked they were still there. I'd have noticed if any had gone.

I shivered, despite the heat, a feeling of foreboding washing over me.

There was one possibility I didn't even want to think about.

I pushed it away. Told myself that it was impossible. There had to be a more logical explanation – the events of the last week had instilled an unnecessary level of fear and paranoia in me.

I set about locking up the house, making sure every window and every door was bolted and double bolted. Windows and doors I may not always have made sure to secure before, because I'd felt secure enough in my own home – in this secluded corner of the world – that I never imagined anyone would ever want to gain entry through. To try to come in.

I wasn't one for drinking, but my nerves were sufficiently rattled to prompt me to pour a measure of Jameson Irish whiskey, from a bottle that once belonged to Paddy. It was so old I wasn't even sure if it was still drinkable, but I sipped from it anyway. Feeling its warmth slide down my throat to my stomach, I grimaced at the taste, but if it helped me to relax that had to be a good thing.

Izzy looked up at me as if I'd lost the run of myself, drinking alcohol, pulling faces, talking to myself.

'Don't you judge,' I chided her, only to be rewarded by the saddest puppy-dog stare in return. 'I'm sorry,' I immediately replied, bending down to pet her and ruffle her fur. 'I'm the worst company in the world right now.'

She curled her body into mine and I lowered my aching bones down onto the floor to enjoy the warmth of her beside me – the non-judgemental nature of her very being, as if there was nothing in the world I could do to disappoint her. If only it were so easy with humans.

The sound of a car crunching on the gravel in the yard made me jump. I got to my feet slowly, my muscles straining at the effort. Then I peeped out of the window to see DI Bradley climbing out of his car. This wasn't expected; I felt my skin prickle. That sense of foreboding again. Nothing good could come from him visiting me this late in the evening.

I opened the door just as he raised his hand to knock, managing to startle him in the process.

'I heard your car pull up, looked out the window,' I said.

He nodded. 'Can I come in, Elizabeth?'

'Of course,' I said, stepping backwards, suddenly self-conscious about the whiskey glass still in my hand. 'I was just having one to steady my nerves. It's been a difficult few days.'

'Well, if I wasn't on duty I'd be asking you to pour me a drink, too,' he said with a tired smile.

'The pressure must be on at this stage,' I said, more than aware I was stating the obvious.

'Very much so. And I'm hoping you can help me again.'

'I'll do whatever I can,' I told him, leading him through to the kitchen, where he sat opposite me at the table.

'I'm afraid there was an incident earlier today, at the home of one of Clare Taylor's friends.'

'One of the girls who received the flowers?' I asked, and he nodded.

I wondered if it was the same woman who Ingrid had mentioned earlier. Whose husband the police wanted to talk to.

'I can't reveal all the details, but I was wondering if you'd look at a picture for me, see if it rings any bells for you at all.'

I shrugged and he took out his phone, drew his finger across the screen, scrolled and then turned the screen to face me.

'This was left at the home of Rachel Walker today. There was an attempted break-in. Rachel has confirmed the identity of everyone in the photo and tells us she believes the girl on the right-hand side of the picture to be your daughter, Laura.'

I knew the picture immediately. It was one of those that had disappeared from my photo album. The realisation was like a kick to my stomach. My eyes were drawn directly to the image of Laura, then to the newly but angrily scored-out face of another girl. Clare. Her face obliterated by angry strokes of a red pen. No trace left at all of her smile, or the confidence she'd exuded back then.

Then I looked at the red circles drawn around the faces of the two other grinning schoolgirls. The angry words written beneath one – a girl with blonde frizzy curls and a look of defiance I'd never seen on the face of my own daughter, despite our many similarities.

I felt tears prick at my eyes. That sense of foreboding from earlier rose into something I could barely contain.

'Is that Laura?' DI Bradley asked.

'It is,' I stuttered, reaching out to touch the screen as if there were a trace of her in her image.

He paused for a moment then showed me another picture.

'If you look here, this was written on the back of it. The names of the girls in the picture. "Julie, Rachel, Clare and me. 1990."'

I stared at my daughter's childish handwriting, the memory tearing at my heart.

'It very much looks as though this photo belonged to Laura,' he said softly. 'Does that look like her handwriting?'

I could only nod. My girl's handwriting. I didn't realise just how much I missed something as silly as handwriting until I saw it in front of me. My hand flew to my mouth as if to try to contain the grief that wanted to spill out.

'I think from this point in the investigation we reasonably have to assume that whoever carried out the attack on Clare Taylor, and whoever's been leaving messages for you, and for those of the friends and family of Clare Taylor, is connected to your daughter and has been able to access her personal belongings. The big question, of course, is who?'

I couldn't speak. I just kept looking at the picture of my daughter. So alive. So full of hope. I thought of the missing space in the photo album.

DI Bradley continued. 'Elizabeth, I know this is horrible and it's bringing up all sorts of memories from a very difficult time. But given what's happened, we'll be looking into Laura's file. We have to question whether the same person who targeted Clare, who's now targeting her friends, could also have targeted Laura two years ago.

'Perhaps she felt threatened by that person. We believe the man responsible to be a very manipulative and narcissistic creature. He's clearly capable of carrying out acts of extreme violence. Did she ever mention feeling threatened by anyone? Scared of anyone? Any information at all that you can give us about the people in her life could break this case.'

The room about me began to sway. The edges became fuzzy. I wasn't sure if I was whispering, talking or shouting.

'But Laura took her own life. She left a note. Nothing about her death, nothing, bears any resemblance to what happened to Clare.'

'And it could be that investigation will find just that,' he said. 'But we can't ignore what's happened and we want to make you fully aware of what's going on.'

I felt the whiskey that hadn't properly settled in my stomach rise. Swallowing it back, I looked at DI Bradley, tried to focus on him and his voice. Tried to think about what he was telling me. What it could mean.

Had someone driven my daughter to her death?

I thought of the picture he'd shown me. What he'd said: 'Manipulative and narcissistic', and 'capable of carrying out acts of extreme violence'. The room swam around me and DI Bradley's voice faded further into the distance.

I was aware of a strange tingling feeling at the back of my neck, the sudden arrival of a sheen of cold sweat on my brow. I tried to focus – on the sights and sounds in front of me, on the familiar smell of home, on the feeling of Izzy at my feet.

A searing pain seemed to hit me like a lightning bolt, right on the top of my head. I wanted to scream but I was already fading. I tried to stop myself from falling, sideways, the darkness growing as I fell.

I was already unconscious by the time my head hit the stone floor with a sickening thud.

Chapter Thirty-Eight

Rachel

Paul looked haggard when he joined us in the hotel. I imagined I didn't look much better. I didn't know what to say to him. Or how to act with him. I couldn't jump straight in asking all the questions I needed to because the girls were with us. They'd been through enough trauma. But it seemed Paul wanted to talk and was in no mood to wait.

Leaving the girls watching the TV in their room, he led me into the second bedroom and closed the door.

'First of all, you know I didn't hurt Clare, don't you? I have nothing to do with what happened to her.'

He looked so sincere. As if it were madness for me ever to have doubted him. I wanted to cling on to that, if only I didn't know for myself how easy it was to convince someone of a lie.

'I'm not sure what to believe any more,' I said. 'I'm not sure if having you here is the right thing. I'm not sure if being here is the right thing.'

'Rachel, you know me. You know I'm not perfect and I'd never pretend to be. But I didn't hurt Clare. I'm *not* a killer.' He spat the word 'killer' out in a whisper as if it burned him to say it. 'I couldn't do that to anyone. I wouldn't. . .'

He looked distraught. The part of me who loved him – and a part of me still did love him – ached to comfort him, but the part of me who was aware that our marriage was falling apart around our ears couldn't bring myself to do so.

He sat down. 'I know you have questions,' he said. 'I know what the police have told you. I know what they've shown you, but it's not what it looks like.'

I snorted. That line.

'I know that sounds like a lie,' he said. 'But I promise you, it's not. Yes, I was in Derry that night and yes, I met Clare for dinner, but it was perfectly innocent.'

'If it was perfectly innocent then why didn't you tell me about it? Where did you sleep, or do I not want to know the sordid details?'

Even as I spoke I knew I was being a hypocrite. I was guilty of betrayal, too, and my emotional betrayal with Michael had started long before we'd become physical.

'Rachel, I slept in my mother's house that night. I didn't tell you because I wanted to get the chance to talk to Clare privately and I knew you'd ask all sorts of questions if I told you outright I was going out for dinner with your friend. But the dinner was just incidental. We were both hungry. It seemed sensible to have something to eat.'

'But why did you want to talk to my friend in private?' I kept my voice low, but there was no mistaking my anger and confusion.

I watched Paul take a deep breath. 'Because I didn't know how to talk to you any more. It seems we can't be in the same room without a row breaking out.'

I bristled, opened my mouth to bite back.

'And I'm not saying that's all your fault, or that it's all my fault, but it is what it is, Rachel, and I thought Clare could help me to reach you.'

'But you can reach me. You just had to pick up the phone

and talk, or sit across the table from me, or ask how I was and listen. . .'

I felt a wobble in my voice then and I was surprised at the emotion I was feeling. Grief. Loss. The loss of him and so much else that year.

'That's the thing, Rachel. I can't, and I've not been able to for a long time. Not since your mother took ill, and then when she died. . .'

Those words still had the power to pull the air from my lungs. I wanted to cover my ears. I didn't want to hear that she'd died. I knew it. I was acutely aware of it every hour of every day. Someone saying it out loud didn't make it any more real to me, but it did make me feel as if I were being punched in the stomach. A visceral physical edge to my emotional pain. Those words. . . those words had the power to reduce me to tears without even realising. I missed her. God, I missed her every moment of every day. Missed being able to pick up the phone to chat. Missed sitting across the table from her, cup of tea in hand, a shared plate of biscuits in front of us. I missed just knowing she was there. This person who loved me unconditionally, who'd been on my side from the moment I was born. I'd never truly known what loneliness was until that first time I wanted to talk to her and realised she was gone. It had only grown since.

I raised my hand. 'Don't!' I said.

I needed him to stop talking about her. I didn't have the emotional energy to think about my mother and just how much I missed her at this moment. How much I wanted her to hold me and tell me it would be okay. That she'd keep me safe. I missed her with an ache so deep that I could only truly allow myself to feel it occasionally, afraid that if I gave in to my grief, I'd fall and never get back up again.

'But we need to talk about it, Rachel, don't you see?' Paul cut in. 'We've been putting off talking about it so much. Arguing over stupid things rather than facing the elephant in the room. You've changed so much. You're not the person you were and yes, I get that you've been through a traumatic loss. But we all have. You lost your mother, but I lost you. Your friends lost you. You're unreachable, both to me and to your friends. To the girls, too, to an extent.

'That's why Clare and I met. She was worried about you as much as I am. We wanted to talk about what we could do to help you. If there was *anything* we could do to help you. She hated seeing you this way. She hated that she didn't feel she could pick up the phone and talk to you, that she couldn't tell you that she was falling in love because you seemed to shrink away from any good news. You must have noticed that you were spending less time with her?'

'Yes, because she was seeing someone. Someone she'd told me about, as it happens.'

'Just not his name, or where he lives. Or how she really felt. And, Rachel, you didn't just see less of each other because she'd met someone. You've become so insular since your mother died. You don't go out. The occasional run, maybe. That creative writing class. But that's it. Where did the Rachel I knew, who grabbed life with both hands, go?'

I wanted to tell him, but couldn't, that that girl was lost and the only thing that made her feel found was spending time with another man. One who seemed to understand her loss and her pain and didn't spend all of his time trying to make her feel as if she should be over it by now.

She'd never get over it.

Michael could understand that. Why couldn't Paul?

I realised I was angry with him. Angry that he didn't try harder. That he ran away to Belfast when things got tough and then turned all the problems in our marriage back on me. It wasn't just me. Was it?

241

Paul spoke. 'Rachel, we were all worried about you. We're all still worried about you. And selfishly, and this isn't something I'm proud of, but selfishly, when you told me that Clare had been killed . . . do you know what my first thought was?'

I shook my head, watched as my husband started to cry. I'd never seen him cry before. Not even when the girls were born.

'Rachel, all I could think was that this would mean there was no way back for us. This would just take you away from me further and look, just look what it's done. We've been at each other's throats since and I know I've been on edge, before you say anything . . .'

'The scratches on your arm,' I said, the one truth that neither of us could escape from. 'I saw them, Paul. That night we . . .'

'That night we had sex. You can say it, you know, Rachel. It's allowed. We're married! We're allowed to have sex *and* to talk about it. I know we barely do any more.'

There was a bitter tone to his words. Had I been pulling away from him? It had seemed to me that we'd pulled away from each other.

'It hasn't been easy,' I said. 'I can't just switch on that side of me, not with everything else.'

In my head, a little voice whispered that I'd found it easy enough to switch it on when I'd been with Michael on Wednesday night. Too easy.

'I know that. I've not pushed you, or pressured you.'

'But you went elsewhere,' I said. 'Didn't you? Don't tell me you didn't. I know what those marks were, Paul.'

He looked to the ground. 'I was afraid we were over. I was lonely. Flattered. Stupid. I didn't mean for it to happen.'

I sniffed.

'I know what you're thinking. It can't just happen by accident. But. . . I didn't plan it, Rachel. That might sound like a weak excuse, or no excuse at all, but it's the truth.'

'Who?' I asked.

'That's unimportant. It was a mistake,' he said, rubbing his eyes with the heels of his hands, shaking his head. 'Does it make it hurt less if I tell you it was just some woman I met in a bar after work? In Belfast.

'I was stressed. I went for a drink and we got chatting. And I felt flattered, Rachel. Wanted, even. I gave in to that. We went back to her place. It was quick, and messy, and it felt wrong. Sordid. The scratches made it more so.' He looked down, rubbed the stubble of his chin. 'Everything about it was a mistake. I wish, with everything in me, that I hadn't done it. And I know you might not believe me, but it was just once, and I've barely been able to look myself in the mirror since.

'Why do you think I've been so short-tempered? I'm so sorry and I'm so ashamed. I don't want to lose you, or the girls. Even if what we've got is broken, it's still what we've got, isn't it? But what you told the police, about the scratches, that you thought for even one minute I could do something so utterly horrific to our friend . . .? It's all just a bloody mess, Rachel. And I want to fix it. I want us to fix it. Despite everything, I still think we can.'

I heard him say the words I wished he'd said weeks ago. Or months ago. That he didn't want to lose me. Or us. That he wanted to fix us. I heard him say those words I'd wished he'd say for a long time. But he'd prefaced them with 'It was a mistake' and 'it was just the once'. And even though I'd known in my heart that there'd been someone else, and even though I was in no position to judge, I started to cry anyway. And my crying soon turned into sobbing.

I felt his arms around me, holding me tight, trying to comfort me, reminding me the girls were next door. I heard him say he was sorry over and over again.

'As soon as I'd done it, I knew I'd messed up,' he said. 'I hate myself for it. You couldn't hate me more than I hate myself.'

'Would you have told me?' I asked him, pulling back slightly. 'If it hadn't been for what happened to Clare? If the police hadn't called you in? Would you have told me or would we just have gone on as we were?'

'If I'm being honest with you, Rachel, I don't know. I can't answer that because what happened, happened. And it changed everything. It made me realise I don't want to lose you. And now there's someone doing their very best to hurt you or scare you, and I'm scared. I'm trying not to be, but I am. But no matter how scared I am, I promise you this. I'll do everything in my power to try to make sure they don't hurt you, or the kids. If you'll let me.'

He held me tightly again and for the first time in a long while I felt a genuine connection between us. It was a fine one, thin, fragile, but it was there. If only I could escape from the fact that I was guilty, too, and I'd also slept with someone else. Someone I still had feelings for. Someone I couldn't stop thinking about. Someone with whom I wondered if I'd ever have allowed myself to get close to if things between Paul and I hadn't slid so far off course.

I just held him, allowed him to hug me, then I closed my eyes and rested my head on his shoulder, trying hard to cut out all the outside noise.

I had no idea at all where we went from here except that in that moment, in that room, keeping the people here with me safe was the only thing that mattered.

Molly ended up sleeping in between us that night. Beth slept in the other bedroom on her own but insisted on keeping the light on and the door open so she could see us. I'm not sure I really slept at all. I jumped at every voice walking along the corridor, at the sound of every car driving into the car park. I'd pushed a chair against the door, making sure the back of it jammed the handle so no one could get in or out, but still my nerves jangled. I wondered if we should have stayed at home, where the police could've kept a closer eye on us, after all.

When it was quiet, instead of drifting off, my mind wandered to what Paul had told me. What the police had shown me. I wondered how Julie was. How Ronan was. Had the police told him they'd been speaking to Paul? Did he think Paul was guilty now?

And Julie – had anyone gone to her house like they had to mine? I suddenly felt sick. She was on her own, with Brendan and the children away to his mother's. Wouldn't she be more vulnerable than I was?

Then again, the picture left at my house clearly said I was next. It still made little sense. I wished I had the photo to look at again. To see if it sparked more memories. I hadn't really absorbed it properly when the police had showed me – not the subtleties of it, anyway. I didn't remember it being taken.

Did I remember Laura trying to hang out with us? Maybe. Maybe she sat on the outside of our group. A memory flickered. A time when she was there, always there. We were trying to discuss something really serious – Julie's crush on Ronan, if memory serves me right – and there was Laura. Listening in. Always listening in. It was none of her business.

Had I told her as much? Something niggled at me. Oh, God! I cringed with shame. I'd told her to get her own life. I remembered it now. Remembered the look on her face as she'd slinked away, face scarlet. Clare muttering, too loudly, that Laura was 'so rude'.

'Who does she think she is?' she'd asked.

We really could be bitches, in hindsight. But these were small incidents. It wasn't like we bullied her. We didn't hurt her. We just protected our own group. It had been none of her business, after all. It was a private discussion, about private things.

But now it was keeping me awake, wondering if she felt it

more. Wondering if there was something I wasn't remembering about the whole sorry episode.

I crept out of bed, lifted my phone and went into the bathroom. Sitting on the floor, I sent a few text messages. One to Ronan to ask how he was, one to Julie to make sure she was safe, and one to Michael to let him know what had happened and to tell him that we were currently holed up in a hotel. I told him it was unlikely I'd be able to see him soon and even sending messages would be riskier than normal. I knew I should've had the guts to tell him it was over. That I needed to be there for my family now. God knows, I wanted to be there for my family, but I wasn't ready to let him go. Not just yet. Not over a text message.

Julie replied to say she'd gone to Brendan's mother's house, too. Once he'd heard what had happened at my house, he'd driven back to insist she go with him. She apologised for the state she'd been in earlier. Said she hoped I was okay.

I was far from okay.

My phone lit up with a silent notification. Michael replied:

Run away with me. I mean it. Let me keep you safe. x

I stared at his words, thought of my family sleeping in the next room. If I just disappeared. . . they'd be safe. Whoever was doing this didn't want to hurt them. He only wanted to hurt me. He'd surely leave them alone if I was out of the picture.

But my girls, they were my life. I wasn't sure life would be worth living if I couldn't be with them. And my husband, who was hurting, who wanted to save us, what would it do to him? I deleted the message from Michael, and crawled back into bed beside Paul, where I lay awake for hours.

Chapter Thirty-Nine

Elizabeth

I woke to the sound of a woman saying my name, over and over. I could just about make out indistinct noises in the background, but it was that one voice – calm, soothing – that gently encouraged me to open my eyes.

Her green uniform, hair tied back. A pretty face, scrubbed clean, no make-up. Blue eyes. Like Laura's.

'You've taken quite a knock, Elizabeth,' she said. 'You've been out for quite a while.'

I tried to speak but couldn't make my mouth work just yet. A voice, male, familiar, was in the background. The policeman. The tall one. I couldn't remember his name. Remember why he was there. This was my house, wasn't it? My head throbbed.

I could hear the whining of a dog. My dog. Where was she? I tried to move my head.

'Steady there, Elizabeth,' I heard the paramedic say. 'No sudden movements. We want to make sure you've not done yourself any real damage.'

She was shining a torch in my eyes, but I tried to close them; the light was too bright.

'Do you know where you are, Elizabeth?' she asked me.

I was sure I did. But my mouth still didn't want to work. The words were stuck in my head. Where was the policeman? Was he with the dog? It was my dog, wasn't it?

'You've had a fall,' the female paramedic said, enunciating each word slowly and purposefully as if I were stupid.

My head was still spinning. There was pain. Like hot knives. Like electric shocks.

'You hit your head. Can you tell us your name?'

I wanted to scream at her that she already knew my name. Hadn't she said it to me already? That was *my* name, wasn't it? Everything seemed to fade in and out and in again. I didn't know any more what was what and who was real, and where was Laura?

I tried to sit up but had barely moved before the paramedic was telling me to stay still and calm.

'She's very confused,' I heard her say to someone.

Maybe the police officer. Maybe Laura. Was she there? Something told me over and over that she was. Or was at least nearby.

'She's getting agitated,' a disembodied voice said.

Of course I was getting agitated. Where was Laura? Why couldn't I hear her voice?

I tried to speak but my stupid mouth still wouldn't move and I knew I was crying, tears of frustration, but I couldn't feel them on my face.

I was tired. I wanted to close my eyes.

'Elizabeth,' I heard and opened my eyes again.

A paramedic. Was it the same one as before? I didn't know.

'Can you stay with me? Try to stay calm and we're going to help you. Can you squeeze my hand?'

I looked at her. I was scared now because nothing made sense. I tried to move my hands but I don't know if I managed it or not.

I was aware of moving. Being pushed. Outside. I saw a dog, looking on from the door where the man stood. The man. Was he the policeman? Was he my husband? Or him? I couldn't find the name in my head as pain washed over me.

The man blurred as they loaded me into the ambulance. I could see him swim in and out of focus until I was sure I was seeing the ghost of someone I used to know.

That boy.

I blinked and he disappeared.

The doors of the ambulance were closed. Through the back window I could see the old farmhouse. It had never looked imposing before. But its shadow against the fading light made me shiver.

'Are you okay, Elizabeth?' the paramedic asked.

I couldn't answer, but even if I could, I doubt I would have known what to say. Something was very, very wrong and I'd never been so scared in my life.

I was so tired that despite the pain in my head, and the noise in the ward outside, I could barely keep my eyes open. I had no idea what time it was, except that it was dark. I couldn't remember what day it was, either. Struggled to remember why I was here.

Memories slipped in and slipped out again just as quickly. Doctors all around me. Soft voices. It was hard to pinpoint which of those memories related to today and which had been pulled from the recesses of my mind.

Someone had mentioned a stroke. I'd tried to answer – my words muddled, slurred. I felt some tingling in my right hand – the pull of the cannula in my vein if I tried to move. My left hand, my left side, continued to be useless.

That policeman, I couldn't remember his name, he stayed

with me for a while. Told me he'd contacted my son-in-law. I wondered why he hadn't contacted Laura. Maybe she was at work . . .

'Don't worry about your dog,' he'd said. 'One of my colleagues has taken her to your son-in-law's house.' He'd looked genuinely worried about me.

Had he been in my house, that policeman? I couldn't remember. Thinking made me so tired. I couldn't keep my eyes open.

When I woke, a nurse was by my side, telling me I was doing well, but I wondered why I was alone. Why hadn't my family come to be with me? Where were they?

A tear slid down my cheek and the nurse wiped it away.

'It's okay to be scared, Elizabeth. You've been through an ordeal. But you're in the best place now and you're getting the gold standard care. I'm told you're a legend around these parts.'

I tried to smile – was aware my mouth wouldn't do what it was supposed to. I kept losing my train of thought. It was as if everything I needed to know was hidden behind a filter that blurred all the edges.

There was something about a photograph there.

An orange T-shirt. Too bright.

And a warning.

Wednesday, 13 June

Chapter Forty

Rachel

Getting out to see Michael wasn't easy. The girls were clingy. Paul had decided to stay with us and not go to Belfast. He'd been attentive, warm even, at breakfast. I'd barely slept all night. I knew I needed to make a tough decision. In my head it was probably already made, but I needed to see him all the same.

I needed to tell him just how complicated everything was. How it was becoming more and more complicated with every day. It had been different before, when I thought Paul didn't love me and no longer had a vested interest in our marriage. Before Clare died. Before I felt my family was threatened from all angles.

Michael's plea to run away with him had been running through my head. Each and every time I thought of leaving the girls, my heart twisted. And in the darkness of that hotel room, my family all so close that I could hear their breathing, the reality of leaving them – hurting them – seemed so alien to me.

Regardless of what had been happening, it had started to dawn on me that I'd been risking it all over the last months without making the effort to fix the broken pieces first. I was to blame as much as Paul was. We'd both let each other down so badly.

I woke to Molly still in the bed beside me, her small, pudgy hand caressing my face as if I were the most precious possession in the world.

'I love you, Mammy,' she said as my eyes flickered open.

Her love was pure. Without motive. Unconditional. In the early hours in a darkened hotel room, it took my breath away.

We decided to go home after that one night. To try to make this very abnormal situation more normal for the girls. We had our alarms in place. The house was safer. The girls wouldn't be going to school or daycare again until everything was settled.

Molly had clung to me as we'd walked in the front door, afraid of every shadow and every corner.

'What if the bad man is here?' she'd asked.

'He can't get in,' Paul had assured her. 'The police have put a big magic shield around the house to stop any bad men getting inside. If they so much as touch it, the police come and take them right to jail.'

Molly had looked at me for reassurance that what her daddy had told her was true. I'd nodded and in that moment, I saw a glimpse of the man I'd fallen in love with. Safe. Secure. Loving. My partner. Not perfect, of course, but then neither was I. I never would be.

In a selfish way, I still wanted Michael. Still tried to run through useless scenarios in my head in which I could have my cake and eat it. But there was no solution that would work. I knew that. When all was said and done, I needed my family more than I needed him. And more than anything, they needed me.

I couldn't seem to sit still. Walked through the house cleaning everything that stood still. Keeping busy until I started to ache. I thought if I kept busy I'd feel less scared. That I'd feel less confused. Less guilty. More sure of myself.

By late afternoon, when the sun was hot and the house so stifling I was sure I was at risk of combusting, I finally decided that I simply had to see Michael, to tell him that I did need the space he'd offered me only a few days before. In fact, I needed more than that.

'I'm nipping to the supermarket,' I said to Paul.

'Is that wise?' he asked. 'I could go instead.'

His voice wasn't harsh. His tone was not argumentative, as it had been before. He sounded concerned – genuinely concerned.

'I'll take that phone the police gave me and I won't be long. Paul, I can't be a prisoner in my own house forever.'

I was fishing through the cupboards, pulling out a selection of 'bags for life' to take with me. The truth was, we did need some shopping, and if I was as quick as I could be around the supermarket, I was sure I could make just a little time to see Michael. I'd text him and ask him to meet me.

'Well, maybe I should come with you,' Paul said, interrupting my thoughts.

I told him that wouldn't be necessary probably more quickly than I should have.

'You should stay with the girls. They need you,' I added. 'Besides, I think I just need some air.'

'I know you're still angry with me, Rachel, about what happened, what I did. And you've every right to be. All I can tell you is that I'm sorry, more sorry than I can ever express. It didn't mean anything. *She* means nothing. She won't be part of my life ever again. It was just a way to release tension and I regretted it immediately. She. . .'

I put my hand up, shook my head. I had no desire to hear any more details. I didn't want to hear any more when I had secrets of my own I hadn't confessed to. Secrets that differed from Paul's because unlike his, mine did mean something. Had meant something. It would have been easier if they hadn't.

I wouldn't feel the need to tell the man I was meeting, face-to-face, that not only would I not be running away with him, I also had to stop seeing him.

'It's not about that. I just need some air, Paul. That's all it is. I've got cabin fever. Claustrophobia. It's daylight. I'll be in a very public place. I'll have the alarm phone with me. If anything happens, I just have to press a button and the police will know exactly where I am. They'll be there in minutes. I'll go to Tesco, to be extra secure. Sure, it's only across the street from the police station.'

'Just be careful,' he said as I picked up my bag and keys. 'We need you. *I* need you.'

He moved towards me. For a second I thought he was going to kiss me, but something held him back. We had a long way to go to attempt to save this marriage of ours. It wouldn't be easy. There'd be no guarantees. We'd have to learn how to talk to each other again. To be with each other. To not fear touching each other.

'I won't be long,' I said. 'I promise.' I smiled, tried to show him I was willing to listen.

I sent a quick text to Michael before I left. Asked him to meet me in forty-five minutes at the old car park at Ness Woods, a small country park about five miles outside Derry, situated off a small, winding country road. That car park had fallen out of favour some years previously when a new one, complete with a visitors' centre, had been opened a few miles down the road. Very few people used the old entrance any more and it was likely to be very quiet at this time of day. We'd be safe.

An immediate reply told me Michael would see me there and that he couldn't wait. I drove off, hoping I was making the right decision.

Chapter Forty-One

Rachel

I hurried around the supermarket in a daze. I kept my head low. I felt vulnerable in a way I never had before, reluctant to draw attention to myself. I threw items into my trolley – the basics to get us through a couple of days – and tried to shut out any unwelcome thoughts.

What if the killer had followed me here? He mightn't be able to hurt me, here in this public place, but he could still get close enough to touch me. To spook me. To find more out about me. More ways to inveigle his way into my life. Could he be the man who'd asked me if the brand of shampoo he was buying was the best for highlighted hair? Who'd said his wife had asked him to pick some up and he didn't want to get it wrong? Could he have been the man who'd brushed into me as I waited at the checkout line? He'd apologised profusely, taking a cursory glance at my trolley. Was that something more sinister than simple nosiness?

I didn't know who to trust, and I found myself fumbling with my purse and bank cards as I paid for my shopping and packed it into bags.

'You're all fingers and thumbs,' the cashier said with a smile.

I gave her a weak smile. A wicked part of me wondered if I should tell her the truth. That she would be on edge, too, if she was possibly being hunted by a killer.

Crossing the car park, I felt my pulse quicken as I pushed my trolley between lanes, hyperaware of the moving cars around me. Aware of doors opening and closing. Aware of the man standing by the trolley station, smoking a cigarette and looking around as if he was waiting for someone. I assigned his more distinctive features to my memory: a tattoo the full length of the calf of his left leg of a footballer mid strike. A Celtic band tattooed on his arm. A red Adidas T-shirt, baggy grey shorts. Sunglasses. Stubble. Short back and sides.

As I loaded the last of my bags into the car, he walked away – waving to a young woman pushing a trolley out of the shopping centre.

I climbed into my car and as I reversed out of my space, I saw a familiar-looking blue car in my rear-view mirror. I couldn't be sure, but I was fairly confident it was the same one that had stopped in the lay-by where Michael and I had last met. There was no one in the driver's seat, but even so, I pulled an envelope and a pen from my bag and scribbled down the registration number.

Trying to settle myself, I set off on the short drive to meet Michael. But as I was still queuing to leave the car park, I noticed the same blue car was second in line behind me. The beeping of a car horn brought me back to my senses. The queue of traffic in front of me had cleared while I was staring through my rear-view mirror. Hands shaking, I drove off.

My eyes darted to the mirror again. The blue car was now directly behind me. I could just make out the shape of a figure driving, the same black hoodie that I'd seen before was pulled up over their head. Was it the same hoodie-wearer who'd been outside Molly's crèche?

I reached my hand across to the passenger seat, felt around for the phone the police had given me. All I would have to do was press one button.

I remembered the police station across the street, so I doubled back on myself. The blue car turned too, continued following me. It was only when I pulled into the lay-by outside the station gates that it sped up and raced past. Trembling, I put my head on the steering wheel and wished for everything to go away. I jumped when my own mobile rang seconds later. It was Michael phoning to see if I was on my way.

Hearing the timbre of my voice, he knew something was up.

'Rachel, are you okay? What's wrong?'

I was shaking so hard by then that my teeth were chattering and I couldn't stop shivering.

'I think I've just been followed.'

I heard a sharp intake of breath. 'Who by? Where are you?'

'Remember that blue car that was at the lay-by the other night? It followed me out of the Tesco car park. I'm sitting outside Waterside Police Station now. I figured if I drove here, whoever it was wouldn't be able to get to me.'

'Jesus, Rachel! I don't like this. Stay there. I'll come to you.'

I shook my head. 'It's too public here, Michael. We might be seen.'

'Does it matter? Can we not just be seen?'

He was pleading and I knew he wanted me to say to him that I didn't care if anyone found out, but I did. I had to care.

'Please, Michael. I . . . I'm sure he's gone now. I'll come to you. It'll be okay.'

With more than a hint of frustration in his voice, he agreed to wait for me. Told me to be careful, just as Paul had done.

My nerves were still on edge as I turned the car onto Oughtagh Road towards the country park. Even the dappled shadows from the trees on the ground had taken on a sinister look. I kept glancing back in my rear-view mirror, wondering if I'd see that blue car again, wondering what I'd do if I did.

When I finally reached the car park, I sagged with relief to see Michael's car. Tears sprang to my eyes when he got out of it and starting walking towards me, enveloped me in a bear hug so tight that it stilled my shaking. I let him whisper that everything would be okay. Let him whisper that he wanted to protect me. I let him tell me he loved me, even though I knew that I was going to hurt him.

'I know in the grand scheme of things we've not known each other that long, but sometimes you just know, Rachel, and I know with you. The thought that someone could hurt you . . .'

His voice trailed off and I looked up into his green eyes, so vibrant against his swarthy skin. He bent his head towards me and kissed me, full on the lips with such tenderness that I wished I could feel like I did in that second forever.

I should have pushed him away. I knew that in kissing him back I was lying both to him and to myself, but I needed this. I needed him. Adrenaline was still coursing through my veins. My senses were still on high alert and I couldn't resist.

I allowed the tenderness of his kiss to give way to passion. I gave myself permission to give in to my body's desire.

'I don't have long,' I whispered to him as his lips snaked their way down my neck.

His hand slid from my waist to my breast, cupping it gently until I gasped with pleasure. I stumbled backwards, felt his body push mine against the side of my car. I could feel he was hard, could tell from the way he hitched my skirt up, pressing himself against me so that I felt the delicious weight of him pinning me to the car, that he wanted me.

I could shut everything out. I could pretend not to be scared. Or hurt. Or confused. I could give in to my base desire just to feel desirable. To feel wanted.

I pushed him back from me for just a moment. Just enough to open the car door. I stood in front of him, lifted my T-shirt over my head and then lay across the back seat.

He bent down and climbed in over me, his hand sliding up the bare skin of my legs to my thighs, pushing them apart. I slid my hands inside his T-shirt to feel the firmness of his muscles, the soft hairs on his chest, and I couldn't hold back any longer.

I unbuckled his jeans, revelled at his sharp intake of breath as I took him in my hand, and then revelled in my own pleasure as he took control, pushed my hands above my head and entered me.

For those minutes, nothing else mattered. There was silence amid the chaos and calm instead of fear. It was the perfect lie.

Chapter Forty-Two

Rachel

'Have you thought about what I said?' Michael asked afterwards. 'Because I was serious, you know. Even though I know it's complicated. Come away with me. We can start again elsewhere and no one needs to know it's us.'

'That's a lovely fantasy,' I told him.

We were still wrapped together, our bodies sticky with sweat.

'It doesn't just have to be a fantasy, Rachel. I know it sounds all romantic and corny, but let me take you away from all this. To somewhere safe. I've got some savings. I can keep us afloat until I find more work. That's the thing with being a carpenter, I have skills and I can travel with them. You can work anywhere. Teach. English or creative writing, or take that time out – you always wanted to write a book. But most of all, just be away from this, from Paul and from this psychopath.'

As pretty as that picture was, it wasn't realistic. Real life was different. What kind of mother would I be to leave my children in the midst of such trauma? How selfish would I be just to walk away? Didn't what Paul and I had – what we'd shared for seventeen years now – didn't that deserve another chance at least?

And what if the killer didn't stop just because I was gone – if he turned his attention solely to Julie, or to my girls?

'I have children,' I said. 'You know that. I can't walk out on them. Especially not now, when they're both so scared. Beth's at a vulnerable age. Molly's just a baby still. I can't walk out. I've thought about it and little else over the last twenty-four hours, Michael, and I can't reconcile with that. No matter what I feel.'

I stroked his face as I spoke, hoped he could see that losing him was far from easy for me, either. Tears welled in my eyes.

He looked at me for a moment, his expression that of someone truly dejected.

'But just now? What was that? If you didn't want to be with me . . .' He pulled back as I pushed myself to sitting.

I blushed. 'I'm sorry,' I said. 'I just lost the run of myself when I saw you. It's not that I don't have feelings for you. I do. You know I do. But it's more complicated than that.'

'It doesn't have to be. Things are only ever as complicated as you make them. You deserve to be happy, you know. *We* deserve to be happy. You deserve not to have to watch your back. To not have to worry about every blue car that drives past you or whoever sends you flowers. You should be able to live a normal life. You should be able to live an extraordinary life. To be loved extraordinarily.'

I let his words sink in for a moment. Tried to find a truth in them that was more important than the truth of my responsibilities to my family and my love for them. A love that was extraordinary in its own way.

'That may be the case,' I said, pulling my T-shirt over my head.

It was startling how soon my skin cooled without the weight of him on me. How my body missed his. I put my hand to his cheek, tilted his head so he was looking directly in my eyes.

'But I can't put my happiness above that of my girls. I don't think I could ever be happy without them. My marriage may have its difficulties, and it may well be over in all but name, but we have to try for them at least. I'm so scared that there are times when I feel I can't breathe. But my girls, they didn't do anything to deserve me suddenly disappearing from their lives. I've made a lot of mistakes in this world, but there's one thing I know I've done right. I've been a good mother. A really loving mother. I can't screw that up, even if it means . . .'

He stared straight ahead, ran his fingers through his hair.

'This is messed up, isn't it?' he said.

I nodded.

It was more than messed up.

'But you understand? What kind of a person would I be to turn my back on my own children? Surely they'd see it as a rejection of them.'

'So you'd rather reject me?' he asked, his gaze still turned from mine.

'It's not like that,' I said. 'You know I care for you.'

My voice was shaky now. I didn't want to hurt him. He'd shown me nothing but kindness, and friendship and love.

'Care for me? When I love you? You just "care" for me?'

There was anger in his voice now. I couldn't blame him. I felt wretched. I shouldn't have come here. I certainly shouldn't have had sex with him.

'Michael, let's not make this harder than it already is,' I said, shuffling to move out of the car.

He climbed backwards, stood in the warm evening sunshine. His clothes dishevelled. His hair messy. Sunlight shining directly on him. He was simply stunning and this, I knew, would break my heart.

'I wouldn't be able to forgive myself if I hurt them,' I repeated. 'When I became a mother I took on that responsibility. That

I'd never hurt them. A mother doesn't do that,' I said, standing beside him.

He moved away from me and I followed.

He sniffed. Kicked at the parched ground beneath his feet, sending small clouds of dust billowing into the air.

'You know what, Rachel. You live in a very privileged world. Some mothers do, you know. Some mothers reject their children, no matter what their children do. That's what real life is like. It's not all sunshine and roses and happy families.'

'You're telling me life isn't just all sunshine and roses less than a week after my best friend was murdered? A year after my mother died much too young from a brutal disease? Do you think I don't fucking know that life is horrific?'

I was angry then. I knew he was hurting. It was written all over his face, but how dare he accuse me of coming from a life of privilege! Of living in some cosseted world where people didn't get hurt! I knew people did. I knew people suffered terrible, awful things. I knew it and it made me want to scream at him.

He was glaring at me, defiant. Like a child himself, about to throw a tantrum. It made me realise just how little I really knew him. It had just been a fantasy. Madness. None of it had been real life.

I shook my head. I had nothing more to say. I just wanted to go home.

'You're as selfish as you ever were, Rachel!' he spat. 'A spoiled, stuck-up bitch who doesn't care who you hurt. You only think you know horror. I've seen it,' he said. 'I've caused it. And it was all that she deserved. Another stuck-up bitch. Oh! her face, Rachel, when she realised. It was almost as priceless as yours is now . . .'

Chapter Forty-Three

Elizabeth

'Some memory loss is to be expected with a stroke of this magnitude,' I heard the doctor say. 'We're confident that thrombolysis was carried out in a timely enough manner to minimise long-term damage, but that doesn't mean there isn't a long road ahead of you, Elizabeth.' He perched himself on the end of my bed, as if settling himself for a long chat. 'We'll be looking at a holistic approach. You'll require an assessment from the occupational therapist, and physio, of course.

'We'll see how things settle or improve over the coming days and check what other support we can offer. See if you need speech therapy. You know we'll be appointing a social worker, don't you? We're aware you live alone and your son-in-law tells me that his house wouldn't be suitable for you as it is, so we need to look at the best options going forwards.'

I took a breath. Every word required effort.

'Want to go home,' I stuttered.

'I know that, Elizabeth,' the doctor said. 'That'll be our aim, but we have to be practical, too. We have to make sure you're looked after. Is there any other family we should be in touch with? Siblings, nieces or nephews?'

I shook my head. My only sister had lived in England for the last forty-seven years and we saw each other once a year at most. Her family were grown, lived in England, too. I didn't have a big family to fall back on. I didn't even feel it fair to worry her by calling. Although my son-in-law had overruled me on that and had insisted she was told anyway.

'She's booking a flight,' he'd told me when he was in earlier. 'Her daughter's coming with her. She wondered, could she stay in the farmhouse?'

I'd nodded, although what she'd make of my ramshackle home was anyone's guess. It had been in a much better condition the last time she'd been over. For Laura's wake and funeral. I suppose I'd let it go since then, even more so since my accident.

Lying in my hospital bed, I couldn't get Laura out of my mind. She was in my thoughts, more so than before. I kept getting a feeling there was something about her that I needed to tell someone. I was sure I'd seen her in the house, when my head had started to spin, even though I knew that wasn't possible. Ever since, I'd felt her with me. Close by. But not close enough to reach.

Maybe it was that life-flashing-before-your-eyes thing people talk about. I'd had patients swear it to me before, when they'd had a scare. That they could see their loved ones waiting for them on the other side. She was there, I was sure of it. Waiting for me.

I wished I'd gone to her. Instead, here I was, the left side of my body numb, more useless than it had been before; the nurses having to feed me and change me and my memory sketchy at best. And what did I have to look forward to? Life in a care home? Old before my time. Or alone, in an empty house, with just the occasional visits from Max and Ava to keep me going.

I was aware they were growing up. In time their old granny, in her fusty old home, would become less and less appealing. They'd be making their own way in life and it wouldn't involve me.

I wished I'd died. I know that's a sin even to think, but it was how I felt. I gave in to self-pity, felt a tear roll down my cheek.

'I know you've been through the wars,' the doctor said, his voice soft. 'Finding that poor girl and now this. DI Bradley filled us in on everything. You must feel overwhelmed! But you're strong, Elizabeth. You're a legend around these parts, and you can and will get through this, and we'll help you do it. The staff think very highly of you; after all, you were one of us for so long. So it's our turn to give back to you now and take care of you as well as you took care of all the patients who came through your care here.'

He couldn't have known I wasn't crying because of how I felt physically – I was crying because I missed my daughter so badly that I didn't think I could endure another day without her. And I was crying because I wasn't a legend at all. I may have been a good nurse in my day, but that didn't make me anything special. I was as flawed, if not more so, as anyone else.

I'd not done things right and I had a feeling all this could be karma catching up with me. I was reaping what I'd sown and I had no one to blame but myself.

'Now, you get a good sleep, Elizabeth. You need to conserve your strength. Physio will be around later to have a little chat with you and no doubt your son-in-law will be in this evening, too. He's very devoted to you, Elizabeth.'

The ward sister who'd been standing at the end of my bed watching the exchange nodded.

'You're lucky to have him. Now, Mrs O'Loughlin, looking at your file, I see your daughter, Laura, is listed as your next of kin.' She spoke so softly, with a look of sympathy that everyone I'd ever spoken to about Laura had worn over the last two years. 'Should we update it? Maybe to your son-in-law?'

I nodded. There was no point in updating it to anyone else. Michael was the closest family I had left. Everyone else had left me.

Chapter Forty-Four

Rachel

It didn't make sense. What Michael was saying. I looked at him as if he were speaking a foreign language. My brain was processing his words but surely he couldn't have really said what he did? Could he?

'You look confused,' he said, taking one step closer. 'I'll spell it out for you, lovely, stupid, selfish Rachel. I killed your friend. I slit her throat while she was looking directly into my eyes. I stood and watched her bleed for a while, flounder around on the ground like a fish. I was the one who left her to die, on the roadside. I didn't expect her to last so long. That she did, that she suffered, just made it all the more rewarding.'

I was frozen to the spot by his words. Paralysed by what he was saying. My brain struggled to reconcile his admission of guilt with the Michael I knew. The Michael I'd fallen in love with.

'No!' I muttered, shaking my head.

The movement seemed to release a burst of adrenaline in me, a surge of fear. His expression was now changed, as if he'd taken off a mask. Grisly, horrid, gruesome. In that second, I knew he was showing me the real him for the first time and it terrified me.

The adrenaline coursing through my veins propelled me into action. I had to get away. The fight or flight response was screaming at me to flee. As fast as I could.

I turned towards my car, only to feel his hand grip my arm and try to spin me back towards him. I pulled as hard as I could, feeling his vice-like grip twist my skin, burn it. The strength of his hold made me fear he could simply snap my arm in two if he wanted.

All I had to do was get to my car. Hit the button on the phone. Signal to the police that I needed them. My location would be sent directly to them. I pulled as hard as I could, even though I could feel my muscles screaming at me to stop. I tried to scream for help, but even if I'd managed it, what good would it have done me?

We were here, miles from anywhere, in a car park barely used by anyone any more, along a quiet country lane.

'Let me go!' I managed, my feet losing their purchase on the dusty ground.

I could feel his body pressing against mine – not in passion this time. No desire. No need. No love.

I felt his arm snake around my chest, pull me backwards towards him. Away from my car. Away from the SOS call of the alarm. There was no tenderness. No love in the way I felt his breath, hot and heavy, at my ear.

'You don't get to reject me, Rachel!' he spat, drops of spittle hitting my skin, making me recoil. 'Not before I've done what I set out to do.'

I felt his hand on my throat and his grasp tightened; the air squeezed from my lungs, my head tilted backwards. I tried to kick out, but my feet were sliding on the ground, my shoes being pulled from my feet, falling off as he dragged me towards his car.

'The more you struggle, the more it'll hurt, or maybe you'd like it to hurt?' he sneered.

I shook my head, again trying to pull away from him. I tried to claw his hand from my throat but he was too strong, using his other arm to immobilise my arms. All the kicking and flailing in the world had me going nowhere. Achieved nothing.

'Please, let me go,' I gasped. 'I've got to go home. They're expecting me. Paul will send the police out if I'm not back. They'll be on their way.'

'Then we'd better get out of here,' he said, reaching his car and pulling open the passenger seat. 'Get in.'

I shook my head, struggled more.

'I said get in!' he demanded loudly, forcefully. His face contorting in front of my eyes to the point that I no longer recognised him as the man he'd been to me just minutes before.

'No!' I shouted as loud as my burning lungs would allow. 'No! I won't. Let. Me. Go!'

'Do you really think anyone'll hear you?' he sneered, pushing me towards the car, trying to force my body to fold into it.

I fought. I fought with all of my might. My heart pounding, my body slick with sweat, pulling against him, using every ounce of my strength. I could feel the gravel on the ground tear at my feet. Had Clare fought this hard? Had she been this scared?

A punch to my stomach folded me in half, drove the air from my body until I was gasping for breath I couldn't find. I looked up at him, at his green eyes that had looked down at me with such love just a short time ago, trying to find some trace of the man I thought he was.

It was gone. There was nothing there to hope for or to cling to. I felt bile rise up and I didn't have the strength to swallow it down. I threw up, my own vomit spattering the ground, his legs, my legs. It came in shuddering explosions of acidic liquid that I couldn't stop.

I felt the car door crunch against my legs as he tried to force me further backwards onto the seat. I saw the shadow of his hand, raised against the sunlight. Tried to move my head as I saw it come at me . . .

Then my head was thrust backwards so forcefully, I felt the grinding and tearing of muscle, could taste blood in my mouth as my teeth slammed into my tongue. The impact of the back of my head hitting the top of the car was the last thing I remembered. That and the feeling of my body giving way beneath me.

Chapter Forty-Five

Rachel

The first thing I was aware of was the pain in my head. It was unlike any headache I'd ever had before. I felt as if my eye socket had been crushed. Even in my half consciousness, I knew something was badly wrong. I felt sick with the pain and there was a foul taste in my mouth. Vomit mixed with blood. My head spinning, I opened my eyes, but it was so dark, I couldn't figure out where I was.

Except I knew he was beside me. I could hear his breathing. Smell him. We were still in his car, but we weren't moving. I tried to orientate myself but wherever we were, there were no streetlights, no sound of passing traffic. We were alone. But as my eyes adjusted I could see we weren't in the car park at Ness Woods any more.

'You've been out a while,' Michael said. 'I was starting to wonder if I'd hit your head too hard before.'

There was a flare as a match was struck and he lit a cigarette. From the brief glow of the flame I could see we were surrounded by buildings.

'Do you not recognise it?' Michael asked, blowing smoke in my direction.

The acrid smell of it made me choke. I needed to run. I needed to get my bearings. I slid my left hand to the door handle and pulled at it, but the door wouldn't open.

He tutted. 'Child lock,' was all he said.

'Please,' I said, my mouth parched. It was still so warm even though it was dark. There wasn't a breath of air in the car. 'Please, just let me go, Michael. I've the girls to get home to. They need me.'

He shook his head. 'Don't you know where you are?'

I could see shadows, shapes emerging in the darkness. It was starting to look familiar.

Michael flicked on the headlights of the car for just a few seconds. Long enough for me to see exactly where we were and to know that there'd be no one within hearing distance. Set back from the road, the abandoned school site at St Catherine's – where Clare, Julie and I had been pupils – had long been boarded up, the grounds left to rot and let nature reclaim while decisions were being made about a new purpose. It had been at least ten years since any pupils had walked through these corridors.

A hotchpotch of buildings of different ages, different designs, now silent and empty of the 1,200 girls who used to walk the corridors daily between lessons. It had been an impressive site in its day, sitting proudly on the banks of the Foyle, but now it felt claustrophobic, creepy, isolated.

'Why?' I asked him.

'You'll find out,' was all he said, getting out of his car door and walking round to me.

I didn't know what to do. Should I refuse to move, force him to pull me out of the car kicking and screaming? Would anyone hear my screaming, anyway? Would it use up whatever energy I had left? Should I try to negotiate with him?

Surely what I'd seen during our time together hadn't been

an act? It couldn't have been. Not all the time, anyway. He'd been so tender. So caring. The long chats we'd shared over coffee. The flowers he'd sent. How tenderly we'd made love that first time. The beautiful words he'd written each week for class. I couldn't think and my head still hurt.

The touch of his hand on the bare skin of my arm made me wince. It was still sore, more than likely bruised by his earlier violence. He didn't respond to my yelp of pain, simply told me to get out of the car. I felt the sting of broken glass on the soles of my bare feet as I stood up. I tried to move, to hop away from the glass, but I couldn't see the ground to see where was clear.

'Move!' Michael sneered.

'There's glass,' I muttered, feeling the soles of my feet become wet with blood.

He didn't speak but pushed me ahead of him, down the covered walkway to the door of what we'd always called the 'Middle Building'. Though the doors were locked and boarded-up, I could see that someone had chipped away at the wooden boarding, smashed the glass within.

Michael slid his hand through the jagged hole in the door and pulled it open, pushing me in and onto the cold tiles of the floor. If it had been dark outside, inside it was darker. No hint of any light, no glow from the moon, all windows covered, electricity long since switched off. I could hear the constant drip of water, felt dust and grit on the floor, now mixing with my shredded foot. Suddenly a bright light, a torch, was shining directly into my eyes. It disorientated me further.

'Up,' Michael said, gesturing towards stairs on my right-hand side.

I remembered my form class, my old geography classroom. I remembered climbing these stairs with a schoolbag filled to bursting with textbooks. The scent of our damp coats in the air. The call of a prefect to stay on the left-hand side – 'Single file, girls!'

We climbed until we reached the second, and top, floor. He seemed to know where he was going, know exactly what he was doing, and that frightened me. This had all been planned. For how long? And why? The why still made no sense to me.

'Please,' I begged again as he pushed me further down the corridor. 'Why are you doing this? Just let me go, Michael. I won't tell anyone it was you. I won't say a word. I'll do what you want. I'll run away with you.'

He didn't speak, just pushed me forwards.

Opening the door of a classroom on the left-hand side, he pushed me inside. With the gentle light of the torch I could see posters, classwork still pinned to some of the walls. The blackboard, with obscenities scrawled along it. A few chairs, lying on their sides. Discarded drinks cans and beer bottles. A mouldy and pervasive smell filled the air, only made worse by the lack of any ventilation.

He walked across the classroom to the door of the small storeroom before waving his torch in the same direction.

'Get in!' he said.

'No!' I shook my head.

'Don't be so stupid,' he said as if he were talking to a child. As if he were asking me to try something fun and I was being stubborn. 'Get in,' he snarled.

I hesitated before he grabbed my arm and pushed me in, my ribs colliding with a wooden shelf as I hit the back of the storeroom. I barely had time to turn around to look at him, when he closed the door and I could hear him move furniture around.

'I'll be back later,' he said through the door.

'Michael, please!' I begged, thumping on the door as hard as I could. 'Don't leave me here!'

He didn't respond, but I heard the sound of his footsteps moving further and further away until there was silence again. Silence and utter blackness.

I slumped to the ground, pulled my knees up to my chest. My head ached, my arm, too. My foot felt as though it were on fire. But aside from the physical pain, my God! I was scared. So incredibly terrified. Terrified and angry for putting myself in this position.

I had no idea what time it was. Were the police looking for me? Surely they'd have traced my car, for what good it would do? I thought of Beth and Paul. How I'd betrayed them by going to meet Michael in the first place. How I'd been so stupid. So reckless.

I cried when I thought of Molly. I'd promised her I wouldn't leave her. I'd promised her the bad man wouldn't get me. That I'd be there for her. She was only three. A baby. She must be so confused and scared right now. I cried more when it hit me over and over again that there was no chance I was getting out of this alive.

I thought of all of Ronan's words, how he'd gone to identify Clare. Who would have the grim task of identifying my body? What kind of state would Michael leave me in for them to identify, or would he leave me here to rot in this building? They might never find me. Or would my body end up like Clare's, locked in a fridge in a coroner's, miles from home? Would my family have to sit in front of the media and plead for my killer to come forward?

Just one week ago, Michael had shown Clare no mercy. If he'd been the man she was seeing, he'd wooed her, too. At the same time as he was wooing me. He'd allowed her to fall in love with him, at the same time as he was telling me he was falling in love with me. Made her think she had a future with him, only to betray her in the most brutal way.

How had I even considered for one second running away with this man? I'd been so very, very stupid. My baby girl was so young that in a few years she wouldn't even remember who I was, how I'd loved her. Would she ever understand why any of this had happened? Would I? And if, by some miracle, I came out of this alive, would any of them ever forgive me?

The putrid smell, as if the very walls were sweating in this heat, filled my nostrils. I was sure I could hear the sound of something scurrying in this enclosed space with me. I was afraid to move. I could barely breathe; my chest was so tight I was sure I'd suffocate in this space. I covered my ears to try to drown out the sound of the scurrying, the dripping of water, but I couldn't drown out the thumping of my heart.

Thursday, 14 June

Chapter Forty-Six

Rachel

I wasn't sure what time it was. There was no way to tell. I thought maybe I could see some light under the crack in the door, but it could have simply been that my eyes had adjusted to the darkness just a little. I knew I'd slept, or dozed at some stage. I knew it because I dreamed that I'd been able to find my way out and run away. Dreamed that I'd been sitting beside Paul and telling him how scared I was but that at least now it was over.

Horror washed over me when I woke, still in this storeroom, my clothes now damp with sweat, blood and God knows whatever else that was lying on the floor. I desperately needed to use the toilet – was determined not to go where I was. I knew it was a silly logic, but it was the one way I felt I could keep control of the situation. But as the hours passed and there was no sign of Michael and the door remained steadfast no matter how many times I'd rammed my shoulder against it, or kicked it, I'd had no choice. I had to pee in the small space where I stood, barely four foot by four foot wide. That was when I truly started feeling all my hope ebbing away.

My heartbeat had settled, though. The adrenaline had stopped pumping in shocking surges through my veins. Exhaustion forced me to sit, to focus on breathing. I was hungry. I was so thirsty I could cry, but in these moments I wasn't in any immediate threat.

The lull allowed me to gather my thoughts. If I could disarm him. If I could plead to his good nature. Surely it couldn't all have been a lie? But then again, he'd lied to Clare. If I could talk to him, reason with him, find out why. Wasn't that what they said to do, get someone who's threatening to hurt you to talk to you, to start to see your humanity. . .? Then again, I'd already shown Michael all of me.

The sound of something rattling, then the heavy thud of footsteps on tiles, awoke both my senses and my fear. I could hear someone approach, someone who was walking purpose-fully, as if they knew where they were going and why. The creak of a door, followed by the sound of the footsteps coming even closer, forced me to try to curl myself into as tight a ball as possible in the darkest corner of the storeroom. It was a foolish and futile attempt to hide, but it was all I had.

'Morning, sunshine. It's another beautiful day!'

I heard his voice through the door as he scraped the furni-ture back. The door opened and I didn't turn my head to look at him. I couldn't bear to see him.

'Now that's not much of a welcome, is it?' he said.

I was aware of him around me, close to me. The smell of him, the heat from his body, the warmth of his breath on the bare skin of my shoulder.

'I mean, I wasn't expecting you to jump into my arms, but maybe a kiss?'

I recoiled further as I felt the brush of his lips on the top of my head.

'Anyway, it's time to rise and shine,' he said, pulling at my arm, ignoring my yelp of pain, dragging me into the main classroom.

It was lighter, but only just. Thin slivers of light cut through the spaces between the wooden boards. The classroom looked no more appealing in the daylight than it had the night before. Clearly, we weren't the first visitors to the abandoned building. There was evidence it had been used as a drinking den. I glanced around, trying to find my bearings. Trying to place exactly which classroom I was in, which way would be the easiest way out – if there was a way out.

'I've brought you some water,' he said, reaching into a rucksack he'd placed on the floor and taking out a bottle of still mineral water.

I looked at it, not wanting to take anything from him. But being so thirsty it was all I could do not to grab it out of his hands.

'Take it,' he said, holding it out towards me.

I hesitated.

'Look,' he said, 'you can take it yourself, or I can force it down your throat. It's really no odds to me; although a part of me would like to watch you choke.'

I took it. The seal was still intact, which offered me a little reassurance, so I opened it and put it to my lips. It was ice-cold and felt so good as it hit the back of my throat. I drank my way through the full bottle, only thinking afterwards that I shouldn't have been so greedy with it. I didn't know when I'd get more. Or if I would get more.

'There are toilets across the corridor,' he said. 'The water's been switched off and well, some of them are a bit smashed up, but if you need to go . . .'

I nodded. If anything, I'd be able to gauge exactly where I was if I got out of the classroom again.

He pushed me towards the toilet block. It was as grim as

283

he'd said it would be, but at least it afforded some privacy. I thought of how I'd been forced to relieve myself in the storeroom and my face flushed red with embarrassment.

'You're not very talkative this morning,' he said. 'It's not like you, Rachel. Normally, you chat away to me. Banter. This is quite disappointing.'

'What are you going to do to me?' I asked as I emerged from one of the cubicles and looked him directly in the eyes. Those green eyes I'd fallen for . . . How stupid I'd been!

'Well, you see, we have a problem. This wasn't supposed to happen like this. Not yet, anyway. I wanted to play with you a bit more. And Julie, too. She's not like you and Clare, is she? Not a slut like you two. It was harder to get under her skin. She's no idea, of course, of who I really am. She thinks I'm just the friendly dad at the school gates. The one who helped to change her tyre when it was flat. She doesn't know I was the one who let the air out, but still . . .'

He was speaking quickly – had an almost manic air about him. I noticed he was still wearing the same clothes as the night before and his eyes were red-ringed, as if he hadn't slept much, if at all. He kept stepping from foot to foot, glancing around him, then back at me. Each time he looked at me he wore an expression as if he'd just seen me for the first time. It was unnerving.

'Back into the classroom,' he said.

I did as I was told and followed.

'Anyway, Rachel, the thing is, I don't quite know what to do with you. I mean, ultimately I do, but things have changed. They haven't followed my plan. So I'm going to hang onto you a for a bit while I work it all out.'

'How long?' I asked. The thought of being here in this space with him was making me feel sick to my stomach.

'I've not quite decided. But don't worry; you'll be safe here until I do decide. This site's deserted. It's the perfect place to keep you, to be honest, and you've got to admit, there's a certain poetic justice to it.'

'I don't know what you mean,' I said. 'What am I supposed to have done – what are we all supposed to have done – to deserve this?'

He shook his head, pulled his fingers through his hair. Then, without warning, he turned and kicked at the door, growling as he did so. I startled and took a few steps back before he turned to look at me again.

'The fact that you don't know,' he said, 'just proves you deserve it. It meant nothing to you, did it? You didn't even notice and you certainly didn't care. So self-involved. Not caring what impact your actions had on others – as long as your life was perfect, that was all that mattered. You and Julie and Clare. All the same.'

'What makes you think my life is perfect?' I asked him. 'If my life was perfect, would I have been falling for another man? You *know*, Michael, you know what I felt for you. You *know* it was real. I believed you.'

'You were putting your own needs above those of your family. You plead and cry "My girls, Michael, think of my girls."' He mimicked my voice as he spoke, 'But what thought did you give to your girls when you were fucking me? And then, like everyone else in your life, I became disposable, didn't I? Pretend it was about them, all you want, but it was about you. You'd had your fun. Christ, Rachel, you begged me to fuck you just minutes before you broke it off.'

He was twisting my words, my actions and my motives. It wasn't like that. Or was it? Had I been too blind, too selfish like he said, to see what I was doing? But even if I was, I didn't deserve this. Any of it. I couldn't hold back my tears as I thought of who I'd hurt because of this.

'You're crying now because I've called out your lies and your selfishness. It hurts to look in a mirror, Rachel, doesn't it? To learn what kind of a person you really are.'

I put my hands over my ears. I didn't want to listen to him. He didn't understand.

He just stared at me, his eyes roaming over my body before he pulled a seat across the room and sat on it.

'You can stand there all day,' he said, 'hands over your ears, but I'll still be here. Nothing will have changed.'

I watched as he delved into the rucksack, pulled out two pre-packed sandwiches and threw one across the room to me.

'Eat,' he said. 'And let's not go through some stupid song and dance with you refusing to eat. You'll be hungry. You'll eat it anyway, no matter what you say, so just cut to the chase and eat it now.'

I lifted the chicken salad sandwich off the floor, fetched the other abandoned school chair and sat on it. I couldn't deny I was hungry, but my stomach was tight with tension. I wasn't sure I'd be able to eat. I took a small bite; it turned to sawdust in my mouth but I knew I needed to keep up my strength. I forced my way through one sandwich, leaving the other in the packet. I wouldn't make the same mistake that I'd made with the water again.

He eyed me suspiciously before reaching again into his bag and rolling a can of Fanta across the floor to me.

I lifted it, popped it open and took a long drink before sitting it back on the ground.

'What now?' I asked him.

'Now,' he said, putting his own drink can down then standing up and brushing the crumbs from his jeans. 'Now, Rachel, we have a little fun.'

Chapter Forty-Seven

Elizabeth

Michael had called to see me that morning. Bringing supplies from home. I blushed at the thought of his poking through my drawers, packing underwear and nighties for me. He'd brought with him a bag from Boots, too – containing toiletries, a toothbrush and hairbrush.

'If you need anything else, just text me and I'll bring it next time I come in,' he'd said.

He'd looked awful. Tired. Stressed. I'd asked him if he was okay.

'The kids are very upset,' he'd told me. 'They're scared they're not going to see you again. Ava slept beside me last night. She cried herself to sleep. I think you being sick has brought up a lot of memories for them of when Laura died. I think I'd fooled myself into thinking they were doing okay now, that they'd managed in that way children do, but then this happens. . .'

From the look on his face, the dark circles under his eyes, I'd wondered if the children weren't the only ones dealing with the ongoing trauma of Laura's death.

'Bring them in,' I'd said, cringing at the slurring of my voice. It had improved, but talking still required a mammoth effort.

He'd looked at me; I could see he was sizing me up. Wondering if it would be any reassurance at all to the children to see their grandmother in a hospital bed, one side of her face still drooping, her left side still weak. Needing to be helped by two staff and a walker to make it to the bathroom.

'I don't want to worry them,' he'd said and I could tell he hated telling me that. That he knew it would hurt me, even if I knew he was doing the right thing.

'In a day or so?' I'd said.

He'd nodded. 'Yes, I think that would be a good idea,' he'd said, but I knew he would be playing it all by ear.

'I'm sorry I can't stay,' he'd said. 'But I've work to get to. I'll try to get in later, but if you need me . . .'

'I know, thank you,' I'd said.

'Your sister'll be arriving later, so you might get a visit from her,' he added.

I'd smiled, a lopsided smile that caused him to frown. I was tired again. I'd wanted to sleep. He was just leaving the room, when I'd felt my eyelids start to droop and I'd drifted off.

'Elizabeth,' a cheery woman, with red hair and ID hanging from a lanyard identifying her as Cliona Barr, said softly. 'I'm Cliona and I've been appointed as your social worker. I think you've been expecting me?'

I blinked at her. She looked friendly. Caring. Ruddy of cheek, wearing a dark green wrap dress and a brightly coloured necklace. She pulled up a seat and sat down.

'I'm here to work on your behalf. To make sure all of your needs are met and that when you're well enough to leave hospital, you have adequate support in place to help with your ongoing recovery.'

She clicked her pen and opened a beige folder before crossing her legs and getting poised to write.

'I've had a look over your notes,' she said. 'And I'll be talking to the multidisciplinary team once they've completed all their assessments. Is that okay?'

'Yes,' I said, 'but you don't need to worry about me. I'll manage.'

My tongue still felt thick in my mouth. I felt as if I sounded drunk when I spoke. Cliona looked at me sympathetically, but I knew by the look of her she wasn't going to be dismissed easily.

'You'll manage, I'm sure of that. But I'm just going to make sure that you don't make yourself worse when a little support can make life easier. You've nothing to fear from me, Elizabeth,' she said. 'I'm on your side.'

Something in the manner of how she spoke made me think I could trust her. I felt comfortable in her company. I found myself welling up – stupid old woman that I was, thankful to find someone on my side. It had seemed as if I'd been fighting against people for too long.

Seeing my tears, Cliona reached over, pulled a tissue from the box at the side of my bed and handed it to me. I dabbed my eyes, tried to compose myself.

'You don't have to be strong all the time,' Cliona said. 'You're not a machine, Elizabeth, and you're not on your own. I've had a good long read of your referral and your file. You've been through the mill in the last few years. Anyone who's been through even half of what you have would be entitled to feel more than a little sorry for themselves.'

A knock on the door to my room interrupted us. We both looked across to where a young male nurse was standing.

'There's a policeman here to see you, Elizabeth,' he said, his face reddening.

I wondered if he thought I was some sort of criminal. I'd have laughed at how uncomfortable it seemed to make him, had I been feeling more like myself.

'He says his name's DI Bradley,' the nurse said.

Cliona spoke. 'I can go and chat to him on your behalf if you want?' she said. 'And if you're too tired, it's okay to ask him to come back another time.'

The nurse coughed. 'Erm, he says it's really quite urgent,' he said, blushing.

Cliona looked at me for guidance.

'He's a good man. If he wants to talk it'll be important,' I said.

She nodded at the nurse and started to gather her things. I reached my good arm out to her.

'Can you stay?' I asked, desperately needing to have someone on my side with me.

She didn't hesitate, not for a moment.

'Of course I can,' she said with a smile, patting my hand gently.

DI Bradley walked into the room looking as though he were carrying the weight of the world on his shoulders. As I saw him, fragments of memory started to come back to me. A photo. He'd shown me a photo. He'd been with me when I'd taken ill. And the photo . . . who had been in it, what it had said. What it had warned.

I felt my chest tighten.

'Elizabeth, how are you?' he asked.

'Scared,' I replied. 'I think . . . you showed me a picture, didn't you? Of Laura? That day at the farmhouse.'

He nodded. 'I did, Elizabeth. Just before you took ill. But something else has happened since . . .'

I felt Cliona squeeze my hand reassuringly before she introduced herself to DI Bradley.

'Elizabeth has asked that I stay with her,' she said. 'I hope that's okay?'

He nodded. 'Of course,' he said before turning to me again. 'Elizabeth, Rachel Walker's gone missing. We suspect she's been abducted. She failed to come home from a shopping trip and her car was found abandoned at a secluded spot at Ness Woods last night. There were signs of a struggle and I don't think I need to tell you that we suspect the person who took her is the same individual who killed Clare Taylor.

'Given how little time he spent with Clare before he left her for dead, we really are under pressure to find her as soon as possible.'

'How can I help?' I asked.

I tried to shift in my bed, felt my chest tightening further.

Cliona whispered: 'Just breathe.'

I clung to her words.

DI Bradley spoke again.

'Elizabeth, the photo I showed you . . .'

He reached into the envelope and took out a picture, wrapped in plastic. I only had to glance at it to recognise it again.

'I had a feeling you were about to tell me something about it, just before you took ill.'

I couldn't speak, just kept looking at it. Drawn to the image of Laura. Her dark shiny hair framing her face. So young. Such a life wasted.

'That picture was taken from my house,' I said. 'From my album. It was one Laura herself took.'

'And who would have had access to your house?'

'No one who'd do any harm to anyone. It's usually only me there. My grandchildren visit once a week.'

'Laura's children?' DI Bradley asked.

'Yes, their daddy brings them for a visit every Wednesday. Sometimes they stay for tea.'

'Does he stay with them? When they visit.'

'No,' I said, shaking my head. 'Well, not usually. He uses it as some time out. He's under a lot of pressure – you know, looking after them. Dealing with everything after Laura died.'

I saw it. Even in my tired and drug-addled state, I saw it. An almost imperceptible raise of his eyebrow. A look between Cliona and him.

'And would he have access to your house at other times? A spare key, maybe?'

'Yes. He helps me out, fixes things when they're broken, does some handiwork. But he wouldn't . . . he wouldn't have taken that picture. You don't think he's responsible for any of this, do you? No. He's not like that. Michael's not like that at all.'

I could feel myself becoming agitated. This was ridiculous. Unthinkable. Not Michael.

'We're not saying that,' DI Bradley said. 'But I think we should talk to him anyway.'

Trembling, I gave the police the details of my son-in-law, his home address, his work address. I felt as if I was betraying him with every word.

'And you're sure there's no one else who could have had access to your home?'

'Yes,' I said. 'Everyone else is long gone.'

292

Chapter Forty-Eight

Rachel

Michael walked around me, sizing me up. I was shaking, my teeth chattering. I couldn't stop tears from falling, even though I didn't want to let him see me cry. I wondered if Clare had been this scared. Had she known what was going to happen?

He stopped after walking around me twice.

'Do you think you're attractive?' he asked, his breath hot on my face.

'What?'

I didn't know where this was leading. His question had disarmed me.

'Do you think you're attractive? Slim, blonde. You always take care of your appearance, don't you? It's important to you.'

I didn't know how to answer. Didn't know what he expected me to say.

'C'mon, Rachel, answer me.'

'I don't know,' I said. 'I'm no different to anyone else.'

'You don't really feel that way though, do you? You think you're beautiful. I've seen how you carry yourself. What you wear. How you interact with others and me. You've a confidence about you.'

He swept my hair back from my face and I recoiled. With his two hands either side of my face, he smoothed my hair flat, twisted it into a knot so tight around his fist that it hurt.

'Pride's a sin,' he said and crossed the room to his rucksack, my hair still twisted around his fist so I was forced to move with him, bent and crooked, the back of my head burning as the hair was torn out by the follicles.

He pulled out a knife and I tried, I tried so hard, with every bit of me, to pull away.

'It's worse when you fight, you know. Clare found that out the hard way.'

'Please,' I begged. 'Please don't do this!'

He brought the tip of the knife close to my face, touched the flat of the blade against my cheek.

'All you ever had to do was be nice, Rachel. That's all it would have taken.'

I was crying, shaking. I was sure my legs would give out from under me. Sure I'd lose control of my bladder. Not that it mattered now. I was aware of how very slowly he drew the knife, still flat, still blunt, around my neck. The image Ronan had painted of Clare – grey, translucent, blood drained from her – jumped into my head. I heard his sharp intake of breath, closed my eyes and let all hope drift away.

I felt the tug of his hand on my hair and then the sensation of lightness, of a release of pressure. The sound of sawing. Through my hair. Cutting it short. Hacking at it until I fell to the ground.

'You're not so attractive now, are you?' he said. 'Maybe I should take a picture. See how you feel about people seeing you at your worst and judging you. See how you like it.'

I could feel a trickle of blood running down my neck. Strands of hair fell in front of my eyes. I looked at my hands, which were planted firmly on the ground in front of me, stopping me from falling further. They were dirty and bruised. My nails broken. I knew I looked monstrous. Bloodied and broken. I turned my head towards him, looked up to where he stood above me, staring down as if I were shit on the bottom of his shoe.

'Why are you doing this?' I sobbed. 'What did I ever do to you? What did Clare ever do? Or Julie?'

'You took my family away from me,' he said. 'And doing this? Well, this is the only chance I've got at getting them back.'

'I took your family away? I don't even *know* your family.' I was confused, wondered if I was losing my mind. I just wanted all this to end. 'I've never intentionally hurt anyone. Nor did Clare, or Julie . . .'

'You remember Laura, don't you?' he said, wiping the knife on the side of his trousers.

'Laura O'Loughlin,' I said. 'From school.'

'This school,' he said, looking around him. 'Did you know she killed herself?' he asked, his voice soft.

'I'd heard,' I told him. 'It's very sad.'

'Do you know how she killed herself? Where she did it? Why?'

I shook my head. 'No.'

He pulled his chair closer, sat down.

'She did it here. At this site. Down by the river, at the railings. She came down here and she cut her wrists then she tied a noose around her neck and hung herself.'

I shuddered. The image in my mind was horrific. Poor Laura. What could have been so bad to end her life, and to end it in such a brutal manner?

'She had two children as well, you know. Just like you. Just like Julie. So when you plead with me to let you go, that your children need you, that's not going to cut it with me. No one cared that Laura's children needed her . . . they still do. But they can't have her. She's been gone from their lives for two years. Seven and nine, they were. Babies, really.'

'So why inflict that pain on other children? On my children?' I was crying again, thinking of my girls. 'Molly's only three. She needs me.'

'She'll adapt,' he said, his tone cold. 'Children are very adaptable, especially when they're younger. Maybe Paul will start a new family with that woman of his. Molly'll get a new mummy.'

'But why us? Why me? I didn't do anything to Laura. I didn't hurt her. Her death has nothing to do with me.'

'You're colder than I ever gave you credit for, Rachel,' he said. 'That you don't even realise. Out of all three of you, you were the one I thought might have been truly good at heart. If you'd agreed to run away . . . maybe . . .' His eyes seemed to glaze over for a moment before he blinked and looked me directly in the eye. 'Each time you excluded her, you made her feel worthless. Every time you rolled your eyes when she talked about her favourite book, or stopped talking when she walked into a room. Every time you all picked her last for games, or left her sitting on her own on school trips, you made her feel she wasn't good enough. That she would never be good enough.

'Do you not remember the time she had her hair cut? Permed. She was delighted with it. Clare, though . . . Clare laughed at her. I always remembered that name. Always remembered how this Clare told her she should sue the hairdresser. You didn't step in. Did you? You let her say it. You must have known it was cruel.

'She started to cut herself, you know, back then. She was broken even then and you three, you just chipped away at whatever was left of her.'

'We were children, for God's sake,' I said. 'We didn't know who we were ourselves. You can't blame us for what happened. It was years ago.'

'Oh I can and I do blame you. You must have known what it was doing to her. You must have known how she was made to feel. What about the time Clare invited her to go with you to the Fifth Year social? Laura was so excited. More excited than I'd seen her in ages. If I remember correctly, a week or so later she asked Clare what she should wear and if maybe she could go shopping with you all for an outfit. Clare laughed in her face. Told her she'd got to be joking, as if you lot would ever be seen with her.'

My jaw dropped. This wasn't true. It couldn't have been. Clare wasn't like that. She was never like that.

'You've got it all wrong. It wasn't us. It wasn't Clare – she wouldn't have done anything like that.'

'No,' he said. 'She was. She had a cruel streak. You can't rewrite the past. I knew this would happen. I think Laura knew too, which was why she never took it further. You and your lot would just have circled the wagons. Made life harder for her.'

'I swear to you on the lives of my children, I didn't know about that. I had nothing to do with it. And no matter what you tell me, I find it hard to believe the Clare I knew had anything to do with it, either.'

He shook his head slowly. 'At least she had the guts to admit it, right at the end. And to think I always thought you were the ballsier of the two of you. But Clare, Clare admitted it all just before. She admitted the name-calling, the jokes, the nastiness over the dance. She even admitted that she'd planted diet pills in Laura's bag with a note telling her to lose weight.'

'No!' I was angry now. I refused to believe it. 'You're lying.'

'I can show you the recording if you like? Clare screaming into the camera, admitting it all. Begging for her life. Here. . .'

He fumbled in his pocket for his phone, but I didn't want to see it. I didn't want anything to do with it. What kind of a sick person records something like that?

'Watch!' he said, pushing the phone towards my face.

I squeezed my eyes shut, held my hands over my ears as tightly as I could, but I could still hear her. Crying. Sobbing. Choking out an apology. It was the most horrific thing I've ever heard and there was no mistaking it – it was Clare's voice.

'Please don't do this!' she begged, her voice tinny and distorted by the phone echoing around the abandoned classroom. 'Please!'

I opened my eyes, caught a second's glance of a bruised face, tear-stained, fear wild in her eyes, and it was all I could take. As swiftly as I could, I reached out and knocked the phone from his hand, sending it scuttling across the floor. At least now it was silent.

Michael just looked at me. His voice icy, calm, he spoke.

'If you persuade a child they're not good enough, if you drive that message home to them, then that stays with them throughout their entire lives. She lived in hell and then she killed herself. What was left of our family imploded. There has to be some form of justice for that, don't you think? Someone has to be held accountable. Someone has to pay.'

'But . . . It wasn't my fault. It wasn't our fault. We were stupid little girls, but that's all we were: children. I'm so sorry for your loss – she clearly meant the world to you. But hurting me isn't going to bring her back. Killing Clare didn't. Killing me won't, either.'

He paused. For just a second I thought I was getting through to him. I saw a shift in his expression, as if my words were sinking in.

'It won't bring her back, but it'll be justice. That'll be a start.'

'The police'll trace you,' I said, anger rising along with my fear. 'They'll find my phone. They'll trace our messages. Get your details from the college. You won't get away with this.'

He smirked. 'Give me some credit. You don't think I've told you the truth about me, do you?'

Chapter Forty-Nine

Elizabeth

DI Bradley had left the room to call the details in to his team that I'd given him.

'What do you think'll happen now?' I asked Cliona as if she had the answers to everything.

She handed me a fresh tissue. The one in my shaking hand had already started to disintegrate from my tears.

'I imagine they'll want to speak to him as soon as possible, especially if there's any chance at all that he may be responsible. They'll want to try to find that poor woman who's missing.'

'I can't imagine he would be responsible. He's a good man. He's always been a good man. I'd have known, surely, if he was capable of something like that . . .?'

'You must try not to get yourself too upset,' Cliona said, a worried look on her face. 'Let's wait until the police have spoken to him. Get all the information. It's not wise to jump to conclusions. I know this is horribly distressing for you, but you're still very vulnerable. I can speak to one of the nurses or the doctor to see if they'll give you a sedative, maybe.'

I shook my head. I didn't want a sedative. I didn't want to be taken away from all this only to have it swoop back in again when I woke, like a fresh cut. I thought of that woman. Clare Taylor. How she'd looked at me. Resigned to the fact that she was dying. I saw the light go out in her eyes. Could someone I'd treated as if he were one of my own really have left a human being in that state – butchered, carved up and left to die?

I shook my head, sniffed. Tried to compose myself.

'No. I need to know what's happening,' I said, even though I was weak and tired and really wishing that right now the light would go out in my own eyes. I'd had enough.

I'd lost too many people to tragedy. Seen too much hurt. In the theatres when I was nursing. On the farm. Losing my husband. Losing my children. Now, I could lose Michael *and* my grandchildren. If this was karma paying me back, she was a cruel mistress.

If only I'd known in the past, when things had seemed so bright, how it would all turn out . . .

I closed my eyes. Remembered the two little people playing in the yard, laughing together. Teasing each other mercilessly but with great affection. I remembered watching them through the window, the smell of my home baking making my tummy rumble. The feeling of my husband behind me, his arms slinking around my waist, him kissing the back of my neck and then joining me in watching our children play.

'This is the life,' he'd said.

I'd never felt as content in my life as I did in that moment. I felt untouchable – how wrong had I been?

DI Bradley came back into the room. I was scared of what he'd say to me.

'We've gone to your son-in-law's house and he's not there. Nor is he at work. Can you think of anywhere else he might be?'

'What time is it?' I asked.

'Just before three,' Cliona said.

'The school,' I told him, my stomach sinking. 'He'll be picking the children up from school. St Patrick's.'

'And his car? Can you describe it? Do you know the vehicle registration? Don't worry if you can't, we can check with the DVLA. This might just be quicker.'

My thoughts were all so jumbled. My brain hadn't knitted all my memories back into place yet. But I knew his car was silver. A Toyota. I couldn't give any more details than that.

'Thank you,' DI Bradley said, putting his phone back to his ear and passing the information on to his colleagues.

He hung up and stood awkwardly at the end of my bed.

'I'm so very sorry, Elizabeth,' he said.

All I could do was nod.

'The children?' I asked.

'My team will be as discreet as possible,' he said. 'They're aware that he's picking the children up and that other children will be present. They'll have informed the school and have liaison officers in place. The children will be looked after, so try not to worry. I know that sounds impossible.'

'Thank you,' I said.

'Elizabeth, I have to ask, have you had any reason at all to suspect Michael before now? Have you witnessed any behaviour that might have indicated a violent nature? His relationship with your daughter?'

I shook my head. No matter how I ran it through my head, I couldn't say that until a few minutes ago I'd ever considered him capable of hurting anyone. He was as gentle as Laura had been. But did everyone have their limit? Did everyone have a breaking point in the right circumstances? Were we all capable of horrendous crimes if pushed far enough?

'And he's the only person you can think of who'd have had access to your home, to your photographs? Who would have known the intimate details of how Laura died and about the flowers. Someone who'd have known about her classmates.'

'I think so,' I muttered, becoming aware of Cliona shifting awkwardly in her seat.

'Elizabeth. . .' she began, but we were interrupted by the ringing of DI Bradley's phone.

He answered it, his eyes on me as he spoke.

'Right, well that's enough for an arrest in itself. Oh. . . okay. Good. Good. Get him booked in and I'll be there as soon as I can. Any mention or sign of her? No? Okay. Right. See you soon.'

I felt as if the air had been pulled from my lungs and I gripped Cliona's hand tightly.

'Michael O'Neill's in police custody now, Elizabeth. And I'm sorry to have to tell you, my team have uncovered some evidence that appears to link him directly to Rachel Walker.'

I didn't think my heart could break any more. Oh, Michael, I thought, what *have* you done?

Chapter Fifty

Rachel

'What do you mean, you've not told me the truth?' I asked Michael.

He raised an eyebrow. 'What do you think I mean? You're a smart woman; you must have figured it out by now. I've been lying to you all this time. People like to write me off as stupid. But I'm not a stupid man.'

He stood up again, walked back and forth across the classroom. He still had the knife in his hand and I couldn't help but flinch each time he came close to me.

He crouched down beside me. 'Don't be scared, Rachel. I'll be gentle,' he said before pulling himself to standing and walking back across the room.

He seemed to be thinking and I heard him laugh before he turned to look at me again.

'You know nothing about me. Nothing about the real me. Michael O'Neill isn't even my real name. I know him, of course. We were good friends, you know. Before Laura died.'

My head hurt. My body ached. I could feel pain shift and move from my arms to my legs to my head. I was just so tired now. What little energy I'd had was seeping from me, as was any hope of being saved.

'So who are you?' I asked.

'I'm not sure I should tell you,' he said, pacing back and forth again.

I was sure I heard the sound of a helicopter in the sky. Most likely the police. Dare I hope they were looking for me?

Michael, or whatever his damn real name was, heard it, too.

'You've got to give them extra points for trying,' he said coldly. He pulled his chair closer to me and sat down again. 'Maybe you could guess who I am. So I've told you I'm not Michael O'Neill – and I have to say I'm surprised you never made the connection between that surname and Laura. Didn't you think it an odd coincidence?'

I didn't want to tell him that until the last few days I hadn't thought about Laura O'Loughlin in years, let alone wonder if she'd married and changed her name. I stayed quiet.

He shook his head. 'Silly, naive, self-obsessed Rachel. Never looks beyond the end of her own nose. Is it any wonder your husband found another woman?'

I wanted to cover my ears. I bowed my head, tried to make myself as small as possible.

'Look at me, Rachel,' he said.

I stayed staring at the floor until I felt the tip of his knife at my chin, urging my head upwards.

'I said look at me!'

I raised my head, blinked and looked at him. This mystery man hell bent on revenge.

'It doesn't matter who I am, don't you realise that? I might as well have stopped existing the day she died anyway. Everything changed. I realised that I didn't matter. All everyone could think about was poor Laura. Even our own mother. It didn't matter to her that she still had one living child. I became invisible to her. Do you know what that felt like, Rachel? To lose my sister, to lose my mother, too? And all of it because of you and your

304

stupid friends. For a long time I wasn't strong enough to do this, but I am now, Rachel.

'I've been planning this for a long time. Watching and waiting. Following you all – playing the game. Do you really think it was a coincidence that it was my mother who found Clare on the road that morning? That was a key part of all this. To give her the justice she'd been denied. I wanted her to see what I'd done to the person who hurt Laura so badly. Now it's time to finish what I started. And my mother will see me now. She'll forgive me for the person I became. I won't be invisible any longer.'

The thrum of helicopter blades overhead distracted me. They appeared to distract him, whatever his name was, too. He looked up and walked to the window, pulling back one of the boards just a fraction to try to see out.

This was perhaps the one chance I'd have. I scrambled across the room, half crawling, half walking as I tried to pull myself to an upright position. The door to the classroom was open and I knew if I could get out, there was just the slightest chance I could get away. I'd have to hope I knew the twists and turns of these corridors and school buildings better than he did.

I was holding my breath, afraid that any noise would cut over the sound of the helicopter and attract his attention. I'd just managed to turn right and start to run towards the stairs, when I heard him bellow my name.

I ran as fast as I could in the darkness, in the dank, sweaty smell of this crumbling building, and I hoped I could outrun him, because I knew without a shadow of a doubt that when he caught me, he'd make sure that I'd never be able to run from him again.

Chapter Fifty-One

Elizabeth

DI Bradley left. Told me that another police officer would come and sit with me, to ask me a few questions. I sat shell-shocked, with Cliona by my side.

'Elizabeth,' she said, 'I'm going to ask you something now that may be distressing for you. But I feel that given everything that's happening, I do need to ask.'

I looked at her. I couldn't imagine anything she'd ask me or say to me could be more distressing than what had already unfurled that afternoon.

'Do you think that anyone else could possibly have gained access to that photo? Anyone at all who might already have a history of violence?' She spoke softly.

I shook my head.

'Elizabeth, I've seen your file. I know about Aaron. What happened to you. What he did. Do you think there's any chance it could be him?'

I shuddered at the mention of his name. I'd not allowed myself to say it, or even think it, since the day and hour he'd left. But no, surely it couldn't be Aaron? He was long gone. He'd left over a year and a half before. He wouldn't dare risk coming back.

I had no idea where he was and I didn't care to know. I never wanted to see his face again. My arm ached, as if the muscles tensed at the memory of that day, and of the days before it.

'He's long gone,' I said. 'He said he'd never be back.'

'Could he have changed his mind? He would have known about the picture, about Laura,' Cliona said. 'He hurt you before, Elizabeth.'

I started to cry. I hadn't wanted to think about him.

'I just think . . . if there's even a chance, you should let the police know. You didn't report the assault last time . . .'

'He's my son,' I said, which I knew was a pathetic reason for not reporting him.

Especially after how he'd left me, but I had known he was hurting. He was grieving just as I was. But in a different way, and I'd closed down, let him down, so he took that anger out on me. He'd been so remorseful. Promised to leave and never come back. Even before he'd been ordered out of the country by shady forces who'd got wind of how he'd left his mother half dead.

'I know,' she said softly. 'But is there even a chance he's come back? I assume he'd have access to your house, too?'

He probably had a key, but I'd have known if he'd been in the house, wouldn't I? And the police said there was a link between Michael and Rachel. So it couldn't be Aaron. He was still gone. I was still safe.

'You know that I'm bound by confidentiality,' she said, 'but in this case, I feel I have to bring this information to the police. Simply because there's a woman in immediate danger.'

I wanted to block out what she was saying. What I was thinking. That a child of mine could be capable of such evil. I knew it was a warped logic, but I could take it if it was just against me. I'd deal with that. But if he'd hurt those women

. . . If he was the sick mind behind those notes . . . I felt sick to my core.

I'd done everything I could to push him out of my head over the last eighteen months. I'd cleared out his bedroom. It was now just filled with boxes, pieces of furniture that no longer had a place in my house.

I'd tried to forget every detail about him, even the good memories. Even the bright smile on his face as a child. All I could see was the hatred in his eyes the night he'd almost killed me.

I still woke from my sleep, my body rigid in shock and pain as I relived how I'd hit every stair on the way down. How he'd screamed at me, spittle hitting my face as he'd told me I was the worst mother God had ever placed on the planet and that Laura was lucky to be dead. 'She probably did it to escape you,' he'd screamed at me as I lay on the floor at the bottom of the steps, as he kicked my already bruised and twisted arm so that I heard it break, felt the jagged bone tear through my flesh.

I'd looked through swollen and bruised eyes to see it jut from my skin. I'd been too shocked to feel pain in that moment. But it had been for just a moment – and then the pain had come screaming in.

The stale smell of beer and vodka on his breath. Drunk again, as he seemed to be every day. I'd simply asked him to get up and freshen up. To think about doing some jobs around the farm. Keep busy. It would do him no good to wallow.

He'd reacted like a man possessed. It wasn't even as if he was looking at me, more like he was looking right through me.

'You never stop,' he'd said. 'Nothing is ever good enough,' he'd said.

I'd walked away, into my room, and I heard him get up, move about. I'd been relieved. Thought that maybe despite his bitter words, he'd heeded something of what I'd said.

But when I'd started to make my way down the stairs, he was there, on the landing, dressed. His heavy work boots on.

'Are you happy now? Is this enough now? Do you need to nag more?'

I should have walked away. I should have kept my mouth shut. I'd learned before that when he was drinking, I did well to keep my stupid mouth shut. But I couldn't help it.

I'd turned to face him. Months of frustration and grief and worry stumbled from my lips.

'Oh, grow up, Aaron.'

I'd felt the full weight of his boot, kicking, pushing me backwards. I couldn't stop myself from falling. I'd tried to grab onto something, anything, as I fell, but when I did manage to grasp onto the carpet, I felt the same boot crush down on my hand. I'd pulled my hand away in pain, losing any purchase I had to stop me from falling, and I slid to the bottom of the stairs, the carpet fibres burning my face as they tore at my skin.

He left me there, on the ground, for two hours. Two hours before he loaded me into his car and, overcome with remorse, sobbed all the way to the hospital. I think he wanted me to tell him it was okay, that I forgave him, but I couldn't. In that moment, and may God forgive me for saying it, but in that moment, I hated him. I wanted him gone.

I was tired of combining grief with fear. I wouldn't let him make me think I'd driven Laura to her death. By the time I was discharged from hospital, he was long gone. Seems word of what he'd done to me had got around and he'd had a visit from a group of 'community activists', who gave him just twenty-four hours to get out of Derry.

'Elizabeth?' Cliona said gently. 'Just in case?'

I nodded, slowly. I couldn't run from the monster I'd created any more.

Cliona filled Constable King in when she arrived a short time later.

'Elizabeth, have you suspected your son might be involved before now? Have you kept this from us?'

Her tone was soft but there was no doubt that she wasn't impressed.

I started to panic. 'I didn't mean to,' I said. 'No, he'd gone. Been warned not to come back unless he wanted a bullet in his head. He was elsewhere. I didn't think of him. Not until Cliona mentioned it.'

But a part of me knew I was lying to myself. A whisper of a memory crept back. Of my being wheeled out of the house on the stretcher. Of the 'ghost' I'd wondered if I'd seen in the doorway. Had it just been too horrific to contemplate? Had I ignored it or blocked it out?

'Elizabeth was diagnosed as suffering from PTSD following the attack she sustained at the hands of her son and the death of her daughter,' Cliona said. 'She may have been unable to make the connection herself.'

Constable King got straight on her phone back to base, relayed the information and the description of Aaron I'd given. She left the room to talk and I broke down once again.

'I didn't think. I just didn't think,' I said. 'What if it is him? What if I could have stopped it all before it happened? If I'd reported him back then?'

Cliona just held my hand. Told me that at least the police knew now. They could look now.

Constable King came back into the room a few minutes later.

'Elizabeth, I know that you aren't well, but it would be very useful to us if you could answer some questions.'

I nodded. I'd do whatever I could. But first I had to know.

'Has Rachel Walker been found yet?'

Constable King shook her head.

'And Michael, and my grandchildren? What's happening?'

'The children are safe. They're being taken to Michael's parents. There's a social worker there and you're not to worry. DI Bradley's also asked me to assure you that your dog'll be taken care of. Officers are going to search your son-in-law's home now and they'll make sure Izzy has a safe place to stay. Mr O'Neill's denying all responsibility or knowledge.'

I nodded.

'Can you think of anywhere that might mean something to Michael? Does he own any other property? Have any storage units? A work space to which only he has access?'

I shook my head. 'Not that I know of. I'm sorry,' I said. 'There are some old outhouses at the farmyard still.'

'Police have been searching those,' she said. 'They've not uncovered anything out of the ordinary.' She glanced down at her notes. 'And his silver Avensis, the Toyota. Is that his only vehicle that you know of?'

I nodded. 'He kept hold of Laura's car, but then . . . well, he gave it to Aaron.'

I saw her eyebrows rise. 'And what kind of car was that?'

I tried to remember. It was red, I knew that much. A Renault, I thought.

'I don't know the registration,' I said. 'But it was a Renault.'

'Any idea of the model?' she asked.

I shook my head. 'Only that it was a saloon car, not a hatchback. And red.'

'That's good,' she said. 'The more information we have, the better our chances at getting to Rachel Walker. We've had a witness come forward who believes she may have seen Rachel with a man who wasn't her husband. She's given a description of his car.'

311

I nodded. 'And you said you'd found a link between Michael and Rachel?'

'We've found that Michael was taking a class at the NWRC in creative writing, which Rachel Walker tutored on a Thursday night. Were you aware of that?'

I paused for a moment. That didn't add up. On Thursday nights, Michael went to a bereavement support group. He never missed it. It was specifically for people who'd been bereaved by suicide. I told Constable King this, gave her what details I could remember.

'He'd even asked me to go with him a few times,' I said, more confused than ever. 'He said he thought it might help me.'

'If you'll excuse me again, I'll just phone in this new information,' Constable King said and left the room.

'You look worn out,' Cliona said to me. 'I think you should take a break.'

'But I'd never forgive myself,' I said, 'if that poor woman's dead and it's because of my stupidity. I'll never forgive myself.'

Chapter Fifty-Two

Rachel

The tiles were slippery beneath my feet. I grabbed hold of the banisters of the stairs to stop myself from falling. I couldn't afford to take it slowly, or watch my step. I had to move as fast as I could. This school, stretched across three buildings, each from a different era, was a warren of classrooms and corridors linking them together. The oldest building, to my right as I ran, had been converted from old outhouses.

There were stairways there to an upper floor that only those really familiar with the school would have been able to find. But if they were blocked up now, I'd quickly run out of space and find myself at a dead end. The newest building, to my left, held what had once been a darkroom as well as a host of storerooms and offices. Perhaps, I thought, I could hide there. But I'd have to run a considerable distance in plain sight to get to it. I knew I had to get to the safest place possible, as quickly as I could. Instead, I opted to run towards the assembly hall at the front of the school.

I vaguely remembered that there was a storage area under the stage. If I could get there, if I could hide out in a place he may not be able to find, perhaps I'd stand a chance. Or maybe I'd just be imprisoning myself further.

On the off-chance the front doors to the school had been breached before, I ran at them, ramming into them shoulder first, trying to get them to move. They didn't budge, but the echo of my body slamming against the wooden hoarding echoed through the cavernous halls and I heard a voice echo back.

'Come out, come out, wherever you are . . .'

The worn carpet was damp and sticky beneath my feet, the building crumbling after years of neglect, the echo of his voice bouncing off the walls making it difficult to assess just exactly where he might be. I looked up, around, hoping for a glint of light. A broken window. A splintered door. If I could get out, I'd be on the main road back into Derry in seconds. It was bright, traffic would be busy.

I rattled the heavy wooden doors to my left, those that led into the assembly hall, and was able to make my way in. The high-varnished sheen of the floor had long dulled. Echoes of my past were everywhere. The faded posters on the wall, the once plush red velvet curtains sagging, moth-eaten. Only the thinnest slivers of sunlight lit the otherwise tomblike space and I swore I could feel the ghosts of times past. Of that first day at school. When I sat on that floor and Clare and Julie sat beside me and we found each other. We found friendship.

We'd never meant to hurt anyone. We'd never realised how Laura was feeling. I'd never thought she wanted to be a part of our group. Or had I? If I were honest with myself, could I realistically say that? Poor Laura. Poor, poor Laura. We were so young and immature and selfish in the way that only teenagers can be. I could see now how we hurt her. It wasn't intentional, but I couldn't deny it. We could've reached out to her but it was easier not to. She was different, wasn't she? Odd.

But my heart ached for her and guilt washed over me. Had

we been partly to blame for her taking her own life, for being so damaged?

Had Clare really done what Michael was accusing her of? I'd never be able to ask her. She was gone. He could say what he wanted. You can't libel the dead. I thought of us all as eleven-year-olds, sitting on that floor. And how it had gone so wrong. Laura and Clare were both gone and I was sure I'd be next. Would Julie be luckier?

And this man, who I swore I could feel bearing down on me, her brother? A man I'd grown to love.

A monster.

I reached the stage, kicked at the doors leading to the under-stage storage. Wept and yelled in pain and frustration when they wouldn't budge, either. My body ached and I wasn't sure I had much strength left, but I wasn't ready to give up yet. I had to keep fighting.

I remembered there was a doorway on the stage itself. I was sure, if I could haul myself up, I could get to it. As long as he didn't know I was here, as long as he wasn't behind me, I could get to it and be safe. I could no longer hear him call me any more. I hoped he'd run down the wrong corridor, was looking elsewhere.

My arm was bruised, useless. But I pushed through the pain to pull myself up onto the stage. I scrambled to my feet and ran to the wings, where I couldn't be seen. Towards the stage door. With every step, all I could think was that I didn't want to die. I couldn't. I couldn't leave my girls. I couldn't let him win.

I reached my arm out to the door, ready to open it, knowing I was close to hiding somewhere where he was unlikely to find me. I was almost there. Almost.

My fingertips just reached the tarnished silver of the door handle, when it moved itself, the latch releasing, the door opening. I recoiled, fell backwards as the door opened fully and the shadow of an imposing figure stood over me, arm raised.

315

Chapter Fifty-Three

Rachel

The light blinded me. Bright, shining directly in my eyes. I raised my arm to shield my face as I tried to push myself backwards, across the stage and out of his way.

'Please,' I called out. 'Don't do this. Please.'

'Miss?' An unfamiliar voice spoke. 'Miss. I'm not here to hurt you. I'm just . . . we had reports of a break-in . . .'

The figure turned the torch towards himself, and I saw a man wearing a slightly horrified expression and a security uniform standing just metres away from me.

'Please, there's a man here and he has a knife. He's killed before,' I stuttered.

The security man paled. Even in the darkness, I could see the colour drain from his face. He lifted a radio from the lapel of his work jacket and spoke into it.

'Call 999 now. Police and ambulance. An armed man and a casualty, here at the old school site. I'm going to try to bring her out. It must be that missing woman they're searching for.'

A disembodied voice muttered something in return as I nodded to him. I couldn't make out what the voice was saying. My heart was thumping too hard. All I could think was that

316

we needed to get out and soon. I was sure Michael, or whatever his name was, would be on us at any second.

The security man took a step towards me, reached out an arm to me.

'Can you stand? Can you walk?'

'Yes,' I stuttered. 'But he's near.'

'We'll get you out of here,' he said, but I could detect the shake in his voice. 'The police have been looking for you.'

He took my hand in his and pulled me to standing, paused for just a second and took in the sight in front of him. I dreaded to think how alarming I looked. He turned, arm raised again with his torch and led me through the stage door to the corridor directly behind it. There was no sign of Michael, but I knew he could appear at any moment.

'This way,' the security man said, motioning for me to follow him towards the end of the corridor.

I knew there was a door there that led outside, but was sure it would be locked tight, too.

'I have a key,' he said, reaching for a large bunch of keys attached to his belt.

He started to fumble through them while I kept glancing at the other end of the corridor. I willed the security man to be quicker, but I could see he was nervous, too. His hands shook as he searched through the keys, which jangled together.

'Can you hold the torch for me?' he asked and I took it, shining it down on the keys as he continued his search.

I almost collapsed with relief when he said: 'Ah, this should do it,' and slid a key into the lock.

We were almost there. If we could just get outside . . .

'Damn!' he muttered, rattling the key in the lock. 'It's sticking. Probably rusted.'

My heart sank.

He pulled the key out and crouched down to look through the keyhole, rattling the door loudly as he went.

Too much noise. We were making too much noise. I felt my fear grow stronger, my legs tremble.

Shoving the key back in the lock, he jiggled it and fought with it, swearing loudly.

'Hurry, please!' I said as he rammed at the door with his shoulder, trying to force it open.

A noise from my left-hand side distracted me. I spun around, pointing the torch to the opposite end of the corridor, and saw my captor bearing down on us, his eyes wild with fury.

Twenty feet away.

Fifteen.

Ten.

Then a tug at my arm as I was pulled through the now open door, onto the stone steps outside. The security man followed, pushing the door closed as quickly as he could, putting the full weight of his body against it to hold it shut while he turned the key in the lock from the other side.

I could hear Aaron scream and curse, smash his fists against the door, but he couldn't get out. Not now. Not from that door, anyway.

But I knew he had his own way in and out, and it wouldn't take him long to reach it.

'This way,' I shouted to the security man as he spoke quickly into his radio.

He followed me down the stone steps and we turned to run up towards the front entrance of the school grounds, where we'd be easily seen by passing traffic.

A white security van was sitting by the entrance and a woman in the same uniform as the man who'd found me jumped out, pulling off her jacket as she ran towards me, wrapping it round me when I reached her.

'He's still here,' I called. 'He'll get us.'

'Help is coming,' she shouted.

And I could hear the thrum of the helicopter blades overhead again and the distant wail of sirens. My legs finally buckled and the two security staff led me to their van, just as the first police car turned into the grounds.

Chapter Fifty-Four

Elizabeth

The ward was quiet when I woke. Cliona had left and Constable King had gone for a break. She'd assured me she'd be back with any news. I'd managed to drift off for maybe half an hour, but although I was exhausted to my very core, I was too filled with adrenaline to sleep any longer.

There were two men in the frame for an unthinkable crime – two men who were both closely connected to me – two men I loved. My son-in-law, who I'd come to rely on, and my only son who, despite his many faults, at one time had been a good and caring man.

And all this had been connected to my beautiful but troubled daughter.

How had I got things so wrong? Had I been a dreadful parent? Was I ultimately to blame for what had gone so terribly wrong in both their lives and mine?

Maybe if I'd been there more for Michael. Maybe if I'd argued with the paramilitary henchmen who'd ordered Aaron from the country. If I'd reported him to the police that time. Yes, he'd have gone to jail, but maybe he'd have received help for his alcohol addiction, counselling for his anger and his grief over the death of his sister. He could have had a true fresh start. I'd been naive in thinking such anger and hatred would only ever be shown against me. That he wouldn't focus it on other people. I'd been stupid to think I was a good mother by letting him go and not pressing charges.

I looked out of the window from my room in the South Wing of Altnagelvin Hospital at the cloudless blue skies, the rolling hills. At the cars moving along the road. A bus. People going about their ordinary business. I heard the chatter of the staff outside my room as they prepared to serve dinner.

And I thought about Rachel Walker. Thought of her family. Wondered if she was alive. Had she survived? Would she bear the physical and emotional scars I did for years to come?

I turned my head at a knock on my door. One of the staff nurses stood there, looking at me sympathetically. No doubt they'd all been made aware of the high drama coming out of my room. I was probably a great talking point in the staffroom.

'Elizabeth, look, we don't normally do this, but we're aware today's been an unusual and stressful day for you. We've a visitor here, says she's your niece? Sister is prepared to let her in for ten minutes, but we'll have to remind her of the visiting hours.'

I nodded. In truth, I'd almost forgotten about my sister and her daughter visiting given everything else that had been unfolding. It was strange it was just my niece who'd come to see me – we'd never been particularly close, but I didn't feel I could turn her away given that she'd travelled so far to see me. Perhaps my sister was tired from the journey. Or resting, maybe. Or, knowing her, she'd taken one look at the farmhouse, pulled on the Marigolds and started with a 'proper clean'.

I used the automatic controls to raise the head height of the bed and waited to see my niece. I was shocked to see Ingrid Devlin walk into the room instead.

'I'm sorry for fibbing,' she whispered as she walked across

the room to me as if we were best friends or co-conspirators. 'I knew they wouldn't let me in unless I said I was family, but I had to see you.'

She pulled a chair close to my bed and sat down. I didn't want her here. She had no right at all to be by my bedside, especially not now.

'Why are you here?' I asked. 'I don't want to see you.'

'I get that you're suspicious of me,' she said. 'But you're my best lead on this story. And I need to get as much as I can.'

'I'm not a "lead",' I told her, reaching for the call button by my side. 'I'm a human being. Not just a story. Constable King'll be back here shortly, you know.'

'Have they told you about the car?' she asked.

'Ingrid, please. Can you leave?' My finger hovered over the call button.

'The car he was driving. The man who Rachel Walker was seeing. I told them, you see.' She looked down. 'I'd been following her. Even on the evening she disappeared. I'd seen her earlier, driving to the police station. I'd seen them before, too, having a rendezvous near the bridge.'

'Ingrid, I don't know what you think this has to do with me,' I said, pressing the button.

'Don't you realise? I was able to tell the police what car he was driving. I know they suspect your son-in-law. My source told me that. But it's not him, Elizabeth. It definitely wasn't him. The man she was seeing was driving a red car. You must be so relieved. If you could just give me a line or two about how police implicated Michael and how wrong they were?'

Her voice trailed off as the ward sister arrived at my door.

'Please,' I said. 'This woman isn't my niece. She's a reporter.'

'Elizabeth, please. Just a line . . .'

'Do I have to call security?' the ward sister asked firmly.

I just turned my head to the side, tried to block it all out.

If it wasn't my son-in-law, Michael, if the man was driving a red car – just like Laura's – that meant the worst of my fears had come true. Aaron had come back. And he was worse than he'd ever been.

I ignored the cacophony of noise, the arguments back and forth between the ward sister and Ingrid, until I felt a hand on my arm and looked up to see Constable King looking down at me.

'Elizabeth, we have some news.'

'It's about Aaron,' I said. It wasn't a question.

She nodded.

'Has he been arrested?'

She pulled a chair over and sat down.

'There was a police operation to arrest him. He'd been holding Rachel Walker in the old St Catherine's building. She managed to escape after site security was alerted to unusual activity. Aaron was left inside the building and we sent our armed response unit in to try to locate him.'

I closed my eyes. Prepared myself for what she'd say next. I already felt it in my heart. Felt that he was gone. Properly this time. Not away to another country.

'During the course of the police operation, our helicopter noticed movement on the top of the building,' she continued. 'We saw there was a man standing there. I'm very sorry, Elizabeth. We sent an officer up to talk to him and, we're truly, very sorry, but before police could get to him, he jumped.'

'He's dead,' I said.

For the second time, I knew this wasn't a question but a statement of what I knew in my heart.

'I'm afraid so,' Constable King said. 'He sustained catastrophic head injuries. Medical teams were at the scene and were with him in less than a minute, but there was nothing they could do. They believe he'd have died instantly. I'm so very sorry.'

The words swam over my head as if I were watching a scene in a TV show.

I took a breath. 'And Rachel? Is she okay?'

'She's receiving treatment. Her injuries aren't life-threatening, but I'm not sure I'd say she was okay.'

I nodded. 'Thank you,' I said to Constable King before turning my head away again.

'Michael's been released without charge. I thought you should know that. He's back with the children. It would appear that Aaron used his name when signing up for the writing course. We obtained a copy of his student ID, which confirmed this.'

I couldn't speak.

I just wanted to close my eyes.

Saturday, 16 June

Chapter Fifty-Five

Rachel

'I'm not sure this is a good idea,' Paul said as we turned the corner and waited for the lift.

'I have to do it, Paul. So many of us are hurt now. If she wants to meet me, how can I say no? She's a frail old lady. She's had a stroke. She's not a threat to me or us.'

He patted my shoulder. 'Okay.'

The door of the lift opened and he pushed my wheelchair through it.

My leg had been broken during the attack. Doctors couldn't understand how I'd been able to run on it, except that adrenaline must have pushed me on. A cracked rib, torn ligaments in my arm, a fractured eye socket, and cuts to my feet and head. I'd been patched up. Stitched back together. Given a headscarf to wear to cover the areas where he'd cut my hair so short he'd slit my skin.

My face was still swollen. I was still in pain. I still didn't want to be left alone. Still needed the light on at all times. Was afraid to sleep. Was still so very angry with myself for falling for him. For putting my family and myself in such danger. But I couldn't have known.

Could I?

Paul had taken the news of my affair better than I could have hoped, but I feared it was just a knee-jerk reaction to the trauma we'd been through. The need we had for things to be okay at that moment. When things calmed down, I knew we'd still have to deal with the massive issues in our marriage. We'd let each other down so badly and broken the trust we'd once shared.

He didn't look at me the same now, nor, if I'm honest, did I at him. It was as though everything had changed. I didn't know if we'd ever get what we once had back. We'd have to be honest with each other. More than we'd ever been before. We'd already talked about seeing a counsellor and he'd agreed to give up his Belfast flat, stay closer to home.

He'd brought the girls to see me the day after I'd been admitted. Molly had been too frightened to come close to me. She told me I looked scary. It had broken my heart to see her tremble at the sight of me, but I knew I had to give her space. She'd come round. At least I had the chance for her to come round. The ache I felt when I thought that I may never have seen her or her sister again was worse than any physical pain I was experiencing.

Beth had held my hand and wept. She'd told me she loved me. Promised she'd do whatever she could around the house until I was fully recovered. It may sound strange, but even as she spoke I already hoped for the day when she'd stomp upstairs and refuse to wash the dishes. Then I'd know things were back on track. That we'd come through this.

I'd only spoken to Julie on the phone. She was still in County Down with Brendan and his family. She had no memory of Clare treating Laura so badly. Or maybe, like me, she had buried them away somewhere. Grateful that it wasn't us. Happy to be in our group of friends and not wanting to rock the boat. The

Clare I knew, the woman she became, would've been horrified to think she could've made someone feel so badly. Clare wasn't a bad person, but in her teenage years she'd made mistakes. We all had.

I didn't tell the Taylor family what Aaron had said. What good would it do to them? It would only bring more pain and God knows, we all had enough of that to contend with. I didn't tell them, or anyone, about the recording of Clare pleading for her life, either. I tried to bury it and hoped it would stay there. The police had yet to uncover Aaron's phone, despite combing the school building for it.

'Are you nervous?' Paul asked, pulling me from my thoughts.

'Yes. I know I shouldn't be. But I am.'

'You can still change your mind,' he said as we arrived on the correct floor and the doors opened again.

'Nope. I need to do this.'

He pushed me through to the ward. I noticed glances from the staff, who no doubt knew who I was. What had happened. How close I'd come to a horrific end.

A woman with curly red hair introduced herself as Cliona, Mrs O'Loughlin's social worker, and led me to her room.

'I'll wait outside,' Paul said. 'Grab a cup of tea or something.'

'Thank you,' I said, looking up at him, noticing how he looked at me, feeling a sadness at what we had done to each other. He turned and Cliona pushed my chair into the room where this woman – who I'd last seen in the kitchen of Clare's house – was resting in bed. She looked smaller. Frail. Older. There was a sadness to her that made my heart ache.

'Elizabeth,' I said, my voice cracking with emotion.

'And you must be Rachel,' she said, taking in my appearance. 'I'm so, so sorry my boy did this to you. And hurt your friend. I didn't think . . .'

'Shush. You've nothing to apologise for,' I said, tears rolling down my cheeks. 'You've lost so much, too. I'm so sorry if anything I ever said or did to Laura contributed in any way to her death . . .'

Elizabeth raised her hand. 'There's no need for apologies there, either,' she said. 'Laura was a troubled person. I don't think any one person or group can be blamed for what happened to her. I had to learn that after her death. It wasn't easy, but there's no other way to think of it without losing one's mind. And don't you think enough people have lost their mind already?'

I nodded.

She gave me a small smile, but her face was as tear-stained as mine.

'Do you have people to help you and support you?' I asked, all too aware that both of her children were now dead.

'Well,' she said, 'I have my son-in-law. Michael.'

I started at the mention of his name. She paused for just a second.

'The real Michael. He's a good man, you know. I have him and my grandchildren. Laura's children, Max and Ava. And Cliona here has been a star,' she said, nodding towards the red-haired woman. 'And you? Will you be okay?'

'I think so,' I said and we sat, looking at each other, thinking of all that we could say but wouldn't.

It didn't really matter now, did it? We just had to learn to live with what had happened and rebuild our lives as best we could.

Wednesday, 20 June

Epilogue

Rachel

Clare was finally laid to rest on a blisteringly hot Wednesday morning. We all felt not only a sense of relief at finally being able to bring her to her final resting place, but also an overwhelming sense of sadness at the unfairness of it all. We knew our grief was only really beginning. We knew it would never really make sense.

Some names scrawled on the back of a random photograph was all it took for Aaron O'Loughlin to choose his victims.

An associate of Aaron's from Wales, where he'd moved after leaving Derry, had sold his story to Ingrid Devlin. He said Aaron had become obsessed with the idea of 'making things right' and rebuilding bridges with his mother. But he'd also talked incessantly about justice. About the need for people to be made accountable for their actions. He'd said he'd do what the police didn't have the guts to.

It wasn't of importance to him that none of us had any real connection with Laura's suicide. He had to be angry with someone, the trauma counsellor who'd been appointed to me had said at my first session.

It didn't really matter though, did it? No amount of

soul-searching or navel-gazing would bring Clare back. She was gone. Her coffin was proof of that. Paul had helped to carry it from the church and I'd felt sick imagining that he could so easily have been carrying my coffin.

Ingrid was there at the back of the church. A suitably sombre expression on her face. I couldn't bring myself to look at her. It had been she who'd been driving the blue car that had scared me senseless just before it had all happened. She'd looked for an interview with me, which I'd politely declined. She'd never hear my side of the story.

Paul and Beth had held my hands tight as Clare was lowered into the ground. Poor Mrs Taylor was buckled with grief. Ronan had to hold her up while Mr Taylor held his composure, just. He was broken. Utterly destroyed. I struggled to be able to look him in the eye. I felt the weight of Clare's death like a stone around my neck. It could have been me. I could have been in the grave beside her. It was only fate or luck or some-thing that I wasn't.

Julie didn't even make it to the funeral. She was still in County Down. Brendan had said she was struggling to cope. She was struggling to come to terms with the fact that she, too, had been taken in by Aaron, who'd pretended to be a father. Pretended to have children at the same school as her own children. That had scared her – how close he'd come to her own children. Just as it scared me. Could he have hurt Molly and Beth, or would he have stopped after he killed me, or Julie? I suppose we'll never know.

As the crowds were dispersing, Ronan invited us back to the Taylors' house for tea and sandwiches, but I was tired. I wanted to be at home. I wanted to escape the pervading sense of grief. I wanted to heal with my family around me.

As Paul pushed me back towards the car, I saw the woman with red hair pushing Elizabeth through the cemetery gates in a wheelchair. We didn't stop to chat — we were too far apart — but I lifted my hand and gave her a small wave. She nodded in acknowledgement and then returned to staring straight in front of her.

Clare Taylor hadn't been the only person laid to rest that day.

Elizabeth

A fresh mound of dirt lay on top of the grave with a grey granite stone bearing the names of my beloved husband and daughter. Soon, Aaron's name would be etched into the same stone in silver.

'He's at peace now,' Cliona said and God, I hoped he was.

I hoped both he and Laura were. I hoped that if there was an afterlife, a greater being overseeing it all, they'd acknowledge Aaron's troubles. They'd understand that I was still a mother who still loved her son. Who hoped to see him again one day.

There were only a couple of wreaths on his grave. It was sad that this was all his life amounted to. One of them was from my sister and her family. Another was from me, a simple display of white roses and lilies.

But the cornflower blue between them caught my eye and my heart started to thump.

'Can you bring me closer?' I asked Cliona.

'Of course.'

I saw it clearly then. A simple display of wild forget-me-nots, their stems wrapped in black ribbon. A familiar white card pinned to them.

'Can you reach that card for me?' I asked Cliona and she did.

She opened the envelope for me, my own hands shaking and still weak from my stroke, and handed it over.

'Can you read it okay?' she asked.

I looked down at the words. In blue ink:

It was all for Laura.

A chill ran through me and I glanced around, suddenly feeling as if someone was watching us. I thought of all the times I'd felt as if I was being watched before. All the times I'd caught a shadow of something and dismissed it as nothing more than my overactive imagination.

The times I now knew were Aaron watching me. Too afraid to come and talk. If only he'd approached me. Maybe I could have got through to him. No one else had needed to die.

But the day was still. No one was there. The only shadows were from the leaves on the trees, the shade from the gravestones.

I shivered.

Acknowledgements

Pulling a book together and getting it on the shelves takes a lot of work – and I am more grateful than words can say to the phenomenal team at Avon who have helped me bring *Forget Me Not* to life.

To my former editor Phoebe Morgan, who oversaw the editing of this book and my two previous thrillers. I owe you a debt of gratitude. You saw something in me and my writing that I don't even think I saw and you took a chance. You have taught me so much during our time working together and have made me a better writer for it. Thank you for bringing your guidance, and patience, to this book and to this author. I wish you all the best in your new endeavour.

To my new editor Helen Huthwaite, who has already mastered calming my nerves, thank you for your support and for taking me under your wing. I look forward to what we can do together.

Thanks also to Sabah, Elke, Molly, Dom, Oliver and all the team at Avon for your enthusiasm, support and endless hard work on behalf of all your authors. You are incredible.

Thanks to Claire Dean for her sterling copy editing work.

Thanks also to the team at HarperCollins Ireland, including Mary Byrne who should be off sunning herself in Italy by the time this book reaches the shelves. I appreciate all your efforts.

For matters relating to the police procedure, rank and protocol, thanks go to Karen and also to my sister-in-law Inspector Penny Jones of the Cheshire Police. Any mistakes are entirely of my own making.

As always, thanks to my agent Ger Nichol – a woman best described by the Shakespeare quote: 'And though she be but little, she is fierce'. Thank you Ger for your unwavering support over the years and the way you have my best interests at heart always. Your reminders to 'mind yourself' are appreciated!

Thank you to booksellers and librarians for getting behind my books. You are rock-stars. Special love and thanks to Bob, Jenni and Dave – royalty of the Indie book trade. And to Heidi Murphy, Maria Dickenson and all at Eason, Foyleside.

Thank you to all the book bloggers and reviewers who do amazing work for very little reward! Especially Mairead at Swirl & Thread and Margaret Bonnas Madden at Bleachhouse Library.

Sincere thanks to my writing friends, who make this journey less lonely and more craic. Thank you Louise Beech, John Marrs, C.L. Taylor, Brian McGilloway, Margaret Scott and Caroline Finnerty and to the wonderful, incredibly talented Liz Nugent who gave me the inspired idea of bringing Ingrid Devlin back in this book, and who during the course of a conversation on a writing retreat gave my confidence a great boost.

While writing this book I was approached by a lovely woman on Twitter with the simple request that, if possible, I name a character after her mother, who passed away in summer 2018. I was only too happy to do so, and so Patricia Hopkins, the

FLO in the book, got her name. With great love to Andrea Molloy for her Twitter loveliness. I hope this small gesture makes things just that little bit easier for you.

To my friends and family, thank you always. Mum, Dad, Lisa, Peter, Emma and assorted partners, little people and dogs, Erin, Catherine, Marie-Louise. Mimi, Auntie Raine, thank you all. And to my Twitter pals, thanks for the laughs.

To my husband, and my two children, and the two cats and the one puppy – thank you again for giving me the time and space to create another story. I love you.

This is a book that, in its very twisted way is about friendship and as such I'm dedicating it to the three friends who have been there for me most of all and continue to be so.

Jim Morrison said: '*A true friend is someone who lets you have total freedom to be yourself – and especially to feel. Or, not feel. Whatever you happen to be feeling at the moment is fine with them. That's what real love amounts to – letting a person be what he really is.*'

Julie-Anne, my oldest school friend, proper Derry Girl, and now road trip buddy; Vicki, my new mum friend and the person I am most 'me' with; and Fionnuala, my writing partner in crime and my soul sister (not to mention a bloody brilliant beta reader) – you all lift me up and I love you x

And finally to you, lovely reader, thank you for continuing to allow me to have the best job in the world.

**If you loved *Forget Me Not*, try
Claire's first thriller!**

Not everyone's life is as perfect as it seems . . .

All she ever wanted was to be a mother . . .

And stay one.